ERABON

QERACH

RANDY C. DOCKENS

Carpenter's Son Publishing

Qerach

Published by Carpenter's Son Publishing, Franklin, Tennessee

Published in association with Larry Carpenter of Christian Book Services, LLC
www.christianbookservices.com

Edited by Robert Irvin

Cover and Interior Layout Design by Suzanne Lawing

Printed in the United States of America

978-1-952025-14-3

CONTENTS

PRONUNCIATION GUIDE

A'iah (ā ī´ ə)
Alpha Centauri (ăl´ fə sĕn tȯr´ ē)
Arnoclid (är´ nō clĭd)
Aphiah (af´ ē ə)
Authocantryx (ôthō căn´ trĭks)
Bicca (bĭk´ kä)
Ca'eb (kā ĕb´)
Chaikin (chī´ kĭn)
Ch'kxl (chə kĭks´ əl)
Ch'kxl'x (chə kĭks´ əl ĕks)
Ch'tsk (chə tĭsk´)
Elnah (ĕl´ nä)
Elyahel (ĕl´ yä ĕl)
E'oa (ē ō´ ə)
Erabon (ĕr´ ə bŏn)
Eremia (ər ē´ mēä)
Felicia (fĕ lĭsh(ē)ə)
Gavrek (gäv´ rĕk)
Hael (hā´ ĕl)
Halayal (hä lā´ əl)
HaShem (hä shĕm´)
Howeh (hăü ā´)
I'ya (ī´ yä)
Jake (jāk)
Jaeyre (jä ĕr´)
Jayahel (jä´ yä ĕl)
Jerim (jĕr´ ĭm)
Kubim (kü´ bĭm)
McNamara (măk nə mĕr´ ə)
Mashiach (mä´ shē ăk)
Mazkir (măz´ kər)

Michael (mī´ kəl)
Mictah (mĭk´ tä)
Myeem (mī ēm´)
Nemit (nĕm´ ĭt)
Neptune (nĕp´ tyün)
Nuke (nūk)
O'em (ō´ əm)
Pentalagus (pĕn tăl´ ə gŭs)
Prahel (prä ĕl´)
Qerach (kər´ ăk)
Qoftic (kŏf´ tĭk)
Ramah (rä´ mä)
Raphek (răf´ ĕk)
Rhicerotide (rī sĕr´ ō tīd)
Seraphia (sĕr äf´ ēä)
Sharab (shăr´ äb)
Ti'sulh (tĭ sŭl´)
Triton (trī´ tən)
Wehyahel (wā yä ĕl´)
Ya'ea (yä ē´ ə)
Yahel (yä əl´)
Y'din (wī dēn´)
Yel (yĕl)
Yohanan (yō´ hă nən)
Za'avan (zā´ ə vən)
Zael (zā ĕl´)
Zaveh (zā´ və)
Zel (zĕl)
Zyhov (zī´ hōv)
Z'zlzck (zə zĕl´ zĭk)

5

ONE

QERACH

When one's heart is seen as beautiful, the outer appearances are viewed the same way. That's how Nuke now thought of his friends. He knew if they were to land on Earth, the populace would view them as freaks, but he had come to adore them. Each were special in their unique way. If he had been told a short time ago he would have such a menagerie of friends, he would have thought the person crazy. Now he couldn't imagine his life without them.

Although Ti'sulh had bluish skin with tentacles for "hair," he thought she had the most feminine and beautiful facial features. He had met her on Myeem, a planet composed almost entirely of water, one of six planets in what the clans here called the Erabon system. Myeem was the planet he landed on when an interstellar gate accident occurring near Neptune flung him into this uncharted part of the universe. Ti'sulh had become a good friend—maybe even more. If they were on Earth, she would likely be called his girlfriend. But while they were close and had even kissed, the thought of them together proved both exciting and engendered a sense of apprehension in him at the same time. While helping him with their mission, the jet she had been flying had been damaged when they had landed on planet Sharab, so she now shared Nuke's jet, sitting behind him.

Bicca, grayish in color with long, bony arms and legs, appeared somewhat insectlike. Nuke had met him on Eremia, a planet composed almost entirely of desert. Bicca sported antennae above his bulging eyes—eyes that could focus on two things at once. That had unnerved Nuke in the beginning. As Nuke thought of this he had to chuckle to himself. It still did make him uneasy—to a certain extent. Yet Bicca had proven to be a good friend more than once. Nuke was happy to have him on this mission.

He found Z'zlzck, from the planet Sharab, to be different from anything he would have imagined, both in name and looks. Nuke's best friend, Michael, had somehow gotten pulled into this part of the universe with him when Michael had tried to assist him during the interstellar gate malfunction. Nuke ended up on Myeem while Michael crash-landed on Ramah, a mountainous planet, and then got sent to Sharab, a planet full of volcanoes; it was on Sharab that Nuke stunningly came across his best friend! There Michael had met Z'zlzck, and the two became good friends. Nuke smiled while thinking about this pair. Michael had died his hair a brilliant yellow just after they graduated from the Academy and prior to their getting posted to serve together on Triton, one of Neptune's moons. Now Michael's hair matched that of the tuft on top of Z'zlzck's head. Yet the similarity ended there. Z'zlzck's profile made his face look like a giant "C." From the front his face looked as though someone had taken a blunt instrument and made a huge indentation in it between his forehead and chin. His mouth was set far back from his chin, and his eyes appeared to nearly dangle from his forehead. Z'zlzck also took some getting used to, but again, this Sharabian had proven to be a loyal friend not only to Michael but to Nuke as well. In addition he looked rather bulky and had an orange-red skin tone. Nuke now saw Z'zlzck as a great friend as well.

Nuke thought back on all the adventures he and Michael had during and after their Academy days. The present adventure, though, clearly topped them all. Nuke also owed his nickname to Michael. Somehow he had a much higher electrical conductance in his skin than anyone his physicians had encountered. Michael told all their friends at the Academy that his best friend had turned "nuclear," so the nickname Nuke stuck. Having this trait always made him feel different; it was something he had tried to hide from others. Yet this abnormality had proved, in a few different situations, to be the one thing that allowed him to survive in this part of the universe.

Then there was E'oa, who came from Ramah, a rocky and mountainous planet. His features appeared rather like boulders comparable to those that peppered his planet. Yet this young royal had a heart of gold. He looked grayish in color but would turn a brilliant purple when he prayed to Erabon, their deity. He, likely more than all the others, wanted all the clans of the Erabon system to reunite and usher in the return of Erabon to all his people. Apparently, all six clans had existed in harmony millennia ago, but civil war had broken out, and each clan separated to a different planet in their solar system. Their ancestors forbade anyone to visit another clan. Yet Nuke had discovered the message of Erabon, and it desired the unity of these clans. To achieve this prophecy, Nuke now helped his friends disobey the words of their ancestors by visiting each planet.

Through varying circumstances, his new friends had come to believe Nuke to be the prophet of Erabon and now were traveling with him to help all the clans reunite and prepare for Erabon's return. In ways Nuke never thought possible, he had fulfilled various prophecies on each of the planets he had visited thus far, and he had discovered the complete message of Erabon to each clan in each planet's temple. His mission now involved getting all the clans reunited in both their belief in Erabon and in his return. As far as Nuke could tell, Erabon was equivalent to the God of the Bible on planet Earth, or at least he now believed that to be the case. Otherwise, he had no idea why he had been brought here nor how he had been able to fulfill prophecies he knew nothing about.

Now here they were, Nuke and these friends, circling the fifth planet in their system, Qerach, which was touted as an ice planet. So far its environment held up to those claims. Nuke spent several minutes flying near the planet's surface looking for a suitable place to land. Yet the wind had picked up so much snow and ice that visibility had become extremely difficult. He pointed to one of the readings on his instrument panel.

"Ti'sulh, watch this monitor, which should filter out a lot of the snow and ice flying around," Nuke called back to her. "See if you can locate anything relatively flat where we can land."

Ti'sulh leaned forward looking at the monitor. She shook her head. "It doesn't look promising."

"Well, just keep looking. I'll circle back around."

A voice came through Nuke's comm device. "Nuke, this is Michael."

"Go ahead."

"My bunkmate, Bob here, just sprang something on me." Nuke smiled. Z'zlzck traveled with Michael in his jet, and

Michael always made jokes about something having to do with Z'zlzck. "Apparently he has the ability to detect heat signatures."

"What? Why didn't he say anything before?" Nuke would never understand why Michael kept calling Z'zlzck "Bob" instead of his real name. But this nickname had become part of their rapport, their banter, since Z'zlzck had saved Michael's life shortly after Michael arrived on Sharab. They were now extremely good friends.

"Well, he said he assumed anyone could," Michael radioed back. "Apparently he saved my life three times from falling into a lava flow through thin-crusted rock back on Sharab. I didn't even know it."

"Wow. OK. So can he save us now? Does he see anything below?"

Silence lingered for a few seconds. Nuke was beginning to think he had lost the signal.

Michael returned to the comm. "He says the mountain below us looks extremely cold. He suggests trying the one over to your three o'clock."

Nuke banked his jet in that direction. "Michael, are you sure it's that one? Its surface looks too steep for us to land anywhere."

"Yeah, but Bob says this mountain has an extremely warm interior."

"Is he sure he's not detecting a lava flow?"

"He says it's too cold for lava but too warm to be nothing."

Ti'sulh leaned forward and touched his arm. "Nuke, I swear this wasn't there before."

"What?" He strained to view the side of the mountain to sync with where Ti'sulh was pointing on the monitor.

"The side of the mountain suddenly has a large ledge," Ti'sulh said.

"Large enough for all four jets?"

She nodded. "And then some."

Suddenly a strobe light was visible. Nuke squinted. "What the . . . "

Ti'sulh looked up and then at the monitor. "That's it. That's the right position."

"Michael, do you see that?" Nuke radioed. "E'oa, Bicca, do you copy?"

All affirmed.

"It seems someone is waiting for us," Bicca said.

"Or . . . " Ti'sulh said, then hesitated.

Nuke turned back toward Ti'sulh's direction. "Or what?"

"Or the beacon is automatically activated when a craft gets near it."

He nodded. Yes, that was definitely a possibility. "Well, there's only one way to find out," Nuke said.

"Michael. E'oa. Bicca. Follow me down."

Again, all three radioed affirmation. Nuke had some difficulty keeping his jet stable due to the wind. He just hoped E'oa could handle the turbulence since the Ramahian had no experience flying in harsh weather like this. The landing area proved much larger than Nuke expected, however, so landing was actually easier than he anticipated.

Once he brought his jet down, Michael and E'oa landed behind him. Bicca landed behind them. Nuke looked through his cockpit canopy. He guessed a whole fleet of jets could have landed on this large ledge.

He looked at Ti'sulh. "How did they get such a landing area on such a steep mountain?"

She shrugged. "I don't know, but I would swear none of this was here on your first pass. Either the mountain opened up, or this area was camouflaged."

Ti'sulh passed a parka up to Nuke. They both attempted to put the heavy coats on—with a great deal of difficulty. They somehow managed in the tight quarters of the jet. "It's going to be cold out there," Nuke said, looking at his instruments. "It's . . . " He furrowed his brow as he tapped on the instrument panel.

"What's wrong?"

He shook his head. "It registered well below freezing just a few minutes ago."

"How cold is that?" T'isulh asked.

Nuke stared at her but then realized, on Myeem, she had never experienced such temperatures. "Cold enough to make liquid water solid," he answered.

Her eyes got wide and she zipped her parker higher.

He tapped the screen again. "While the outside temperature is still cold, this says it's warming slightly. It's now only a few degrees below freezing."

He looked at his other instruments. "Air seems fine. Breathable." He looked at Ti'sulh. "Ready?"

She nodded. He pushed an icon on his control panel and this broke the canopy's seal; Nuke pressed another, and the canopy retracted. He breathed in a deep lungful of air—cold, slightly moist, but refreshing. He climbed out, helped Ti'sulh out, and both descended the short length of stairs to the ground. Or, rather, the deck.

Nuke did a three-sixty as the others walked over. Z'zlzck looked up and pointed. "The wind and snow are blowing, but nothing is getting to us."

13

Michael nodded. "Must be some type of force field or something." He looked at Nuke. "I swear the temperature is warming up."

Nuke nodded. "Yes, that's what my instruments were saying."

"Well, that's very hospitable of them." Michael wasn't smiling as he said this. He looked around warily.

Ti'sulh looked up. "I see the strobe light isn't on any longer." She looked around. "I'm surprised no one is coming out to greet us."

Nuke nodded. "Or put us in prison."

Michael laughed, nearly under his breath. "Forever the optimist, I see."

"Just realistic," Nuke said, devoid of any real emotion.

E'oa pointed. "There seems to be some type of portal in that direction."

They all walked toward where E'oa indicated. The portal opened with a *swoosh*.

Each briefly looked at one another, then walked through. The temperature was even warmer. Nuke guessed he could probably take his parka off, but he left it on.

Michael turned in a circle. "It looks almost like some type of control room or control tower."

Nuke nodded. "But where is everyone?"

E'oa looked at Nuke. "Maybe this place has been abandoned."

Ti'sulh shook her head. "If that's true, why is everything still functional?"

"Maybe certain things work automatically," E'oa said.

Ti'sulh shrugged. "Maybe."

They walked farther into the large room. Multiple holographic displays could be seen throughout. Most were blank or had swirling colors intermingling with each other. Nuke assumed this to be the Qerachian version of a screen saver. A few were simply clear. One was a solid blue with a blinking blue light at the top. Nothing else looked distinguishing about it, though. Yet as Nuke looked, the monitor turned to swirling colors like the others. Nuke's eyebrows shot up as he glanced at Ti'sulh.

She tilted her head slightly. "That wasn't creepy at all." As she stepped ahead, she added, "Maybe that was the one controlling the strobe light."

Bicca had walked ahead and motioned for them to step to where he stood. Another portal stood before them that opened into some type of lounge area. There were multiple seating arrangements, some tables, and what Nuke assumed to be a bar area. And there was something else: all sorts of colorful jars with various liquids in them.

Michael kept turning. "This is getting creepy," he said quietly.

Nuke nodded, and also said softly, "I feel like I'm in the beginning of a horror film just before something really bad happens."

At that moment, another *swoosh* occurred behind them. All jumped and turned. Nuke's eyes widened. Standing at the portal was a feminine figure. Nuke thought her gorgeous and eerie at the same time. She appeared rather tall—taller than any of them, somewhat thin, but not out of proportion. She was dressed in white and had long white hair and white skin— very white, devoid of all color. Yet she looked beautiful at the same time with delicate feminine features. She seemed to have what looked like glitter on her cheeks and eyelids.

But what really drew Nuke's attention were her eyes. Her irises were a brilliant purple. She also had one purple streak in her hair on her right side that ran from her scalp to the tip of her long hair. The purple strand carried to her hips. The rest of her hair appeared as white as snow and only went to the middle of her back.

All six of the visitors remained frozen in place for what seemed like minutes but was likely only seconds. Finally, the woman smiled and stepped forward.

"Ah, I see the time has arrived."

Nuke stared at her and blinked. "What . . . time?"

"Four clans and two red-bloods. What else could it be?"

Nuke cocked his head and continued to stare. It dawned on him he could understand her, which meant his comm already understood Qerachian vocabulary. *Their language must be close to that of Myeemians,* he thought. Yet while he understood the words, he was not sure he understood their meaning. "I'm afraid we don't understand. And . . . you are?"

She continued to smile. "Oh, forgive my manners." Her hand went to her chest. "I am Halayal." She gestured toward Nuke. "You are here for Erabon's return, no?"

Nuke nodded but didn't say anything. He really didn't know what to say.

"Good. I thought so."

She turned ever so subtly and waved them forward. "Come. We have much to discuss."

TWO

MISUNDERSTANDING

Halayal led them to what appeared to be some type of conference room. The table, somewhat serpentine with its surface increasing and decreasing in width along its path, looked made of ice, but it wasn't cold to the touch. The six pedestals of the table radiated lights of blue, purple, gold, crimson, white, and clear up and throughout the table surface.

She gestured to the table. "Everyone, please have a seat. I'll ask Yahel and Jaeyre to join us." She paused and gave a slight nod. "It is fortuitous you come on the heels of The Name Celebration. We celebrate him, and then you arrive." She turned and stepped from the room.

Nuke looked at the others as he sat. "Anyone know what's going on here?"

Everyone shrugged. Michael chuckled. "I guess your reputation precedes you."

Nuke smiled but didn't like the implication. On almost every planet he had been accused of being a Qerachian. Now, here on Qerach, he failed to see the similarity. While they did look more like him anatomically than the other clans, he thought they still looked quite different from him. He shrugged mentally. Maybe those on other planets had just been speaking in general terms.

Halayal returned with two individuals, one man and one woman. The other woman, who Nuke assumed to be Jaeyre, looked almost identical to Halayal except her eyes and strand of colored hair were a deep crimson. The man, evidently Yahel, had noticeably short hair, still all white, but had the same long strand of hair which, for him, started behind his ear and carried down to his hip. Yet his irises and strand of hair looked like some type of clear crystal. Diamonds were the first things that came to Nuke's mind. His whole presence, devoid of color, made him look even more eerie.

Yahel came forward and shook each of their hands. "I am so happy to meet each of you." He kept looking from them to Halayal. No one said anything as they, like Nuke, were stunned at his appearance. Yet he seemed extremely friendly. Jaeyre only smiled and nodded at them.

Halayal gestured for all to take a seat.

Yahel grinned. "You have come at a most opportune time."

Halayal gave him an almost imperceptible shake of her head. He looked shocked for a brief second but recovered with a grin. "We are just incredibly happy to see you. We have studied your prophecy for so long."

Nuke raised his eyebrows. "Oh? Which prophecy would that be?"

Jaeyre gave a thin smile, although it looked forced. "Yahel, we first need to verify a few things."

Yahel expressed shock. "But they are all here, just as the prophecy indicated."

Jaeyre shook her head. "Not all."

He pointed at Nuke and his friends. "But they are in the order of our planetary system. Aphiah comes after Qerach."

Jaeyre turned to Yahel with a stern look. "We must consider the words of the prophecy with great care and not with a cavalier attitude."

Yahel shot back an irritated look and tone. "That is *not* what I am doing."

Halayal held up her hands. "Please, let's not argue in front of our guests. We are likely confusing them."

Nuke nodded. "Yes, I'm afraid you have. Could we start with what prophecy you are referring to?"

Yahel's genuine smile returned. He started to speak, but then looked at Jaeyre, his smile vanishing. Still, she said nothing. So he looked back at Nuke, his smile returning. "The prophecy goes: *The one who comes in my name will come with those who speak for their people.*"

Nuke nodded. "I see. Somewhat specific, but vague enough for further interpretation."

Jaeyre gave a slight nod. "I see you understand the gravity of the situation. Many interpretations of these words have yielded some . . . conflicting . . . opinions."

Ti'sulh leaned forward. "Well, I for one can state unequivocally that Nuke proved to be the prophet of Erabon on Myeem by fulfilling specific prophecy."

Bicca nodded. "Same on Eremia."

"And Sharab," Z'zlzck said.

E'oa nodded. "As well as on Ramah." He glanced from one of the Qerachians to the other. "So what specifically do you have doubts about?"

Jaeyre shifted in her seat. "Well, you have two red-bloods in your midst, and we . . . "

An "ahem" came from Yahel.

Jaeyre's eyes shot to Yahel and then back to Nuke. "Some have thought the prophecy implied someone from each planet would arrive."

E'oa shook his head. "But from what Yahel has said, that does not seem to be a specific requirement for either this one"—he pointed to Michael—"not to be here, or someone from Aphiah to be here."

Jaeyre gave a slight nod with a tense smile. "Granted. Yet, as I said, many have thought the prophecy implied that." She tilted her head slightly. "Perhaps . . . " She glanced at Halayal and then back to E'oa. "Perhaps we were mistaken."

E'oa nodded as though that answered the question. Yet Nuke had a feeling Jaeyre's doubts were not gone. He had a sinking feeling he would have to prove something on this planet as well. He wished, for once, a planet's leaders would believe him.

"Well," Bicca said. "Once your council gets to know us, perhaps your confidence will increase."

The three Qerachians looked at each other with a questioning look. Halayal looked back at Bicca. "Council?"

He nodded. "Yes. Those who are in charge and govern for your people."

Halayal had an unsure look, yet she seemed to try and mask, with a smile, what she really was thinking. "Oh, we are three of six who look out after the well-being of our people." She gestured toward the door. "The others are, even now, attending to such duties."

Nuke gestured toward her. "And they, the other three, are like the three of you?"

Halayal nodded. "Yes, one other female and two other males." She sat up in her seat. "Do . . . do you wish me to retrieve them for you?"

Nuke shook his head. "No. No, that will not be necessary. I assume the others have different colored eyes and streaks of color in their hair?"

She nodded slowly. "Yes. Is there something wrong?" She gestured between the three of them. "We each share a representative trait of Erabon. Howeh is all white, Zaveh is gold, and Elnah is blue."

Nuke nodded. "You represent the six characteristics of Erabon."

"Yes," Halayal said, acting somewhat enthused that Nuke recognized this. "Seeing the color of each other is a constant reminder we are to reflect Erabon's character in our lives."

"All of your people are this way?"

Her enthusiasm waned. "It is true of all who believe." She stood. "Yet I know you are weary from your travel. Perhaps we should pick this up later."

Nuke furrowed his brow. He wondered why she changed subjects so rapidly. Yet he wanted to understand more, so Nuke decided to press the issue a little further. "Perhaps we could meet and dine with some of your people later. You know, establish a rapport with them so they can grow to understand and trust us."

Halayal looked confused once more. "Dine? You mean with the six of us?"

Nuke tilted his head. "Well, yes, but I thought we could meet others of your people as well."

He saw the three of them exchange confused looks.

Nuke held up his hands. "Only if that is all right, of course." He squinted. "Is . . . is something wrong?"

Yahel shook his head. "The six of us are the only ones who eat. There are no others who dine."

Z'zlzck cleared his throat. "Excuse me, but I saw heat signatures of many people here. Are they not Qerachians?"

Yahel's eyebrows lifted. "Oh, yes. We have thousands of Qerachians here."

Ti'sulh held up her hands. "Wait a minute. Only six out of thousands of Qerachians actually *eat*? How . . . how is that possible?"

Yahel gave a dispassionate shrug.

"Because they are in stasis."

THREE

STASIS

Nuke stared at the scene before him. He put his hand up to the now transparent walls of the conference room trying to be sure what his eyes were showing him was true. He glanced at Ti'sulh. She looked back with mouth slightly open and shook her head. Nuke looked back. All he saw were row after row after row of Qerachians in stasis pods as far as he could see. All were in some type of suspended animation within the confines of a sophisticated mechanical device keeping them alive in their unconscious state.

Halayal pointed. "As you can see in the distance, our fellow companions are monitoring the needs of our citizens." She stood a little straighter as if proud. "They ensure all their vitals are within specified parameters, their bodies get all the nutrients they need, their muscles are exercised with electrical stimulation, and they even help stimulate their minds by providing pleasing, vivid dreams for them."

Jaeyre nodded. "As you can see, we are very diligent in taking care of them."

Nuke nodded. "Yes, I see. But my question is: why?"

Yahel's jaw dropped slightly. "Why? Because we love them and want the best for them."

Michael turned and looked at him. "Yahel, not to be rude, but why is this the best for them? Wouldn't living their lives, interacting, having families, and living . . . life, be better for them?"

Halayal stepped forward. "Don't judge us until you understand us. Everyone here consented to their stasis—not just us."

"But still, it just seems . . . wrong." Nuke looked at her. "Help me understand."

Halayal looked at Jaeyre, who nodded, and then back to Nuke. "Come with me."

She led them down a long hall. Nuke was amazed at the décor. Everything appeared white, but interspersed in strategic places were dashes of color: red, blue, purple, and gold, as well as clear crystalline structures which made everything look vivid. They entered another large room. This one had no furniture.

Before anyone could ask a question, Halayal closed the door and spoke. "Mazkir, display events of Stasis Day."

Nuke whispered to Michael. "Hebrew again."

Michael nodded; he whispered the word in English. "Recorder."

The whole room morphed into one of the most realistic holograms Nuke had ever seen. There seemed to be a room full of people with a panel of six individuals up front behind some type of large table. Each had a different colored iris and strand of hair. The panelist with purple irises was talking to Halayal; Nuke noticed she was standing next to him as this scene played out. This was apparently a scene from Halayal's past.

Nuke noticed Halayal seemed upset. "But sir, how long are you expecting this to last?" She looked from one panelist to another. "This could be for years. Are . . . are you sure this is the right time to embark on such an endeavor?"

"Remember what Erabon has told us," the man said. "We must not hesitate to unite."

Halayal nodded. "Yes sir. I remember what he has told us. And you're sure this is the prophesied course of action?"

The panelist with blue eyes leaned forward. "We are at the maximum since the dawn of our history." Halayal stood in silence. "I fear we will never be so strong again," he continued. "The risk of not doing so now is too high."

Halayal nodded. The blue-eyed panelist motioned for others to come forward. Jaeyre, Yahel, Howeh, Zaveh, and Elnah each came and stood in front of their similar-eyed counterpart. Each panelist put a hand on the shoulder of their counterpart. The purple-eyed panelist lifted his other hand. "Erabon, we pray—"

The hologram dissipated and everything went dark. No one said anything for several seconds. Nuke heard the door to the room open. He saw strips of emergency lighting lining the hallway.

"Follow me," Halayal said, this time in somewhat of a commanding voice.

She led them back the way they had come.

Nuke asked the question he knew everyone in his party was wondering. "What's going on?"

No one replied. Once they got back to the conference room, Halayal opened the door. "Go in here and wait until I return."

Nuke and his friends did while Halayal and her companions went on.

The conference room wall remained transparent. They each went to the wall to try and see what was going on. Only emergency lighting lit the floor below. Yet all stasis pods looked active as the monitor next to each was lit.

Michael was the first to speak. "What just happened?"

Z'zlzck replied. "Their power went out."

Michael rolled his eyes. "OK. I repeat. Other than the obvious, what just happened?"

Nuke shook his head. "No idea. But they seemed frightened by it."

"Yes," Ti'sulh said with a nod. "Their actions went beyond concern."

Nuke turned and paced and then came back to the transparent wall. "Something else is going on here. There's something they're not telling us."

"I agree," E'oa said. "What they tell is not the complete truth."

Nuke nodded and stared through the window. He saw the three whom he had seen monitoring the stasis pods and the three others they had met were now on the floor in the middle of the stasis pods. They were discussing something in an animated manner. Each were gesturing and pointing to different points of the room. Yahel turned and ran from the group, picking up speed as he went. Halayal looked up to where the six visitors were gazing through the wall. She lifted her wrist and pressed something. The wall through which they were gazing turned opaque. They were now facing the wall but unable to see anything.

The only light in the room, the emergency lighting along the floor, pointed to the room's door. Nuke went to the conference table and sat; the others did the same. Michael drummed his fingers. "What are they trying to hide?"

Yes, Nuke thought. *What are they trying to hide?* "That's exactly what I intend to ask Halayal when she comes back," he said.

After a minute or so, the lights came back on.

After several more minutes the door opened and Halayal entered. Jaeyre came in behind her. Yahel came running up and stood next to Jaeyre.

Halayal gave a weak smile. "Sorry for the disturbance. Come with me and I'll show you to your quarters."

Nuke shook his head. "Halayal, what is going on here?"

"The storm. It interfered with our power source. It's . . . being worked on."

Nuke looked at the others. Jaeyre gave a slight nod, but Yahel had a pensive look, his lips pursed.

Nuke cocked his head slightly. "Halayal, please tell us the truth. Truth is always the best path."

Halayal sighed. "I will tell you in detail tomorrow. I . . . I don't have the time right now." She turned. "Follow me."

Nuke looked at his companions. Some shook their heads; others shrugged. What was he to do? He couldn't force them to be honest. Complying with their request seemed the best option for now.

Halayal led them down another hallway. Jaeyre and Yahel both bowed slightly and went down a different one.

Nuke looked back. The two of them once again were in an animated discussion. There was clearly disagreement between them.

Halayal turned a corner which led to an open area with seating and what looked like a small bar area. Off from this area were several doors. She turned to them. "Each of these doors is the entrance to a resting pod. I'll check back with you first thing tomorrow." She abruptly turned and left.

Everyone looked at each other. Nuke shrugged and sat on one of the sofas. Ti'sulh sat next to him. Michael and Z'zlzck sat in chairs opposite them.

E'oa stretched. "I think I'll go ahead and just head to bed."

"But . . . what about dinner?" Michael asked, looking around as if expecting something to eat to be waiting for them. He sat with a thud.

E'oa shook his head. "I don't think that is going to happen." He shrugged. "I'm too tired anyway."

"Me too," Bicca said. "See you in the morning."

They picked the first two doors. There was a slight *swoosh*, the door opened, and they entered.

As those remaining sat, Nuke looked at Z'zlzck. "So, Z'zlzck, what do you think so far of your first off-planet excursion?"

Z'zlzck produced a slight chuckle. "It seems secrets abound everywhere."

Nuke nodded. "I just wonder what theirs is."

"While this was the largest concentration of life-forms, this area was not the only source," Z'zlzck said.

Michael nodded. "She seemed a little hesitant to imply not everyone other than the six of them were in stasis."

Ti'sulh put her hand to her chin. "You think there's a connection between that fact and what happened tonight?"

Nuke nodded slowly. "Maybe." He tapped his knees with his hands. "Well, let's get some sleep and tackle this . . . whole confusing situation tomorrow." Remembering what happened on the previous planets, he chuckled. "Who knows? This may be the only night we have for a good night's sleep."

Michael shook his head as he stood. "It won't be good with my stomach growling all night."

"Sorry, my friend." Nuke said, patting Michael's upper back. "It's only one night. I'll work on getting that corrected in the morning."

FOUR

THE DARK ONE

When Nuke woke, at first he had trouble remembering where he was. Nothing looked familiar. The night before slowly came back to him as he sat up and then stood. Automatically, his bunk retracted into the wall. With the room so small, this allowed more space for him to move around. In the corner was, apparently, some type of shower, or so he assumed. It looked rather small. On the wall was a diagram of a humanoid with feet wide apart bending over with hands on the wall. Under this was a highlighted button. Nuke then noticed two gray tiles on the floor and wall.

Nuke raised his eyebrows. He disrobed and stepped onto the two gray tiles on the floor. He then saw something transparent, but blurry, develop around him. As he slowly put his hand against it, he felt a slight tingling sensation with pressure pushing back. He assumed this was to keep the water from the shower contained.

Nuke looked at the wall in front of him and saw two additional gray tiles. Placing his hands on the tiles, a shower head protruded from the wall between the tiles and slightly higher.

He felt silly standing with his arms parallel to the floor and his legs wide apart.

Several types of twirling brushes came forward and scrubbed his body, including his face and head. At first he grimaced thinking the brushes might hurt or perhaps tickle, but they were extremely soft and actually comfortable. They were evidently self-soaping. After this, jets sprayed water all over his body; the spray seemed to come from every direction. Next came warm air, and this dried him completely.

The forcefield then dissipated.

Nuke stepped out, combed his hair, dressed, and headed out to the seating quarters. Ti'sulh was already there seated with Halayal.

Halayal looked at Nuke as he sat. "Did you find everything to your satisfaction?"

Nuke nodded. "Different, but quite nice."

Halayal looked somewhat surprised. "Oh, you don't have resting pods like these?"

Nuke smiled and shook his head. "No, I'm used to things being a little more manual."

Halayal nodded. "I see. Well, we have found this way more efficient, both in time and use of water."

Nuke held up his hands. "Oh, I'm not complaining. The experience was nice. Extremely nice."

Ti'sulh handed him a cup with colorful pills. He gave her a blank stare; he had no idea what this meant. *Am I supposed to take these?*

"What's this? Vitamins or something?"

Ti'sulh chuckled. "Something."

"Yes," Halayal said, "this is your morning nutritional supplement. From what I could tell, your physiology is similar to ours, so I've given you what we would take. The other clans are in our database, so I knew what to supply to them."

Nuke nodded but gave Ti'sulh a raised eyebrow.

She just smiled in return and handed him a glass of water. "Enjoy."

Nuke gave a forced smile, dumped the contents of the cup into his mouth, and swallowed, chasing them down with a big gulp of water. "Yummy."

Ti'sulh laughed.

Halayal gave a sheepish smile. "I'm sorry. This is how we provide our nutritional needs. Ti'sulh was just telling me how you typically have meals." She shook her head. "I'm sorry we can't accommodate that. But this is . . . "

Nuke finished the sentence with her. "More efficient."

She nodded.

Michael stepped into the main area next. He sat next to Nuke. "Some shower, huh?"

Nuke nodded. "Takes some getting used to."

Michael's eyes went wide. "Tell me about it. I bent over to scratch my leg. That's when the brushes came out." His eyebrows went up. "Woo!"

Nuke had just taken another swallow of water and almost choked as he burst into laughter. He coughed several times.

Ti'sulh quickly turned his way. "Nuke, are you all right?"

He gave a dismissive gesture, coughing again. "Yeah, fine. Michael just surprised me with what he said."

Michael chuckled and patted Nuke on his back. "Sorry, buddy. Didn't mean to make you choke."

Nuke jabbed his shoulder. "Yeah, but you're not sorry about it either."

Michael laughed again.

Nuke handed him a cup he had seen sitting on a table; there were more cups, obviously, for the rest of the party. The cup Nuke picked up had the same pattern of pills as was in his. "Here, just eat your breakfast."

Michael's eyes widened. "What, no toast and eggs?"

"Oh, it's in there," Nuke said. "I think it's the yellow and white ones."

Michael shook his head. "This place is certainly different." He downed the pills in the cup and swallowed some water Nuke also handed him.

The others came into the main area within a few minutes. They too were surprised with their breakfast, but no one complained—not much, anyway. Z'zlzck made a comment about being too full. Everyone—except for Halayal—laughed. Z'zlzck apologized to her, and she seemed satisfied he had not been serious or too disappointed.

After everyone finished their supplements, Halayal stood. "I'll have these dispensed in your resting pods each morning."

Nuke stood. "Halayal, we appreciate your hospitality, but we really need to understand what is happening here."

Halayal's smile vanished. She nodded. "Yes, I know. Please follow me back to Mazkir."

They headed down the hallway, and when they arrived at the room, Yahel was waiting for them.

Halayal didn't seem happy to see him there. "Yahel, what are you doing here?"

He glanced from her to Nuke and back. "Halayal, may I speak to you?" He paused, but she didn't immediately respond. He tightened his face. *"Now?"*

She sighed and nodded. "Very well." She gestured for the six to enter. "I'll be right back."

Nuke stood in the doorway to keep the door open as the others entered. He kept looking at the two Qerachians now in animated discussion some distance away. He walked over. Their conversation came to an abrupt halt.

"Is something wrong?" Nuke asked. Neither of them said anything, but both looked pensive. "Maybe it's something I can help with."

Yahel looked at Halayal with raised eyebrows. She just stared at Yahel while biting her bottom lip. After a few seconds she sighed and made a quick gesture his way. "Fine, Yahel. Go ahead. Bring them to me when you're done. I'll go tell Jaeyre." She shook her head as she walked off.

Yahel gestured back toward the room. "I think you need to know the whole truth."

Nuke nodded and followed him back inside. When they entered, the others just stared at Nuke but didn't say anything. Nuke gave a slight shrug.

Yahel looked slightly upward. "Mazkir, explain the Dark Ones."

Everyone glanced at each other and then back to Yahel. Nuke knew this couldn't be good.

The computer showed several scenes as it explained. "Seven hundred cycles ago, Shael refuted his belief in both Erabon and his return. Over time his hair and eyes turned black. After several opportunities to recant, he was banished to the outside elements."

The computer showed the man's hair gradually change. His golden eyes were the last to go black. Once his eyes were all black, he truly had an evil look. This was the first time Nuke had seen a visual change in someone not believing in Erabon. *Is their physical look a reflection of their inward belief?*

Nuke started to ask a question. Yahel held up his hand. "Mazkir, tell of the Dark Period."

The computer showed several scenes of others being banished. "Over the next four hundred cycles, a period of discontent and doubt emerged, fed by the rebellion of the Dark Ones. This continued until the time of Elyahel, who rejuvenated belief in Erabon. His eyes reflected the hearts of those with whom he spoke. Many Dark Ones turned when they saw their own darkness reflected in his face. Many, but not all, Dark Ones turned back to Erabon."

Nuke sat up straighter at the last image the computer showed. Although several people were shown whose hair turned from black back to white, the last person looked exactly like Yahel. All images then dissipated, and the room again appeared empty.

Nuke spoke first. "Yahel, that last image . . . "

Yahel nodded. "Yes, I was once a Dark One."

FIVE

THE UNEXPECTED NEWS

Nuke and the others just stared at Yahel for several seconds.

Yahel held up his hands. "I know it's a lot to take in. I'm sure you have questions."

Ti'sulh took a step forward. "Yahel, that incident you just showed us. How long ago did that occur?"

"Almost three hundred cycles ago."

Everyone's eyes widened. Nuke managed to whisper, "Three hundred?" He shook his head. "How is that even possible?"

"I was the last one to turn before everyone was placed in stasis. Because of my history with the Dark Ones, some thought I would be able to help predict their actions."

Ti'sulh shook her head. "But that still doesn't explain how you have lived over three hundred cycles."

Yahel gave a slight smile. "Well, we have always had a long life span, but the nutritional supplements we take helps slow the aging process." He looked at each of them. "We didn't know when the prophet of Erabon would come, so we had to take every precaution."

Nuke ran his hand across his mouth. This was certainly a lot to take in, but there were still so many unanswered questions.

E'oa spoke up. "But why put everyone in stasis?"

Bicca nodded. "And why are the Dark Ones still attacking?"

Yahel looked shocked at Bicca's question.

Bicca shrugged. "Why else would so much fear be on your faces?"

Michael gave a slight gasp as though a bright light had just been switched on. "You fear the Dark Ones will overtake this place before Erabon returns."

Yahel sighed. "Yes. Let me try and explain." Everyone looked at Yahel with great expectancy.

"Well . . ." Yahel seemed somewhat fidgety. "With the banishment of Shael, everyone thought that would be the end of things, that the harsh elements would do him in. But that act backfired. Others became critical of his banishment. Some of those began to turn and went out seeking him." He shrugged. "For a while, that seemed to have been the end to the rebellion." He shook his head. "But it wasn't. Those banished managed to somehow survive and establish a colony. That led to the Dark Period. They would capture certain ones of us, ones they thought were on the fence, and try to turn us." He hung his head. "That included me." His eyes watered and the moisture against his crystal irises made them glow. "Those who didn't turn, returned, but many remained, causing their numbers to grow and their survival to be more successful.

"Then, Elyahel grew up in their midst. He appeared different from the other Dark Ones. Although his hair and eyes were dark when he was little, they slowly changed as he aged. He made people see their inward selves. Many had a change of heart. Therefore, because of that and because he looked more like us here, they banished him from their camp and he came here. Elyahel being here helped those considering turning to recant as they saw how ugly they were on the inside. Some of the Dark Ones, like me, had been captured from raids made on the facility here. Elyahel met with us and most of us came back to Erabon." He shook his head. "I . . . I just couldn't believe I was that dark on the inside. I was unhappy with the way things were run here, but I really didn't think I was that far from Erabon and . . . and so dark."

Nuke folded his arms across his chest. "OK. That explains some things, but why put everyone in stasis? If I were a Qerachian here at the time, I would have thought Elyahel was the prophet of Erabon. I mean, look at what he did and could do."

Yahel's eyes watered once more. The sparkle in his eyes was uncanny and made Nuke uneasy. "We became desperate, after . . . his demise."

Ti'sulh gasped. "Demise. You mean . . . "

Yahel nodded.

She shook her head. "How? Why?"

Yahel tried to talk but couldn't get his words out. He cleared his throat. "Our elders devised a test to ensure not just anyone could claim to be the prophet of Erabon and fool the community." He sighed. "I guess after Shael, they had become a little paranoid."

Nuke shifted in his stance, uncrossing and then recrossing his arms in front of his chest. "So what happened?"

"The temple was sealed."

Ti'sulh shook her head. "Why?"

"The elders felt the prophet of Erabon would be able to enter the temple and open it from the inside if that person was, indeed, the true prophet of Erabon."

Ti'sulh put her hands to her temples and shook her head slightly. "But that just denied more people access to the temple and to Erabon. Isn't that the opposite of what they wanted to accomplish?"

Yahel shrugged. "I'm not sure clear minds prevailed at the time. Anyway, many believed Elyahel to be a true prophet of Erabon and persuaded him to take the challenge and enter the temple." Yahel shook his head. "He . . . failed."

Bicca stepped closer. "What happened, Yahel? You're making it sound more serious than just failing."

Yahel's eyes watered again. This time a few tears fell from his cheeks. "He froze to death."

Everyone's eyes widened. A quiet "What?" escaped Nuke's lips.

"The temple is composed of ice. After being sealed in an ice chamber, he was somehow supposed to get into the temple and open it from the inside." Yahel wiped the tears from his cheeks. "It never happened."

E'oa sighed. "It seems they wanted a type of miracle to force everyone to believe."

Yahel nodded. "Yes, I think so. As you saw, after that the elders felt they were fulfilling Erabon's prophecy for us not to hesitate but to act. Putting everyone in stasis was the way they believed they could accomplish that.

Ti'sulh tilted her head sightly as if weighing his words. "Stasis? But, if your lifespan is as long as you say, who considered such technology needed?"

"Oh," Yahel said. "It was originally used for vivid dream excursions. The elders thought this technology effective for fulfilling Erabon's request of them as those on Erabon's side would be preserved. Because the number of the Dark Ones had decreased due to the efforts of Elyahel, and with everyone in stasis, the Dark Ones could not increase their ranks. Then it would only be a matter of time before they would die out. Yahel paused. "Or so we thought. At that point, the whole planet would be ready for his return."

Nuke waved his hands. "Wait. You're saying your job was to keep everyone in stasis until all the Dark Ones died out?"

Yahel gestured to him. "Or until the prophet of Erabon came."

Nuke's body jerked more rigid. Yahel expected *him* to solve their problems? He swallowed hard. "You expect me to solve the disunity among your people?"

Yahel nodded. "Of course. The prophet of Erabon will destroy all the Dark Ones, we bring everyone out of stasis, and we are then ready for Erabon's return."

Nuke's jaw went slack. "You want me to . . . " He swallowed hard again, his throat now constricting, making it hard to get his words out. " . . . *kill* the Dark Ones?"

Yahel nodded. "Yes. Before they kill us."

SIX

QUESTIONS

Nuke sat on the sofa outside his resting pod waiting for the others to come out for the morning. He had taken all his supplements but one and was now chewing on it; he was glad for the option to actually munch on something rather than just swallow it. He wasn't sure how, but the supplement had a type of peanut butter taste and chewy texture. The taste and texture were actually quite satisfying. What surprised him, though, was he never felt hungry during the day. Whatever these supplements contained really did meet whatever his body required.

Ti'sulh was the first to join him. She came over, sat beside him, and placed his hand in hers. "So, prophet of Erabon, what are your plans?" She gave a slight smile. "Ready to kill some Dark Ones?"

Nuke's smile vanished. "I can't believe Yahel even suggested that."

Ti'sulh shook her head. "Sorry. I shouldn't have said that. I know that's not what you want to do."

He patted her hand giving her a slight smile. "I know. But I can't believe he feels they have followed the prophecy Erabon left to them." He shook his head. "It doesn't fit at all with his prophecy."

Ti'sulh nodded. "Yes, going into stasis doesn't quite seem to fit with, *'Hesitation to unite through Erabon will make the hope of your soul go numb.'"*

Nuke sighed. "They're focusing on hesitation to act rather than hesitation to unite." He turned to her. "And have they even read his other words to them? If so, how could the idea of killing the Dark Ones even enter their thoughts?"

Ti'sulh cocked her head slightly. "They have reached desperation. Because the Dark Ones have tried to kill them, retaliation is somewhat logical, even if not appropriate."

Nuke tilted his head back and forth. "I suppose. We have to figure out how to reach the Dark Ones."

Ti'sulh's eyes widened. "Is that possible?"

Nuke shrugged. "We have to at least try."

"Any ideas?"

"Well, yes. But I don't think you're going to like it."

Ti'sulh's eyebrows shot up, but before she could say anything, Michael walked up with Z'zlzck just a step or two behind him.

Nuke laughed. "You two now in sync with each other?"

Michael patted Z'zlzck's shoulder. "I guess great minds just think alike." He turned to Nuke with eyebrows raised. "So, what happened to yours?"

Nuke laughed. "Well, since I was up before either of you, I guess that makes mine even greater."

Michael smirked. "Or just off."

Z'zlzck raised his hands. "Let's cut it off there before I get pulled in to referee."

Michael patted Z'zlzck's shoulder again. "See, Bob, I told you you'd be a good diplomat." He turned back to Nuke with a smile. "So, oh Great One, what's today's plan?"

Ti'sulh interjected. "He was just about to tell me how to get the Dark Ones back on our side."

Michael's eyes widened. "I'm all ears."

Z'zlzck nodded. "Me too. What's your plan?"

Nuke looked at each of them in turn and finally said, "I need to get captured."

All three gave him a blank stare, their mouths slightly open.

Michael slowly shook his head. "I take back my compliment. That has to be the stupidest idea you have ever had."

Nuke sighed. "Just hear me out. I'm not going to be a part of killing off these Dark Ones."

Michael shook his head, his index finger twirling, pointing at each of them. "We're not asking you to, but . . . getting captured? You have no idea what they would do with you."

Nuke sat up straighter. "Well, I'm open to other ideas. Got any?"

Michael sighed. "Well, no. Not yet, anyway."

Ti'sulh held up her hands. "Let's try and find out more information before we do something rash. We've heard from Yahel, but not from the others. I for one would like to hear Jaeyre's side. She and Yahel seemed to be in heated discussions. What's her story?"

Nuke raised his eyebrows and tilted his head slightly. "Makes sense."

Michael nodded. "Yeah, it's time for a heart-to-heart talk with all of them."

Ti'sulh gestured toward the hallway with her head. "Well, here's our chance."

Nuke turned and saw Halayal approaching. He also heard the other pod doors opening. In fairly quick succession, Bicca and E'oa stepped into the main room.

"Good morning," Halayal said with a smile. "I understand Yahel gave you a lot of information to digest yesterday."

Nuke nodded. "Yes, he did. But I think we need to have a discussion with all of you."

Her eyes widened. "Oh? In what regard?"

"I'm not sure we have the whole story. We would like to get the perspective of all of you."

Her smile vanished. "Why? Yahel's answers are not satisfactory?"

"Maybe too satisfactory," Nuke said. "There are two sides to a story. I'm not sure we have heard the full story."

Halayal sighed. "OK. Follow me to the other side of the facility. There is a conference room where we can talk and still monitor the stasis pods."

The others had been listening. Their facial expressions revealed they too remained confused. E'oa spoke up. "Halayal, may I ask you a question?"

She looked at him and nodded. "Of course."

"What are you truly afraid of?"

She cocked her head. *"Afraid of?"* She shook her head. "I don't know what you mean."

"I think you do," E'oa said. "You and your companions have been talking around the truth ever since we arrived. Yahel has told us part of it, but clearly his explanation is not the whole story."

Nuke's eyes widened. E'oa had not been part of their earlier conversation, but it was clear he was perceiving things the same as Nuke had yesterday.

E'oa continued. "Don't think partial truth is actual truth. A lie can be defined many ways. Partial truth can as easily be defined as a partial lie. Both are usually meant to either deceive or manipulate. Is that what you are trying to do?"

Halayal's face was one of shock. Nuke knew that, if possible, she would have gone pale, but since she was already nearly of that coloration, her frozen demeanor was enough of a telltale sign.

"Please understand," she said. "Our mission is to protect our fellow citizens. We must be sure before we . . . tell all, so to speak."

Nuke nodded. "Yes, we understand that. But we also know, as well as you, that you are running out of time. Your hesitation, and lack of trust, may be your downfall and ultimate ruin. You think you are fulfilling Erabon's prophecy to you, but I fear you are doing just the opposite."

Halayal's posture stiffened as her head jerked back slightly. "What? What are you saying?"

"You said your elders told you failure to act would be your downfall, but Erabon's words were actually about failure to *unite*."

"But we have united," she said emphatically. "All in stasis are in one accord—with Erabon."

Nuke shook his head. "But you haven't achieved the unification of *all* Qerachians."

Her eyes widened. "All? You mean . . . "

Nuke nodded. "Yes. The Dark Ones."

She took a step back. "You're not serious. Impossible!"

E'oa spoke up. "The words of Erabon always sound simplistic, but they are never easy to fulfill in their original intent."

"But how do you know this was meant for all Qerachians and not just the ones who are faithful to him?"

"Because," Ti'sulh began in a quiet, compassionate voice, "we have read all the words of Erabon. That is why we have come. That is why Nuke, the prophet of Erabon, is here. So you can know all the words of Erabon given to all the clans. Only when you have all the words of Erabon can you fully understand his intent."

Bicca nodded. "Yes, it seems we have all distorted his words to us when we focus only on the words given to us as individual clans."

Halayal put her hands to her cheeks. "But how can we know this? The temple is sealed."

Nuke reached out and took Halayal's hand. "You have to trust us."

The lights went out again—and emergency lights came on.

Halayal's eyes widened. She looked visibly shaken. "Come. We must help the others." She took a few steps and then turned. "Follow me." She shook her head. "The others won't like this, but I don't think we have a choice at this point."

Nuke looked at the others and then back to her. "What do you mean?"

"It's easier to show you." Then she repeated herself, this time with more desperation in her voice: "Come."

SEVEN

HIDDEN AGENDA

Nuke and his friends followed Halayal down multiple hall-ways and through several portals. Soon they were running through the stasis pods, trying to keep up with her. As he hurried through the room, Nuke glanced at the pods as he moved quickly by them. The Qerachians were immersed in a type of liquid. Some appeared to be moving around, but he assumed that was due to muscle stimulation to keep them from atrophying. He couldn't tell about their eye color as their eyes were closed, yet he did see several distinct colors of hair strands. The bottom two-thirds of the tubular pods were translucent, making seeing any details difficult.

Once they reached the other side of the room, they met up with the other five. Nuke could see the shock on their faces.

Jaeyre was the first to speak what was likely on all minds. "What are *they* doing here?"

Halayal held up her hands, patting the air. "It's all right. I asked them to come."

Jaeyre cocked her head, but Halayal replied, "We can use their help."

Jaeyre paused, then gave a hard nod. "Fine." She looked at Nuke. "Each one of you travel with one of us."

Yahel grabbed Nuke's arm. "Come with me."

Nuke ran with Yahel to the far side of the room. He looked back and saw his friends pair off with one of the Qerachians; they all headed in different directions. Nuke turned back to Yahel. "What are we doing, actually?"

Yahel glanced back. "The Dark Ones have infiltrated our security. We think at least one of them is in the building."

Nuke's eyes widened. "And you want to . . . what? Capture them?"

Yahel nodded. "Yes. We need to know what they know so we can better prepare ourselves." He shook his head. "I'm afraid we no longer know what we're up against with them."

"What do you mean?"

Yahel stopped running and turned to look in all directions. He then pointed down another hallway. "This way."

"Why this way?"

Yahel didn't respond. He just turned to run once more. Nuke kept following, unsure of what they were supposed to accomplish. As they passed another corridor, Nuke saw the foot of someone who had headed down an opposing corridor.

Nuke stopped abruptly. "Yahel! Yahel! This way."

Yahel stopped and turned. "What?"

Nuke motioned. "I saw someone down here."

Now Nuke led and Yahel followed. Nuke turned the corner in the direction he had seen the person run. As he turned another corner, he stopped and pointed at someone entering a ventilation shaft farther down the hall. He looked at Yahel, who nodded. They both ran to where they saw the person climb up and into the shaft.

"Give me a hand," Nuke said as he gestured with his hands what he wanted Yahel to do.

Yahel put his hands together. Nuke stepped into them and Yahel lifted Nuke so he could grab the edges of the open ceiling. Once Nuke had pulled himself up, he turned to reach down and pull up Yahel, but the Qerachian was no longer there.

Nuke stuck his head down and looked both ways. He said in a loud whisper, "Yahel? Yahel? Where are you?"

No reply. He shook his head, turned, and crawled down the ventilation shaft looking for—he presumed—a Dark One who evidently had gone this way. Yet the farther he went, the more confused he felt. *Where did Yahel go?* Did he already know where this Dark One had gone? If he did, why didn't he communicate that? Something didn't feel right.

The shaft was almost completely dark. After several minutes, Nuke came to a cross-sectioning of the shaft. One way looked dark, the other had some light, so he went that way. Evidently a panel had been opened. When he arrived, he stuck his head down, but didn't see anyone. He slowly lowered himself from the opening and then dropped to the floor. As he looked around he realized he was standing inside someone's living quarters. There was emergency lighting next to the door to indicate its location. He could vaguely see some type of sofa, but the rest of the room lay in dark shadow. He went to the door but found it locked. He thought that odd. Why would someone come to an unoccupied locked room? *Or is it not unoccupied?*

Hearing a slight noise, Nuke quickly turned and faced the darker corner of the room. "Is anyone there?"

Light suddenly illuminated the dark corner and revealed a young man sitting on a bed. Nuke jumped because of the sudden light as well as the sheer surprise of seeing someone. Hearing another noise behind him, he looked back, but a bright light blinded him; still, he could tell the source came from the opening in the ceiling.

"Hello."

Nuke turned back to this young man who looked grown—and yet quite young. His hair was noticeably short and extremely white. As Nuke got close to him, his appearance at first reminded him of a younger version of Yahel. His eyes seemed to be clear crystal, like those of Yahel; his long lock of hair had the same look. Yet this man's eyes also looked different from any he had seen on anyone here. Nuke saw various colors within the man's irises, almost like a prism: purple, blue, red, and gold. They were quite beautiful and mesmerizing, and the more he stared into the man's eyes, the brighter the colors seemed to appear.

Nuke stood in awe. "Who . . . who are *you*?"

The man shook his head. "No. The question is, who are you? What do you see?"

"Your eyes. I've never seen anyone's eyes like yours."

"How so?"

"They appear to be like a prism giving off colors of purple, blue, red, gold."

The man smiled. "It's nice to meet you, prophet of Erabon."

"And . . . you are?" Nuke knew this man was kept in a locked room, even though, supposedly, everyone rested in stasis except for the six he had already met. Nuke shook his head. *More secrets.*

The man with the light dropped to the floor and walked over. Nuke saw the face of the one with the colored eyes morph into golden-colored eyes when he looked at the second man.

"What's going on here?" Nuke demanded.

The man on the bed looked back at Nuke. His eyes were multicolored again. "What did you see?"

"Your eyes. They went from multicolored to golden-colored."

The man on the bed looked back at the other man and smiled. "You are not too far from the path."

The man chuckled. "Yeah, well, we'll see about that." He lowered the light he held.

Nuke gasped and took a step backward. The man's eyes were pitch black as well as his hair. "I demand to know what's going on here." Nuke pointed. "You're . . . you're a Dark One." He also realized this man looked much older than any he had seen so far.

The man's chuckle turned into a laugh. "You're astute." He looked back at the man on the bed. "Are you sure he's the prophet of Erabon?" He shook his head. "He seems pretty confused for someone who is supposed to save us all."

Nuke squinted his eyes and was beginning to ask another question when the door opened. There was Yahel. He looked from one of them to the other. A smile came across Yahel's face. "Good. I see everyone has met."

Nuke's jaw went slack. *Did he plan this? Why?* "Yahel, what's going on here?" He pointed his finger between the two men in the room. "And explain these people."

Yahel looked behind him and then back to Nuke. "We don't have a lot of time. The others may be here any minute. You just have to go with me on this."

Nuke shook his head. "Not until I know what's going on."

Yahel walked closer. He gestured to the man on the bed. "This is Elyahel—"

"What?" Nuke was dumbfounded. His head started to spin. "You mean the one . . . "

50

Yahel nodded. "Yes. Sorry about what I said, but I needed your other companions to think as I stated so as to not blow my cover story."

Nuke shook his head repeatedly. "Yahel, you're not making any sense."

Yahel pointed to the other man. "And this is Hael."

The man gave Nuke a nod. Nuke nodded slightly in return and turned back to Yahel. "But why is he here?"

"I have come to take Elyahel and the prophet of Erabon to my people," Hael said.

Nuke's eyes widened. He spun back toward Yahel. "You set up my kidnapping?"

Yahel nodded. "I'm sorry, but it's the only way I know to save everyone." He pointed at Nuke. "You said we should not abandon the Dark Ones. I agree. The others do not."

Hael interjected. "Our numbers are few. As you can see, I still doubt, but if the two of you . . . " He looked from Nuke to Elyahel. " . . . can save my people, it's worth the gamble." He shook his head. "I warn you, though. My people will not be easily convinced."

Yahel put his hand on Nuke's shoulder. "Please, go with them." He looked back at the door. "We're running out of time. If they get the power back on, you all will be trapped here."

Nuke looked from one of them to the other trying to weigh his options. He didn't feel right about simply letting the Dark Ones die out. Plus, who knew how long that would be? This war between the two could go on and the Dark Ones, even though small in number, could eventually kill the power to the stasis pods. It seemed his best bet was to go with the two men.

He looked back into Yahel's eyes. "Tell everyone I'm OK."

Yahel nodded, and a smile crept across his face. "Thank you." He then put an ear communicator in Nuke's hand. "Use this to contact me, but remember, any communication attempt can be detected, so be sure your news is something critical. Otherwise, this mission will not be successful."

Nuke nodded. "I understand." Yet his heart ached to know how distressed Ti'sulh would be. The others would be concerned, but she would worry the most.

Yahel led them down the hall to one of the outer walls.

Hael put some type of tracker on both he and Elyahel. "This emits a signal for the transferrance device to lock onto."

Yahel then had them don heavy fur parkas. Hael pressed something on his wrist, and the next thing Nuke knew, Yahel and the facility blurred and he felt weightless.

EIGHT

THE DARK ONES

When Nuke materialized, two other Dark Ones were there. He couldn't see their hair due to the fur parkas, but their eyes were completely black. He had an eerie feeling seeing them—it seemed almost like greeting demons. Yet when he looked at Elyahel's face, his eyes morphed from crimson to purple as he greeted them.

Both he and Elyahel followed the others on a type of personal sled that reminded Nuke of the Segway vehicles still used by some on Earth. This device, however, traveled over snow and ice. Nuke had no idea where they were headed, but he traveled next to Elyahel's sled while following the Dark Ones.

The sky looked clear, devoid of clouds, with hardly any wind present. Nuke had to admit the planet looked beautiful in all white against the blue sky. He decided it best to try and carry on a conversation with Elyahel. The sleds were moving at a decent pace, and yet they didn't make much noise across the soft snow and ice, allowing conversation to take place.

Nuke wanted to explore more. Something didn't seem quite right with Yahel's story about this man.

"Elyahel, is the story about you trying to enter the temple, but then freezing, really true?"

He nodded. "When they finally pulled me out, I must have looked dead. I was told my heart rate was extremely faint. My body took quite some time to recover."

That would explain the myth of him being frozen to death, Nuke reasoned, but he still had more questions. "But you still look so young. If what Yahel said was true, that occurred around three hundred cycles ago."

Elyahel nodded. "Just about."

"But you look younger than those younger than you."

"I lived with Shael only a brief time before I was sent back to the community. The nutritional supplements really decrease the aging process." Elyahel shrugged. "Because of my special ability, I guess, they started giving them to me before they do others." He leaned close to Nuke. "The supplements inhibit procreation, so most take them only after they have a family."

Nuke's eyes went wide. Halayal had not said anything about this!

Elyahel smiled and patted Nuke's shoulder. "Don't worry. The ones Halayal gives you do not have that property."

Nuke nodded but felt a huge internal sense of relief. A thought then came to him. "Is that why they expected the Dark Ones to die out, because they were expected to not procreate?"

Elyahel nodded. "It was unknown at the time this effect would wear off when supplements were stopped." He tilted his head. "Or for some, anyway—depending upon how long they had taken them."

Well that answers one of my nagging questions, Nuke thought, but he still had another. Nuke glanced between

Elyahel and the path. "Why weren't you put into stasis with the others?"

Elyahel laughed. "Insurance policy, I guess."

Nuke scrunched his brow and shook his head.

"People see themselves as they will be before they physically change. Halalyal, Yahel, Jaeyre, Howeh, Zaveh, and Elnah meet with me each morning to be sure they are not becoming Dark Ones," Elyahel said. "Their allegiance starts to change before they physically change."

"And if they do?"

"It's easier to keep them from turning if they haven't fully turned. Once a Dark One, they can change back, but it's difficult. Once a Dark One mates with another Dark One, their offspring only see themselves as a Dark One." He shook his head. "I've never seen one revert back at that point. To my knowledge, they are lost." He shrugged. "Yahel doesn't think so. He thinks the right impetus will make them revert."

Nuke saw Hael pull off to the side next to a giant snow drift and stop. The others did the same. Nuke and Elyahel came up behind them.

"What are we doing?"

Hael looked at Nuke. "We are about halfway. We will stop, rest, and let the sleds recharge with the sun."

Hael passed out what looked like some type of jerky. Nuke wanted to ask what it was but thought better of doing so. He didn't want to appear ungrateful, yet he didn't feel hungry. The supplements he had taken that morning left him still feeling full.

Nuke went over and sat next to Elyahel to find out more information. The three Dark Ones sat together and talked in whispers, so Nuke couldn't overhear them.

Elyahel took a bite of his jerky and motioned for Nuke to do the same. "I know you're not hungry now, but when the supplements wear off, you'll be twice as hungry." He tilted his head slightly. "Another motivation to keep using the supplements."

Nuke thought the jerky had hardly any flavor, but he found chewing something actually quite satisfying. After a few bites, Nuke reengaged Elyahel in conversation. "So, is Hael in favor of reverting back?"

"He's likely in favor of his folks not dying out."

Nuke cocked his head. "What do you mean?"

"Living out here is harsh. There are no supplements to inhibit the aging process. While I'm still alive, Shael has been dead for many, many cycles. Most of those living out here were likely born out here, so the number with any allegiance back to the community is few. Looking into my eyes will likely work only on those who remember the community. Those born out here will likely need more persuasion if that is even possible." He gestured to Nuke. "I think Yahel assumed you would be able to supply that."

Nuke's eyes widened. "What? I'm supposed to supply what? Some type of miracle for them to believe?"

Elyahel cocked his head. "Something like that, I suppose."

Nuke shook his head. He wasn't sure if coming out here would prove to be a good idea after all.

Hael came over. "We continue onward."

Both Elyahel and Nuke stood, got back on their sleds, and followed behind the group once more. The rest of the journey went more quietly. Nuke had run through his major questions, so he spent time thinking about what kind of miracle would help these people believe in Erabon and his return. He found himself with nothing.

After another half hour or so, Hael again stopped his sled. They entered a large indentation in the side of one of the mountains and stored their vehicles. Behind this was another entrance. Nuke followed the rest of them in and found an exceptionally large opening containing various sized abodes. Tents, and other structures looking reminiscent of igloos on Earth, were scattered randomly except for a few groupings. Nuke assumed these to be living quarters for the people. Their living out here looked much more primitive than what those in the main mountain community experienced.

The other two men went their way while Hael led Nuke and Elyahel around various tents toward the middle of the sea of dwellings. Hael held back the opening flap of perhaps the largest tent and gestured for them to enter.

Nuke stopped short once he stepped inside. It was certainly less primitive than he had anticipated. Hael motioned for them to sit. Nuke sat on a chair which looked remarkably similar to the one he had used that very morning.

Likely seeing the surprised look in his eyes, Hael replied, "We have replicators which can make almost anything we need—except for food."

Nuke nodded but was unsure what to say. He thought it somewhat cruel. The Qerachian elders were evidently willing to allow them to die comfortably. Yet he also realized this type of civil war was not about showing good graces to each other.

"So what are your plans for us?" Nuke asked.

Hael sat across from them and shrugged. "That is up to you."

Nuke started to question this. "What do you me—"

Another man entered, and he was obviously angry. "What have you done?" He gestured toward Elyahel. "And why have you brought back that relic, and . . . " Now he gestured toward

Nuke. "And what is *that*?" The man stared him up and down with a look of repulsion and yet curiosity.

Nuke stiffened. He had never been referred to as a thing before. *How degrading.* He didn't like this man already.

Hael gave a slight smile. "This is the prophet of Erabon."

The man gave a huff and shook his head. "You are a fool." He gave Hael a stern look. "If you weren't my father, I'd have you given to the arnoclids as an appetizer."

Nuke had no idea what an arnoclid was, but he didn't imagine it was anything good.

"Jayahel, please."

Jayahel folded his arms and looked at his father sternly. He gestured toward Nuke and Elyahel. "No one believes in this anymore. All those with regrets have reverted long ago." He pointed to Hael. "Maybe you and your two sympathizers want to go back, but no one else does."

Hael stood, his voice now stern. "I do not want to go back. I want to save our people. I thought you did too."

Jayahel glanced at Nuke and Elyahel again and then back to Hael. "And how do you plan to do that?" He shook his head. "You were in their facility and you brought back two useless . . . people rather than shutting their place down and letting us all enter." He pointed his index finger into Hael's chest. "That would be how you save our people."

Hael stood straighter, his tone still stern. "Respect your elders."

Jayahel matched his tone. "Then provide your wisdom rather than this foolishness."

"I want to save us all, not just a few."

Jayahel smirked. "So why bring these two here?"

"Elyahel shows our potential. The prophet of Erabon brings us hope."

"How?"

"He will fulfill the prophecy of Erabon."

Jayahel laughed with derision. "That's your plan?" He turned, putting his hand to his head. He turned back with anger on his face. "You and your myths. Now who's the child?"

Hael's voice got quiet. "Jayahel, you used to believe."

Jayahel's tone became even more acidic. "Yes, when I was a child. But I grew up. Why didn't you?" He turned to leave.

"Jayahel . . . "

Jayahel turned with a jerk. "Fine. Then this . . . this *prophet* of Erabon can fight Zael."

Hael's eyes widened. "But Jayahel . . . "

Jayahel held up his hands. "If he is the true prophet of Erabon, then he should have no issues."

Hael stood quietly and said nothing more.

Jayahel turned to Nuke. "Prophet of Erabon . . . "

"Nuke."

Jayahel stopped, stunned. "What?"

"My name is Nuke."

"Nuke, prophet of Erabon, you will face Zael tomorrow morning. Rest until then." He turned and stormed from the tent.

Nuke turned to Hael. "What was that all about?"

"Tomorrow, you fight Zael."

"Why? To fulfill some type of prophecy?"

Hael nodded.

"What prophecy?"

"The one who spills the blood of the prophet of Erabon will kneel before him."

Nuke's eyes widened. "What?" He shook his head. *What type of prophecy is that?* Nuke sat and put his head in his hands. Things never seemed to get easier.

NINE

FIGHTING ZAEL

Nuke woke, shivering. He wasn't used to sleeping in a giant igloo. He had been given thermal blankets, but they had fallen off him somehow in the middle of the night. Just as he tugged them back over himself, he saw Hael entering his area.

"Here's some nutrition before your event today," the Qerachian said.

Nuke sat up and groaned. "No need to sugarcoat it. You mean my blood being spilled?"

Hael grimaced as he handed Nuke something that looked like the jerky he had eaten the day before. "I didn't want to phrase it like that," the Qerachian said.

Nuke sighed and took a bite. The jerky tasted just as bland as before. "How big is this Zael, anyway?" he mumbled through his chewing.

Hael was quiet for a few moments. "The largest Qerachian in the compound."

Nuke sighed. He had been afraid that would be the case. He put his head in his hands and shook his head.

Within a few minutes, Jayahel walked in. "We are ready."

Nuke stood, put the remaining jerky in his mouth, and took a deep breath. The event was earlier than he had expected, but waiting wouldn't make him any more ready. "So, how am I to do this?" he asked, looking at both Hael and Jayahel.

Jayahel turned. "Follow me."

Jayahel led him outside. A huge semicircle of people had formed. One large Qerachian stood in the center. He had discarded his parka and stood wearing a sleeveless vest. Nuke removed his parka and continued to follow Jayahel. Thankfully, no wind blew, and the sun was shining. The air felt brisk but tolerable.

Nuke noticed Zael remained stoic and offered no introduction or greeting. As Nuke scanned the faces of everyone in the crowd, it became obvious no one wanted him here. He now was doubting whether coming had been a wise idea. Despite those thoughts, it was too late to back out now. He said a quick, inaudible prayer asking for wisdom.

Nuke then noticed Zael standing next to two pickaxe-type instruments stuck in the snow. Jayahel pointed to them. "These are your only weapons other than your wit and strength."

Nuke stared at the implements and then looked at Jayahel. "How long do you fight?" He was wincing on the inside, afraid of the answer, but needed to ask anyway.

Jayahel replied, "You fight until you can fight no more."

Nuke swallowed hard. Things were definitely stacked against him. Zael, immensely muscular and taller than he, didn't seem to have an ounce of fat on him. He was simply big. Nuke had no idea how to come out of this successfully—or even alive.

Jayahel looked at the crowd and spoke loudly. "Hael has led Elyahel back to us along with . . . " He gestured to Nuke. "This—supposedly—prophet of Erabon."

The crowd laughed. Someone in the crowd yelled, "At least the first part of the prophecy will come true." The crowd laughed even more, and louder.

Zael picked up a pickaxe and hefted the implement to his shoulder in one swift movement. "OK, prophet of Erabon. Let's get to it."

Nuke picked up the second pickaxe. It felt heavier than he anticipated. He tried to act as if it wasn't.

This didn't fool Zael, and a smile spread across his face. "Having trouble there, prophet?"

"Nuke."

Zael got a blank expression on his face.

"Nuke. My name is Nuke."

The smile returned to Zael's face. "OK. Prophet Nuke. You ready?"

Nuke wanted to scream "No!" but simply nodded instead. It just seemed odd. In a time of such technology, here were two men standing with archaic weapons trying to kill each other. All because of what? Because he wanted to help them. None of this made sense, and that made the whole duel surreal.

That surrealism lasted only moments as Zael swung his pickaxe over his head and brought it down toward Nuke in one swift motion. Now everything was very real. Nuke held up his pickaxe with both hands to block the blow. While this was successful, the force of the swing knocked him to the ground. Zael chuckled along with several in the crowd.

Zael didn't hesitate long but came around again with his swing. Nuke's eyes widened. He ducked between Zael's legs just as the blow came down where he had been. Nuke used his pickaxe to knock Zael's feet out from under him, causing the large Qerachian to fall forward and hit his head on the axe-head part of the pickaxe. When he stood, a clear liquid dripped from his forehead. Nuke assumed that to be the color of his blood. *No wonder these Qerachians look so white,* Nuke thought. *Their blood is colorless.*

Zael approached, now patting his palm with the pickaxe head. His look of anger had turned into a murderous gaze. Nuke swallowed hard. A wicked grin came across Zael's face as he lifted the pickaxe as a golfer on Earth would prepare to swing a club. Nuke knew he was to be the ball. He jumped back and blocked the huge swing at the same time. He heard a tremendous crack. One of the pickaxe heads went flying. The other lay in the snow not far from him. The blow had broken both pickaxe handles.

Zael had swung so hard he lost his balance when the two pickaxes collided, and he dropped to one knee. Without thinking, Nuke jumped on Zael's back and wrapped his arms around his neck. He hoped to make Zael go unconscious before he could do anything. Zael stood to his feet quickly, though, and swung Nuke back and forth as he twisted his body. Zael managed to pry Nuke's arm from around his neck, peel him off, and fling him to a landing spot several meters away in the snow. Nuke's arm hit the head of one side of the pickaxe causing a deep gash in his upper shoulder. He cried out in pain. A red stain remained in the snow as he stood, and blood now trickled down his arm. The crowd gasped. Nuke could feel his skin start to prickle.

Zael picked up the pickaxe handle and came toward him. Nuke thought Zael looked as large as the rhicerotide and as fierce as the authocantryx he had fought on Sharab. *Rhicerotide. Authocantryx.* A thought came to Nuke. He just had to find a way to execute it. Blood dripped off his arm making red spots in the snow. Nuke tried to block the pain from his mind.

As Zael approached, he picked up the other pickaxe handle which had fallen out of Nuke's hand when he was cut. Zael swung both handles wildly. Nuke jumped back from one swing, which came near his abdomen. Zael continued his swing with his other hand, and this scraped across Nuke's hand. Nuke went to his knee from the excruciating pain that made him go weak.

Zael now stood over him, both arms up and wide. Before Zael could come down on him with the two pickaxe handles, Nuke made a decisive plunge: he jumped on Zael's torso and locked his legs around his abdomen. Zael, shocked, dropped the pickaxe handles and tried to pull Nuke off him. Nuke could feel his skin prickle even more. What he had done to the authocantryx on Sharab he now wanted to do to Zael. Nuke put each palm on Zael's temples. Zael screamed. He tried to pull Nuke's hands away, but Nuke's skin prickled even more as he felt his heart rate skyrocket. He knew he had to make this work or die—and Nuke was determined to make this work.

Zael's screaming grew louder and louder; it was as though his strength was being sapped from him. He kept turning and screaming. Nuke pressed as hard as he could and squeezed with his legs to keep from losing his grip on Zael. After a few minutes Zael stopped turning. He fell to his knees. Nuke let go with his legs but kept his hands on the Qerachian's temples. When Nuke saw Zael's black eyes roll into his skull, he let go. Zael slumped but remained kneeling. Nuke's blood-stained handprint remained on the side of Zael's face. Nuke looked around and saw red blood strewn across the white snow.

Nuke stood breathing hard. He slowly turned looking at the crowd and then saw Jayahel approach. Several members of the crowd were now kneeling. When Jayahel touched his arm, he flinched.

Jayahel let go immediately, but then gently put his hand back. "OK. OK. You're fine now," he said quietly to Nuke.

Nuke slowly looked at him. He found it hard to believe the ordeal was over, that he had survived.

Jayahel led him back to the large tent in the middle of the complex. A doctor entered and used some sort of medical device to heal his wounds; this reminded him of what the medic on Eremia had used. In a short time all the blood had been cleaned and the wounds closed with hardly a scar.

Once the doctor left, Nuke went to his designated igloo, collapsed on his cot, and fell asleep in a matter of minutes.

TEN

TURNING THE TIDE

"Nuke, Nuke."

The voice sounded distant. Nuke felt his body being shaken. As he began to come awake, he tried to focus on who was speaking to him and shaking him awake. He squinted. "Elyahel?"

"You must come. It's a miracle. A miracle, I tell you. Praise be to Erabon."

Nuke slowly sat up, rubbing the back of his neck. The reason for him being so tired and sore came back to him. *Zael*. He had survived. That was miracle enough for him. He looked at Elyahel, who seemed to be almost dancing.

"What are you saying? What miracle are you talking about?" Nuke asked.

"It's Zael. Yahel was right after all." Elyahel lifted his arms and looked upward. "Praise Erabon. May his miracles continue."

Nuke still had no clue what Elyahel was talking about.

The Qerachian's attention turned back to Nuke. "Come." He motioned for Nuke to follow him. "Come see. Come see the miracle Erabon brought through you."

Nuke stood but remained confused. "Miracle through me?" He shook his head. "I don't understand."

Elyahel smiled. "You will." He motioned again. "Just come see."

Nuke cocked his head slightly with raised eyebrows. "OK. Lead the way."

Elyahel walked more quickly as he weaved his way around various tents. It dawned on Nuke that although they were within the mountain, he could still see well. He looked up and saw large anti-gravity orb lights. They apparently were synchronized to the amount of light outside the mountain. He assumed the time of day to be early morning. He turned a corner and came to an abrupt stop as Jayahel stood at the entrance to a tent.

Jayahel nodded. "You have given us something to consider."

Nuke gave him a curious look but followed Elyahel into the tent. Once he entered, his eyes widened and his jaw dropped. The man looked the same size as the one he had fought, but he now looked totally different. His eyes and hair were no longer black. His hair was now a bright white and his eyes were a brilliant blue to match the longer lock of his hair.

Nuke glanced at Elyahel. "Is this . . . "

Elyahel nodded with a wide grin on his face.

"How? How did this happen?"

Elyahel gestured toward the man. "Zael was touched by Erabon and is now restored."

Zael genuflected. "Nuke, prophet of Erabon, I ask your forgiveness."

Nuke waved his hands. "No, no, no. Please stand. Please stand." *Is this really him?* He turned to Elyahel. "Is this really the same man I fought?"

Elyahel nodded enthusiastically.

Nuke turned back to Zael. "Tell me what happened."

Zael gestured for Nuke to sit, so he sat in a chair opposite from him.

Zael gave a slight shake of his head. "When Jayahel told me you had arrived and wanted me to fight you, I was delighted to do so. I didn't want you here and I wanted to send you back. Dead or alive. It didn't matter to me."

"Why? What made you hate me so much?"

"You represented those who had abandoned us and the myths they had created."

Nuke thought that curious as the story Halayal told was that Zael's ancestors had abandoned her beliefs.

"So, what changed that perspective?"

Zael gave a slight chuckle. "Our fight did not go as planned. When you placed your hands on my temples, the pain became excruciating, but my mind had a conversation with itself, if you will."

Nuke cocked his head. He didn't understand.

Zael shook his head. "It's hard to explain, but it was like a voice told me my thinking was wrong. My distrust was not with the White Hairs, but with Erabon himself."

This was the first time Nuke had heard that term. Their term was more specific than Halayal's term for Zael's people. White Hairs described a physical characteristic. Dark Ones seemed to convey an inward characteristic and not just the physical.

Zael nodded toward Elyahel. "When he came to see me, I saw Erabon's potential for me in his eyes. At that moment, I knew I wanted Erabon's favor. I wept and felt the coldness in my heart melt. Sometime later, I noticed the change in my hair. When I looked at myself in a mirror, I then saw the change in my eyes. The change in my outward appearance matched the change Erabon had done within me."

Nuke nodded but was unsure if he fully understood. He put his hand to his chin. "And you were born a Dark One?"

Zael nodded.

"Had you never looked into Elyahel's eyes before?"

Zael nodded again. "But I only saw myself as a Dark One."

Nuke looked back at Elyahel, whose face now beamed, and he gave a quick nod. Elyahel evidently knew what he was thinking. Nuke gestured toward him. "But you said . . . "

Elyahel nodded. "I know. I know." He grinned. "Sometimes it's nice to be wrong. Apparently, no one is lost forever. All can return." He threw his hands up. "Praise Erabon."

Nuke turned his attention back to Zael. "Why only you? I know Hael has doubts, but he hasn't turned."

Zael shrugged. "I don't know. All I know is Erabon changed me from the inside out."

Nuke looked back at Elyahel. "So what happens now?"

Elyahel shrugged. "It's up to Jayahel. I think he is meeting with others even as we speak."

Nuke nodded. Based on all this, it would seem there was hope in reuniting everyone. But he had no idea how close he was to achieving that goal. Would others respond as did Zael, or would they be resistant?

At that moment, Hael entered. "Come with me. All three of you."

They followed him out. "What's happening?" Nuke asked.

Hael kept walking but replied, "Jayahel has called a meeting for everyone to attend." He stopped and turned to them.

"Get prepared for questions." His eyes went to each of them. "All three of you will be asked to give an account, I'm sure."

Nuke's eyes widened. "You mean they still have doubts?"

"They have questions. Almost all were at the fight, but not all."

"And that makes a difference?"

"For skeptics, it always makes a difference."

Nuke shook his head and sighed. Why was each step so difficult? He glanced at the others and continued following Hael.

ELEVEN

TESTIMONY

Nuke had a déjà vu moment as he saw the crowd which had gathered outside. This time, though, he didn't see any weapons in the snow and Zael was standing with him, not opposing him. He noticed the looks on the faces of those in the crowd also looked different. He experienced hate before. Now the faces in the crowd carried both anticipation and confusion with most whispering to each other and receiving nods and shrugs in return.

Jayahel spoke first. "Everyone, you've heard what has happened to Zael. I will let him speak first to give his perspective as to what happened." He gestured for Zael to step forward.

Zael looked extremely uncomfortable standing before everyone. He was undoubtedly more a doer than a speaker. Still, he seemed to gain confidence as he began, and then went on. "My friends, I can't say I really know what happened, except I have been changed."

"How is that possible?" someone from the crowd shouted.

Zael shrugged. "I don't know. All I know is when this prophet of Erabon had my head in his grasp . . . " He pointed to Nuke. "Erabon spoke to me. Then, later, when I looked into the eyes of Elyahel, I saw how I could be. I yielded to the pull of Erabon and I now stand before you changed."

Whispering spread through the crowd.

"Do you believe me?" Zael asked in a plea to the crowd.

Nuke saw a few within the crowd nod, several shook their heads, and others whispered between each other.

Zael pointed to someone in the crowd. "Prahel, you have known me all my life. Surely you believe me."

Prahel took a step forward. "I thought I did." He shook his head. "But I'm not sure I do anymore. This . . . " He swept his hand up and down toward Zael. "This is not the Zael I know."

"But that's the point, Prahel." Zael looked over the crowd. "I think this is the point Erabon is making to us. He is offering us the ability to change—to come back to him."

"Are you now a prophet of Erabon too?" someone yelled. There was some laughter from the crowd.

Zael shook his head. "No. No, I am not claiming that at all. I am simply someone who responded to the touch of Erabon. If he is willing to do this for me, who is no one important, he is willing to do the same for you." His gaze fell back on Prahel.

Prahel stared back. "And why should we believe you?"

"He's brainwashed," someone else yelled.

The man next to him nodded. "This prophet of Erabon has brainwashed him."

Zael held up his hands. "No, no. I had just as much hate for him as you do now. This is just as surprising to me as it is to you." He shook his head. "I don't know why Erabon chose me as the first to come back to him. I think it's to show you don't have to be special; you just have to be willing."

Prahel held out his arms with a shrug. "Willing to do what, Zael? Willing to concede the White Hairs are correct? That they are not responsible for banishing our ancestors? Why . . . why would we go back to them?"

Zael shook his head. "It's not that way, Prahel. Yes, the White Hairs were likely responsible for the banishment of our ancestors. That was wrong. Yes, a crime, but not unforgiveable. While the White Hairs may have abandoned us, we were the ones who abandoned Erabon. We are the ones who have turned our back on him. He is now forgiving us and letting us come back to him. If he can forgive us, we can forgive the White Hairs."

"Never!" someone in the crowd yelled.

Nuke began to notice, though, that many in the crowd now did not seem to agree with this dissident. Zael's words seemed to have struck a chord with many. Maybe Zael had made the first crucial step.

Zael pointed to the man who just yelled. "And what would change your mind?"

"Have this prophet of Erabon enter the sealed temple! Make him achieve what Elyahel was unable to do," he said.

Many in the crowd began nodding, including a number who, seconds ago, Nuke thought had been reached by Zael's words.

"I agree," another Qerachian yelled. "We will return if the temple can be opened."

Zael sighed. "Your hearts are as cold as the sealed temple itself. As if me standing before you today is not enough of a miracle for you."

The man yelled out again. "We deserve a miracle! If you want us to follow, then we deserve a miracle we can believe in."

Zael shook his head.

Elyahel stepped forward. "If a miracle is what you desire, then a miracle you will receive. We will return to the White Hairs and Nuke, the prophet of Erabon, will enter the temple."

Nuke felt nauseous. He knew he likely looked suddenly visibly pale. What was Elyahel doing? Why would he say such a thing without his consent? Yet Nuke couldn't say no to this. Not considering everything Zael had told the people. Yet he somehow had to get out of this. Freezing to death was not on his to-do list.

Hael stepped forward and raised his hands. "That is enough for now. We will consider all that has been spoken today and get back with you on our next steps."

The crowd slowly dispersed with many still talking and discussing what they had heard. Many kept glancing back at Zael. His change was so radical, Nuke couldn't believe this would not somehow impact them. His transformation was not something that could happen on its own. They had to know that. Nuke reasoned their resistance was just obstinance. They would rather ask for another miracle, thinking it could not happen, than change.

Nuke saw Elyahel talking with Zael and walked over to join them. "Elyahel, why did you say such a thing?"

Elyahel looked at Nuke as if he didn't understand the question. "Why wouldn't I?"

Nuke's head jerked back. "Why *wouldn't* you? Well, for one, you never asked me. Second, you said it at a time I could not refuse. And third, you may have just sentenced me to my death."

Elyahel stared at Nuke and then said, "Do you believe yourself to be the prophet of Erabon?"

Nuke nodded.

Elyahel shrugged. "Then you have nothing to fear. The prophet of Erabon is the who can enter the temple. My fate was doomed because I was not the prophet of Erabon. Since you are . . . " He gave a broad grin. "You will be successful. Everyone will see and believe." He nodded. "It's a good plan, no?"

Nuke shook his head. "No."

Elyahel scrunched his brow.

"Look, Elyahel, this plan of yours, while it makes sense to you, was done without my consent. I need to feel comfortable with it before you make such a claim."

Elyahel patted Nuke's shoulder. "Oh, I see. Just talk to Erabon. You'll see. This is what he wants you to do."

Nuke gave Elyahel a stern look but said nothing more.

Zael smiled. "I believe in you, Nuke. Erabon has convinced me you are his prophet. Now it's time to convince the others." He pointed at Nuke. "For *you* to convince the others."

Nuke sighed. "Let's go see what Hael and the rest of the elders have to say."

TWELVE

ZEL AND YEL

By the time Nuke reached the tent of meeting for the elders, all were present. Nuke stopped short once he entered; he hadn't expected everyone to already be on site. Jayahel motioned for them to sit. He sat next to Hael while Elyahel and Zael sat next to him.

Jayahel gave them a slight nod and began addressing the elders. "Well, we have a decision to make. We can either send Zael back to the White Hairs . . . "

Zael's eyes widened as he glanced at Nuke. Clearly, this was not an option he had considered.

" . . . or we can all go back to the White Hairs and ask for Nuke to enter their temple."

Elyahel raised his hand about halfway. Jayahel looked at him with eyebrows raised.

"Correction," Elyahel said. "*Our* temple."

Jayahel furrowed his brow.

"You said 'their temple,' but it's our temple. It is for all Qerachians."

Jayahel frowned but nodded. "Yes, of course." He turned back to the elders. "What is your council?"

One of the elders began to speak. "I have the same sentiment as many about what the White Hairs did to our ancestors. Yet . . . " He looked at Zael. "I have known Zael his whole life—always devoted to our cause." He shook his head. "I don't know what caused him to change his appearance—and his heart—but he would never willingly deceive us." He looked back at Jayahel. "I vote we go back to the White Hairs and get this . . . "—he paused and pointed to Nuke—"prophet of Erabon to enter the temple."

Jayahel looked at Nuke. "Are you willing to enter the temple? It must appear that we are not forcing you to do so. You must enter willingly."

All eyes turned to Nuke. He swallowed hard. He never expected he would have to make this decision so soon without further thought about the request. After saying a quick prayer in his mind, he nodded. "Yes, I will enter voluntarily."

Jayahel nodded. "OK." He looked back at the other elders. "Does anyone oppose?"

Most shook their heads. Only one other elder spoke up. "I don't like it, but I'll go along with it. But I think we should leave half of us here—just in case."

"No!" Elyahel's tone was emphatic. "To be effective, all must personally witness the miracle." He gestured toward the doorway. "You just witnessed the unbelief in those who did not personally witness Zael's change." He pointed to Zael. "Even though the evidence of the change is in his visible appearance, it did not persuade them." He pounded his right fist into his left palm. "We must have everyone there to witness this."

Jayahel rubbed his mouth and chin. He nodded slowly. "Yes, Elyahel, while I don't want to agree with you, you have a point. Yes, we should all be present."

Jayahel looked back at the elder. He simply cocked his head with a shrug. "Very well."

Jayahel slapped his legs and rose from his chair. "OK. Settled then. We leave day after tomorrow." He turned to Zael. "Can you get the arnoclids ready? We will likely need them, and I don't know anyone with more control over them than you."

Zael nodded. "Of course. I'll be sure they are ready."

Nuke looked from Zael to Jayahel. Did he hear that right? While he didn't know what an arnoclid was and had never seen one, based on the previous discussion between Hael and Jayahel, it sounded as if they were wild creatures. Did they tame them?

Once everyone dispersed and was outside the tent, Nuke caught up with Zael. "Tell me about these arnoclids."

Zael smiled. "Want to see them?"

"*Them?*"

Zael nodded. "I have two of them. I've raised them since they were only a few weeks old. Their mother was killed, and they were all alone. They are friendly to me, but not necessarily to others."

"So why take them on this trip?"

"If we take everyone, we will need supplies. They can help pull them."

Nuke cocked his head. "Pull them?"

Zael nodded. "We have a giant sled which we can load, and they pull. We can take more that way than loading the arno-

clids down. Plus, they function better pulling than carrying."
He motioned for Nuke to follow. "Come on. I'll show you."

Zael led him around tents to the outside of the mountain. Once outside, they traveled another ten minutes to a giant corral-type structure. Zael gave a whistle. Two large animals exited from inside a large snow dune located in the corner of the corral. Nuke's first instinct was to step back. In one way they were beautiful, but they were also quite intimidating at the same time. They were solid white except for their long tails, eyes, and two long, slender extensions, like long tentacles, protruding from the bottom of their ears—all of these were golden in color. The extensions, and their tails, seemed to move constantly. The creatures were probably about twice as long as they were tall. Nuke couldn't get over the enormity of their presence.

"Zael, they're beautiful. But intimidating."

Zael nodded. "Aren't they, though? I've always admired them."

As they got closer, Nuke realized they were almost twice his height. They reminded him a little of the authocantryx on Sharab as they moved in a sleek, lithe way like a giant cat, but the way their eyes focused on him sent shivers down his back. *Great. They could probably devour me in one bite.*

Zael climbed the corral railing as the first one came close. The creature stopped and looked at Zael like he didn't recognize him.

Zael laughed. "It's OK, Zel. It's me. I just look a little different." He held out his hand toward the creature.

The creature sniffed a couple of times and then came closer. Zael wrapped his arms around its neck as far as he could, buried his face in its fur, and shook his head back and forth. The creature nuzzled him in return. The two of them had a noticeable closeness.

The other creature came up and Zael did the same to it as well. Zael turned and motioned for Nuke to come up beside him. Nuke swallowed hard. He thought this risky as he could be gone in no time if one decided to turn on him. With Zael present, though, he hoped that wouldn't happen.

"Now don't act scared," was all Zael said.

Nuke gave a short laugh. "Easier said than done."

"Just concentrate on their beauty," Zael said.

"I admit they are beautiful. But I bet they're just as deadly."

"Oh, Zel and Yel are usually pretty docile with me."

Nuke's eyes widened. "Usually?"

He tilted his head back and forth a few times. "They can be a little . . . agitated . . . sometimes." Zael laughed while seeing Nuke's hesitancy. "Oh, it'll be fine. Come on."

Nuke climbed up next to Zael and put his hand where Zael petted Zel. "Oh my. The fur is so soft and thick. It feels wonderful."

Zael grinned. "Want to ride Zel?"

Nuke raised his eyebrows. *Ride? Are you serious?* He wasn't sure if he wanted to take that risk. "Will they even allow it?"

"Well . . . " Zael shrugged. "It depends if they like you or not. So far, they seem to." Zael gestured. "See if Zel will nuzzle up to you. Wrap your arms around his neck and rub your face in his fur. See what he does."

Nuke got on the other side of Zael and ran his hand over the creature's fur. The animal at first took a step back.

Zael patted the creature's neck. "Easy . . . there. Easy there." He turned to Nuke. "Hold your hand out so Zel can get your scent."

Nuke looked at Zael with eyes wide. "He could just as easily take it off."

Zael chuckled. "Oh, Zel won't do that. Will you, boy?" He patted the creature's neck again. "No, I know you won't."

Nuke swallowed hard and did as Zael asked. Zel sniffed, took a step closer, and rubbed against Nuke's hand. Nuke patted the creature's neck. Zel took another step forward. Nuke wrapped his arms around the animal's neck, buried his face in the fur, and then raked his face back and forth through its thick, soft fur. Nuke found the feeling amazing. The softness reminded him a little of the pentalagus, the rabbit-like creature on Ramah. Zel responded by nestling into Nuke. Finally, a creature he didn't have to fight, and one that reciprocated good feelings.

Nuke felt the skin of his hands start to prickle. He looked up. Zel's long protrusions under his ears were rubbing against his hands. This was a different kind of prickle, though. It somehow felt soothing.

He heard Zael laugh. "Well, I'll be," the large Qerachian said.

"What?"

"He has never done that with anyone else." He patted Nuke on his shoulder. "I think you've made a good friend."

"What does he normally do?"

"They tolerate me holding onto them to guide their direction, but this is more like he is bonding with you."

"Are they electrically charged?"

Zael nodded. "That is one way they defend themselves— and why many feel they are too dangerous." He shrugged. "If I had not gotten these before they were older, they would never allow us to be around them."

Nuke again rubbed his face into Zel's fur. He climbed higher on the fence. Zel bowed somewhat to allow Nuke to get on its back. Nuke climbed up and found a solid perch.

He heard Zael laugh again.

"What's so funny this time?"

"Watch this." Zael wrapped his arms around Yel and then flung himself up and over the creature's neck to land on its back.

Nuke grinned. "Very impressive. I guess not everyone would have the strength to do that."

Zael chuckled. "No, and no one—and I mean no one—has ever gotten on an arnoclid the way you just did."

Nuke's eyebrows went up. "Really? Doing so seemed pretty instinctive. I mean, I was wondering how to get on the creature's back and wished the animal would bow down to allow me on. And it did."

"I guess you've made a bigger connection with Zel than I thought. Now he's sensing your thoughts—or at least your moods."

Nuke thought about this. There was some type of connection with the creature, but he wasn't sure that meant the animal was reading his thoughts. "No, I think it's just intuitively sensitive to my needs."

Zael shrugged. "Whatever you're doing, it's definitely working. See if you can make Zel walk around the corral."

Nuke patted the creature's neck. Zel's head tentacles went up his coat sleeves and wrapped around his arms. He could feel his skin prickle, but again, the feeling was soothing. Zel turned and walked around the corral. When he got back to Zael, the Qerachian's mouth was hanging open.

"Nuke, I have never seen anything like that before. No arnoclid has ever bonded with anyone like Zel has with you."

Nuke grinned. "At least someone likes me."

Zael threw his head back and laughed. "It has no axe to grind with you."

Nuke grimaced. "Bad pun, Zael. Bad pun."

"I rather like it myself," Zael said with a satisfied look.

Nuke laughed. "So now what?"

Zael shrugged. "Well, I think it's very clear who rides Zel back to the White Hairs' community."

Zael dismounted Yel in nearly the reverse order he had mounted the beast. Zel again bowed slightly, allowing Nuke to step back onto the corral railing. Zael just shook his head while chuckling. They each petted the creature in front of them and then headed back to where the others were preparing for the trip.

THIRTEEN

CLASH OF THE ARMOCLIDS

he next morning Nuke helped the others get everything loaded onto the giant sled and assisted Zael with hooking up the arnoclids. No one else seemed willing to help with that chore. Everyone seemed completely afraid of the large beasts. Nuke saw many wide-eyed people staring at him as Zel acted quite docile with him. Their mouths fell open when they saw Zel bow slightly to allow Nuke to step on its leg to climb on its back. The ultra-muscular Zael did his usual swing-up technique to get atop Yel.

Once they all started moving, Nuke saw several of the children run and climb onto the big sled the arnoclids were pulling. Occasionally the sled jostled as it went over an ice bump and one of the kids would fall off. At first Nuke was concerned, but the kids just dug their way out of the snow, laughed, and ran to jump back on the moving sled. Everyone else traveled on foot, so the pace was a good bit slower than Nuke had expected.

Nuke rode Zel and Zael was on the back of Yel. Thus, Nuke had only Zael to talk with. "Zael, why is everyone on foot and not on the sleds?"

"This big sled sets the pace. Since we must move more slowly than the smaller sleds, so does everyone else," Zael said. "The other sleds are stored on this one in case they are needed. We will have to camp overnight before we get to the White Hairs' mountain."

Nuke nodded. He didn't really mind except he longed to see his companions again—especially Ti'sulh. He considered the fact that both he and Zael were on the arnoclids and away from the others a good thing for now since the two of them were the centerpiece controversy of this whole adventure. Nuke found that to be true when they made camp for the night as well. No one came near he and Zael except Elyahel and Hael.

While there was nothing to make a fire out of, Hael brought a small pyramid-type device which soon glowed red and produced heat for the four of them to sit around and warm up from the coldness. As he sat there with his newfound friends, Nuke looked at the sky, now filled with stars, which looked like diamonds against a black backdrop. Aphiah had just cleared the horizon and slowly climbed into view. While only the size of a baseball, the planet did provide effective visibility as the light reflected against the white snow. He stared at the small ball in the sky for several minutes; he had never seen anything like it. Aphiah's glow wasn't steady but continually waxed and waned in brilliance. While mesmerizing, he had no idea what caused the effect.

Hael brought each of them more of the jerky Nuke had eaten several times before. He wasn't sure if this was all they ate, or if it was just convenient for the trip. He didn't ask; he didn't want to insult or sound ungrateful.

"Hael, why does everyone shun us?"

Hael didn't answer right away but chewed on his jerky for several seconds. "Well, for several reasons, I think. Many are skeptical, some are downright against you, and some are curious but fear those who are against you." He shrugged. "Don't take their actions too personally. You on the arnoclid has almost everyone more curious and willing to think you are quite different." He laughed. "Especially when they would never even try to approach one."

Elyahel nodded. "While all of that is true, I know many of those against you are trying to convince everyone you have sway over Zael."

Zael scoffed. "Those who really know me know that's not very likely."

Hael nodded. "I think it's more about them not wanting to believe than it is about them knowing you and your tendencies."

Zael sighed and shook his head.

Nuke felt sorry for his new friend. Not believing and mistrusting an outsider was one thing, but they had known and lived with Zael his entire life. One would think they would trust him more. He reached over and patted Zael on the back of his shoulder. Zael nodded and gave a small smile.

All four of them slept in the same tent that night. Zael woke Nuke early to get the arnoclids ready so they would not be the ones to hold up getting underway. Zel nestled into his chest as Nuke reached where he was standing. The animal's hot breath felt good on such a chilly morning but also caused steam vapor to surround Nuke like a cloud. He patted Zel's neck and rubbed his face into its thick, soft fur, which helped warm his face from the chilly morning air.

Not long after the caravan got underway, Nuke heard a reverberating roar in the distance. The large noise bounced off the mountains making the echo sound even more ominous. Nuke looked at Zael with eyes wide. "What was that?"

Zael had a worried look. "That, my friend, is a wild arno-clid. It sounds agitated."

In the far distance, Nuke saw several figures scrambling quickly up the mountain face. He heard the unsettling roar again. Zel and Yel began to get antsy and started snorting and pawing the snow.

Both Nuke and Zael patted the necks of the arnoclids. Nuke tried to give assurance to Zel. "Easy there, big fella. Easy there." He rubbed his arm across a tentacle. That seemed to supply some comfort.

Zael hopped down from Yel.

"What are you doing?"

"I'm unhooking our arnoclids. It's not wise to have them harnessed to the sled if they're agitated." He shrugged. "Who knows what they will do? I don't want all our goods strewn all over the side of the mountain."

Jayahel and some of his companions came and took the smaller sleds off the larger sled.

Zael helped them. "What do you plan to do, Jayahel?"

"We should go and help those fleeing from the wild arnoclid."

"Who are they?" Nuke pointed toward the distance. "I saw them flee up the side of that far mountain."

Jayahel shook his head. "I'm not sure, but they may be from the White Hairs' camp."

Nuke's eyes widened. "I thought you didn't care about the White Hairs."

Jayahel paused and looked up at Nuke. "Well, if we're going to go there and talk about making peace with them, it would look pretty bad if we didn't try to help them when they are in distress, wouldn't it?"

Nuke swallowed hard. "You mean they're from where I came?"

Jayahel nodded. "Those are the only White Hairs I know."

Nuke quickly turned back and looked at the far mountain. He heard the roar again. *What if Ti'sulh, Michael, and the others are in that group?* His heartbeat quickened and his palms got sweaty.

Zel rubbed its tentacle over Nuke's arm and seemed to become more agitated. He was undoubtedly feeding off Nuke's anxiety.

"Whoa there, prophet. Keep him calm," Jayahel said to Nuke.

Nuke looked at Jayahel with irritation. "Easier said than done."

The roar grew louder. Nuke could feel the sound start to reverberate within his chest. It reminded him of the rhicerotide roar on Sharab, but this roar was somehow more grating on his nerves. The finish to the roar had an irritating high-pitch squeal to it. Nuke looked up and saw the creature in the distance now heading up the side of the same mountain he had seen the others scramble up earlier. He couldn't help but think perhaps Ti'sulh was in trouble. Zel became more agitated and, without warning, took off toward the distant mountain with a gallop.

"Whoa, Zel! Whoa!" Nuke tried to make the beast stop, but his words had no effect. Zel wrapped its tentacles around

Nuke's arms and kept galloping. Nuke wasn't sure if the creature was trying to keep him steady or just feeding off his feelings.

Nuke looked back and saw many of the smaller sleds following, but the distance between him and them kept widening. He didn't see Yel coming, so he assumed Zael had somehow kept him there, which was probably a good thing.

Nuke turned to look back in the direction Zel was headed. The fast gallop caused his face to be heading directly into the wind. The fur parka helped keep his ears warm, but not his nose and the main part of his face. Nuke lowered his head to put his face in the fur of Zel's head, but he also tried to look forward to see where Zel was taking him. Although he knew an encounter of the two arnoclids was likely, he had no idea how it would turn out.

As Zel got closer to the mountain, the roar of the wild arnoclid got louder. Even before they arrived, the roar had become nearly deafening. Once they reached the base of the mountain, Zel didn't stop but continued up the mountain slope. Now being along it, and looking up its side, the mountain didn't appear as smooth as it did from a distance. There were footholds for Zel to land on, but the incline was steep and perilous. Nuke looked farther up the slope and saw the arnoclid standing on a small plateau with a number of Qerachians even farther up the same slope on a small outcropping. The arnoclid apparently couldn't go higher. Nuke assumed that was why the creature was so irritated.

When the creature heard Zel approach, the arnoclid turned and gave another ear-piercing roar. The animal's mouth opened so large Nuke felt the creature could likely swallow him whole. Zel returned the roar and the stance, his large teeth now glaring at the other creature. The other arnoclid now seemed to ignore the Qerachians on the ledge and instead focused on Zel. The arnoclid approached, but slowly, almost as if the creature was sizing up its tactics for how to attack. While both arnoclids looked almost identical, Nuke noticed this creature's tentacles and tail were a solid black rather than golden like Zel's.

Once the creature got close to Zel, Nuke heard a crackling sound. He turned quickly to see its source. Nuke's eyes grew wide. The end of Zel's tail had split into several smaller tentacles and sparks were emanating from them. These creatures were even more dangerous than their looks showed.

The plateau was just wide enough for the two arnoclids to pass each other, and this allowed Nuke to feel the hot breath of the other creature as Zel walked past it. Nuke looked to his left and swallowed hard. One misstep and they would be falling to their deaths—or, at least, his death. He didn't see how that could be avoided with the jagged rocks jutting through the snow below.

The two creatures seemed to be sizing one another up. Nothing happened between the two until they had almost walked past the other. Then, in a blink of an eye, Zel's electrified tail, in whiplike fashion, hit the other creature in its snout. Nuke heard a loud pop. The wild creature roared in anger. The noise, so incredibly loud, started two avalanches, but not near their location. Nuke breathed a sigh of relief but again remembered how precarious his position was. The creature turned to avoid another hit from Zel's tail; the animal then attacked. Zel whipped around in a split-second to face the creature, but its front paw slipped over the edge of the plateau causing Zel's right front side to go down quickly before Zel was able to recover. Nuke knew he would have fallen off if Zel's tentacles hadn't held him fast.

The other creature, seeking to take advantage of Zel's slip, pounced. The creature pushed Zel's face into the snow leaving Nuke's face now barely centimeters from the giant creature's teeth. Nuke leaned back, but his face was pelted with some of the creature's saliva as the animal roared once more. He would have covered his ears, but Zel held fast to his arms.

Before the creature could advance, Zel regained his footing and suddenly stood, forcing the other creature up. This exposed the underside of the wild arnoclid and Zel headbutted the creature's body into the face of the ledge and, at the same time, let go of Nuke's right arm with its tentacle and used it to grab the creature's neck and squeeze. The wild creature's black tentacle reached forward, grabbed Nuke's left leg, and lifted him off Zel. Nuke then felt Zel let go of his left arm and grab his right leg. Before he could react in any way, the creature wrapped its other black tentacle around one of Nuke's arms. Zel let go of the creature's neck to grab Nuke's other arm, now causing Nuke to be suspended in the air, terrifyingly, between the two arnoclids. He heard a scream from above. *Ti'sulh!* She was here.

The other creature began pulling on Nuke, stretching him. He yelled in pain. Zel took a step forward to ease the tension, but the creature took another step backward to maintain it. Nuke knew if either of these creatures made a misstep, he was a goner. He felt the current in the other creature escalate. Nuke's skin prickled as he tried to match the current. His heart rate was escalating as well as his anxiety. Both creatures reacted in kind and became more agitated and roared at each other. Nuke knew his only chance was to calm himself. But he had no idea how to do that.

While stretched and hung between these two creatures, Nuke closed his eyes and willed himself to focus. He prayed and focused on Erabon. *God.* If they were one and the same, then it didn't matter which. If he was indeed the prophet of Erabon, this was just another test. Erabon would see him through. His anxiety calmed. He felt his skin prickle even more, apparently reaching a point of being greater than the current of either creature. He willed calmness inside himself. The creatures responded in kind. Slowly, the tentacles around his legs were released. He was now suspended between the two creatures with arms outstretched. Both creatures slowly bowed . . .

He felt his feet touch the snow and then the creature's other black tentacle gently wrapped around his head, almost in a sort of comforting embrace. The creature gave another roar—though now more muffled and relatively quiet, almost as if giving a warm greeting.

The creature released him entirely, turned, and headed down the mountain.

Zel wrapped his other tentacle around Nuke's other arm and returned him to his back. Nuke looked at those above on the ledge. His attention was immediately drawn to Ti'sulh. She had a huge grin on her tear-stained face. He looked down. Several Dark Ones were scattered along the mountain. Many were kneeling on one knee with heads bowed.

FOURTEEN

BACK TO THE MOUNTAIN

Nuke sat on the back of Zel for several minutes trying to digest what had just happened. He put his head on the arnoclid's neck and buried his face in its soft fur. He patted its neck. "Thank you, my friend. Thank you." He rubbed the creature's long tentacles.

Zel gave off what seemed to be a grunt of contentment.

When Nuke looked up, there, nearby, was Ti'sulh. She was smiling. She appeared to want to come closer but looked terrified of the giant creature in front of her.

Nuke held out his hand. "Don't be frightened." He held onto one of Zel's tentacles and the creature knelt. "Just step onto its leg and I'll pull you up."

Ti'sulh approached warily. She took a cautious step up onto the creature, which grunted, but didn't do anything else. He saw Ti'sulh swallow hard, but when her gaze caught his, she climbed with more confidence. He took hold of her hand and pulled her up. She settled behind him.

Ti'sulh hugged his torso. "I missed you so much. That was so awesome . . . and so frightening."

Nuke nodded and chuckled. "You can say that again." He twisted his torso so he could look at her. "I've really missed you also." She kissed his cheek before he turned around; the kiss made him feel warm throughout.

When he turned, he saw Yahel standing where Ti'sulh had stood moments earlier. "Nuke, it looks as if you were successful." He took a step closer, but Zel stood and Yahel took a step back, eyes wide.

Nuke gave a slight chuckle. Because he had no special connection with Yahel, Zel apparently didn't sense a need to be hospitable.

Nuke gave a nod to Yahel. "Somewhat. At least they have all come. That's, hopefully, at least a good start." He shrugged. "Some still doubt."

Yahel grinned. "After what we all just witnessed, I'm sure that number will dwindle." He turned and gestured with a head motion. "I'm glad Jaeyre and Howeh were here to witness this."

Nuke looked in the direction Yahel had indicated. Both Jaeyre and Howeh were talking with Jayahel.

"They gave me a difficult time after you left," Yahel said. "I told them you would come through." He smiled broadly. "They will have to believe me now."

When he looked up again, Jayahel motioned for Nuke to lead the way back down the mountain. Instinctively, Zel stepped forward. Yahel stepped out of the way, as did everyone else. Zel made no noise, and did not get distracted, but simply headed back down the mountain. Many just stared at them. Some bowed their heads as they passed.

"Are the others back at the mountain?" Nuke turned to ask Ti'sulh.

Ti'sulh rubbed his shoulders and nodded. "Yes. They wanted to come, but Halayal was insistent they stay and help them out."

Nuke nodded. It made sense they would need help with only a few people to take care of everything. "But she let you come?"

Ti'sulh was quiet. Nuke gave a quick glance back. "You told her you were coming and wouldn't take no for an answer?"

She smiled and put her head against his right shoulder. "Something like that."

Nuke laughed. "I know how convincing you can be when you want to be."

"Who's that?" Ti'sulh was now pointing toward the base of the mountain.

Zael stood there waiting with Yel.

"That's Zael. A friend—now." He laughed. "I'll explain that sometime soon, I hope."

"How can he be a Dark One? The others have such . . . creepy eyes. He . . . Zael, did you say?"

Nuke nodded.

"Zael looks normal—like all those back at the mountain."

"He has quite the story to tell," Nuke said. "I'm sure he'll tell you once we get back with the others."

Zael smiled as Nuke and Zel approached. "I see you survived."

Nuke nodded and smiled back.

"And have recovered another in your short travels as well," Zael added.

Nuke's smile got bigger. "Yes. Zael, this is Ti'sulh, from—"

"Myeem," Zael said, interrupting. "Yes, I know our clans quite well." He gave a slight bow. "I have always found Myeemian women to be the most beautiful of all our clans." He gave a slight shrug. "After Qerachian women, of course."

Ti'sulh gave a slight bow with a muffled, "Thank you."

Nuke laughed. "You go from trying to beat me up to trying to butter me up."

Zael grinned. "Oh, I would never say anything against someone who just bested a wild arnoclid."

Nuke threw his head back and laughed. "Zael, you kill me. You really do."

"Or almost did," Zael said with a grin. "But now I'm glad I did not."

Nuke nodded as he kept laughing. "So am I, my friend. So am I."

The others were gathering around them now as most had arrived at the base of the mountain.

Jayahel approached. "Let's get your arnoclids hooked up again to the sleds. We should try to make more ground before the day is over."

"Sir," Zael said. "Now that we have some of the White Hairs with us, why don't you and the people head back with them on your faster sleds? You should all likely reach there just after nightfall." He looked at Nuke and then back to Jayahel. "Nuke and I can follow along with the larger sled and supplies and meet you there sometime tomorrow."

Jayahel looked at Yahel and Howeh. "Are you fine with that arrangement?"

Yahel nodded. "Yes. That way you can get your little ones out of the elements more quickly."

With minimal conversation, they all headed back to where the supplies had been left. A few of the men with the women had been left behind to keep watch over the supplies and children while the rest were gone. The chatter picked up considerably once they got back. Nuke wasn't sure what everyone said, but he noticed several people pointing toward him and talking rapidly. The others would nod, give him a quick glance, and sometimes the hands of the women would cover their mouths and they would shake their heads. Nuke found these actions a little disconcerting, but he tried to simply ignore them.

Jayahel raised his hands. "OK, everyone. Mount up quickly. We have a lot of ground to cover in a short amount of time."

Everyone mounted their snow sleds quickly, taking only a few basic supplies since the plan had been announced that Nuke and Zael would be coming behind with everything else. In only a matter of minutes, even before Zael and Nuke had the arnoclids once again hooked to the giant sleds, the group was out of sight.

Zael looked over at Nuke with raised eyebrows. "Was it something I said?"

Nuke shook his head. Ti'sulh giggled, and this made Zael seem quite pleased with himself.

Once back on their arnoclids, Zael, Nuke, and Ti'sulh followed the tracks of the others. The strides of the large arnoclids allowed them to cover ground quickly even though they got off to a slower start than the others.

Nuke had Ti'sulh sit in front of him. "If your nose gets cold, just put your face into Zel's fur," he said.

She nodded. "It is soft." She put her head into his neck fur. She sat up again. "And wonderfully warm. That would make a nice blanket."

Zel gave a grunting noise.

Zael laughed. "Careful what you say. Zel and Yel are extremely sensitive creatures."

Ti'sulh patted Zel's neck. "That's all right, Zel. I didn't mean it literally." She rubbed his fur again. "I just like your fur, that's all."

Zel gave another grunting noise; he sounded more satisfied this time. All three of them laughed.

"Since we have time, Zael, why don't you tell Ti'sulh how you went from a Dark One to a White Hair."

Zael scrunched his brow. "I prefer the term, enlightened Dark One." He shrugged. "White Hair has been such a derogatory term for so many years, it's hard to think of myself in that way."

Nuke nodded. Ti'sulh put her head back on Zel's neck but managed to turn to face Zael. "So, you were born a Dark One?"

Zael nodded. "Yes, I looked just like the others you saw today only a few days ago, before I met your friend here, Nuke, prophet of Erabon."

Ti'sulh raised her head to glance back at Nuke before turning back to Zael. "So, what happened?"

Zael explained, in great detail, all that occurred. At times Ti'sulh gasped at what Zael said. Often she would glance at Nuke. He would nod to signify Zael spoke the truth, and she would simply shake her head. Nuke knew a lot of Zael's story was hard to believe even though true.

As the sun set, they camped on the lee side of a large snow dune to avoid wind. Zael fed the arnoclids from some food stored on the sled.

Meanwhile, Ti'sulh set out to gather as many stones as she could find. "See if you can find some large ones," she said to Nuke.

Nuke turned up his brow. "What for? These aren't like the stones on Sharab that can burn by themselves."

Ti'sulh stood bracing her back with her hands from the load she had just laid down. "Just gather them, and I'll show you."

Nuke shrugged but did as she asked. Stones were hard to find since the snow covered everything. He found a few large ones and placed them next to the ones Ti'sulh had gathered.

Ti'sulh stacked the stones with larger ones on bottom and smaller ones on top to form a type of pyramid. She then opened her backpack, took out a jar, and poured an extremely viscous liquid over the stones. This coated them and then slowly dripped into the crevices. After a few minutes, she lit the liquid to create fire. The substance burned slowly but gave off intense heat.

When Zael came back, he smiled and sat next to them holding out his hands for warmth. "I haven't had one of these fires in a long time," he said.

Nuke nodded. "We have something similar to this where I come from, but it doesn't put out this much heat."

Ti'sulh gathered some of the snow, melted it in a pot Zael pulled from the sled, and then dumped in something from a pouch in her backpack. In a matter of minutes the aroma caused Nuke's stomach to growl.

"Ti'sulh, what is that? It smells delicious." His taste buds were quite ready for something besides the jerky he had eaten for many days now.

Ti'sulh shrugged. "I'm not exactly sure. It's some type of soup, I think."

"I thought Halayal said they only ate supplements."

Ti'sulh nodded. "That's what they prefer to use, but I did find these in one of their supply rooms. Coming out into the snow, I thought this might prove useful."

After a few minutes she gave each of them a cupful. Nuke blew on the hot liquid, to him looking like some type of vegetable soup, and sipped it. He could feel the warmth travel down to his stomach. The flavor was good—not the best he had ever eaten, but quite good considering his options. Plus, this had the benefit of warming him from the inside out. Satisfied sounds slowly escaped his lips.

"I agree," Zael said with a smile. "I'll sleep well after this."

After a few more stories were shared, the three climbed into their thermal sleeping bags and fell asleep. Nuke woke once during the night. The night air was still, beautiful. The fire, still burning, wasn't as bright, but it gave off a good deal of heat. He was grateful to Ti'sulh for bringing it.

The next morning Ti'sulh split the remainder of the soup. The fire, now essentially out, nonetheless kept the stones hot enough to warm the soup. Being warmed from the inside out again felt wonderful. As Nuke and Zael hooked up the arnoclids once more, Ti'sulh dumped snow on the hot stones. Steam rose briefly, but soon all was cold again.

Nuke looked up; there was hardly a cloud in the sky. While barren, the white-against-blue backdrop looked quite beautiful. He was thankful they would reach the base camp sometime today. He was tired of roughing it and wanted a few comforts again.

In the middle of the afternoon they saw the "home" mountain in the distance. Both Nuke and Zael tried to get Zel and Yel to travel just a little faster.

FIFTEEN

MORE DOUBT

As they approached the mountain where his group first arrived, Nuke wondered how they were supposed to get inside. Ti'sulh pointed out a large indentation at the base of one side. It was large enough to create a makeshift stall for the arnoclids.

As Zael fed them again, he said, "I'll come and check on them at least twice a day to be sure they are doing fine." He looked at Nuke. "Maybe you can help me exercise them occasionally."

"I'd like that," Nuke said. He appreciated the bond he and Zel had established. This creature was one of the few animals he had encountered that bonded to him so readily. He turned to Ti'sulh. "So, is there an entrance from here?"

"Something like that." She led them deeper into the cave-like opening.

Nuke's eyes got big. He knew he shouldn't be surprised by now. But he still found it odd these clans had such advanced technology but didn't apply it to every aspect of their lives. There, somewhat hidden in the rock of the mountain, stood a body displacement unit. Nuke shook his head. "If I didn't know what I was looking at, this device would almost blend completely into the rocks."

Ti'sulh nodded. "I think that was the point."

Nuke had Ti'sulh go first, then Zael, and he went last. When he rematerialized, he found himself not far from where he had encountered Elyahel the first time. They found their way back to the large area containing all the Qerachians in stasis.

Nuke realized Zael wasn't keeping up with them. He turned and saw him slowly turning, looking, in amazement. "Are you OK, Zael?"

As Zael did a three-sixty, he replied, "I had heard about this place, but never thought about what it would actually look like." He went to the nearest stasis pod and looked in. He glanced back at Nuke. "They look so peaceful." He shook his head. "Resting in peace while so many suffer." A tinge of anger could be heard in his voice. Nuke realized there was still a lot of mending to do.

They meandered through the sea of stasis pods toward the conference room on the far end. Nuke looked up. He could see several people engaged in animated discussion. Jayahel's arms were flying wildly. Nuke sighed. Things did not seem to be going well.

He saw Ti'sulh glance from the conference room to him. "In hindsight, maybe we should have arrived with them."

Nuke shook his head and sighed again. "I'm not sure that would have made a difference."

Ti'sulh raised her eyebrows. "What do you plan to do?"

"I don't really know," he said, giving a weak smile. "As usual, I'll wing it."

She wrapped her arms around his nearest arm. "I trust you and Erabon to find the right solution."

He patted her hands with his free hand but didn't say anything. He looked over at Zael, who had a pensive look. "Everything OK, Zael?"

Zael's gaze jerked Nuke's way as though he had been shaken out of deep thought. "What? Oh, yeah. I'm fine. I was just thinking."

Nuke's eyebrows raised. "About?"

Zael gave a slight shrug. "Oh, about our future. After what happened to me, I now know Erabon is real. Otherwise, I can't explain what happened to me." He glanced up at the conference room. "I was just wondering how to get them to understand that fact." His voice got low, almost like thinking out loud. "I think we're too buried in the past to see the possibilities of our future."

Nuke thought about that. *Is that the key?* Could he get them to put behind all the bad that had happened with their ancestors and blaze a new trail with the hope of Erabon's return?

Once they neared the conference room, Nuke could hear the muffled sounds of someone talking loudly. He couldn't make out what they said, but this person was clearly upset. As he opened the door, the cacophony of the argument slammed his eardrums.

" . . . I don't have to *do* anything. As far as I'm concerned, you are guests here—and uninvited at that." Halayal's voice, at first uncharacteristically high for what Nuke knew of her, trailed off as she stared at Zael. Her attention whipped back to Jayahel. "Did you exit someone from the stasis pods? How . . . how could you?"

Jayahel responded with what was clearly sarcasm. "Yes, we're taking over the place," he said dryly. "There's way more of us than of you, you know."

"Whoa. Whoa. Whoa!" Nuke held up his hands as he stepped into the room. "Let's take things down a notch, shall we?"

Both looked at him. If eyes were daggers, he would have been dead.

Nuke gestured for everyone to sit. "Why such animosity?" he asked as people found chairs. He saw Jayahel, Elyahel, Hael, and Yahel, but none of the others. "And where is everyone else?"

As he was sitting, Yahel said, "The others are on the lower tier. They're resting—quite comfortably. Jaeyre and Howeh are . . . seeing to their needs, along with Bicca, E'oa, and Z'zlzck."

Nuke saw Jayahel roll his eyes.

Yahel seemed to ignore this gesture and continued. "Zaveh and Elnah are keeping watch over the stasis pods. Michael is helping them."

Jayahel added, "And no, we did not open a stasis pod."

Nuke looked from Halayal to Jayahel. "What's with all the hostility?"

"Well, for one," Halayal said, exasperation in her voice, "you bring them *all* here . . . " She overemphasized the word *all*. " . . . without warning, and without us even being able to vet them as to their intentions." Her attention turned back to Zael and she pointed toward him. "And who is this?"

Jayahel's attention whipped her way. "I've explained our intentions. And *this* . . . " He pointed to Zael. "This is Zael, one of the members of our clan."

Halayal huffed. "And I'm just supposed to believe you?"

Nuke held up his hands again. "OK. OK, now. Let's just start from the beginning." He put his hand on Zael's shoulder. "Zael, here, is one of the reasons we are all back here."

Halayal turned up her brow and shook her head. "What?" She looked from Zael back to him. "What are you talking about? He's not a Dark One."

"But I am. Was," Zael said. He took a deep breath and briefly explained all that happened between him and Nuke and what happened to him afterward.

Halayal's eyes seemed to grow wider with each sentence. "How is that even possible? Those born Dark Ones cannot turn." She looked to Yahel as if for support.

Yahel gave a slight shrug. "That's what we thought. But Zael, here, has proved us wrong."

Halayal put her hand to her forehead. "This is too much to grasp." She glanced at Jayahel again. "So all of our assumptions were incorrect?"

"Apparently."

She shook her head. "This changes everything." She looked deep in thought. "So, why did only this one change?" Her attention turned back to Jayahel. "Why didn't others change?"

Jayahel shook his head. "I . . . don't know."

Zael leaned forward. "I think I can answer that." Everyone's attention snapped in his direction. "I think it's because I had an encounter with Erabon. I don't think it's enough to just see something astounding. One needs to encounter him. When Nuke had his hands on my temples, I truly believe I and Erabon were in communication."

Halayal's head jerked back. "What? You want Nuke to put his hands on everyone's temples?"

Zael shook his head. "No. I don't think it's a prescriptive thing. But my people have encountered two amazing events now, so I think they are ready for an Erabon encounter."

Halayal cocked her head. "And you expect them to do that, how?"

"By entering the temple, of course."

Halayal's eyes widened. "I . . . I don't have the authority to grant that."

Zael sighed. "Then who does?"

"The Council of Six."

"Well, convene them, then."

"Impossible." Halayal squirmed in her seat.

Zael sat back in his. "And why is that?"

"They're in stasis."

Zael looked at Jayahel with a slight nod, as if to prod him to jump into this discussion.

Jayahel gave a slight grimace and turned to Halayal. "So, my people aren't important enough to take your council out of stasis?"

Nuke closed his eyes, inhaled a breath, and breathed out slowly. He could see this escalating into another argument. He held up his hand. "OK. Before we start accusing anyone of anything, let's get all our facts on the table." He turned back to Halayal. "What's the downside to taking them out of stasis?"

She gave him an indignant look. "I can't put them back into stasis once they are taken out. And they gave us specific instructions they should only be woken once we know Erabon is returning."

Yahel jumped in. "But Halayal, we have the prophet of Erabon here. The prophecy states he comes before Erabon's return."

She looked from Yahel to Nuke and back; she appeared nervous. "I know, but do we . . . I mean . . . " She looked back to Yahel. "Do we really *know* he is?"

Yahel sighed. "Halayal, if you saw what I saw, you wouldn't have any doubt. Plus . . . " He pointed at Zael. "We have another miracle right in front of our eyes."

"But how do we really *know*?" Halayal asked again.

Jayahel puffed himself up. "What? You think we are lying? Everyone here but you feels this is the right step. You think we brainwashed everyone we've come in contact with?"

Yahel raised his arms and let them fall to his side. "Really, Halayal? How preposterous."

Her gaze shot to his. "Yahel, we have to be certain. The Council's words were quite clear."

"Well, I *am* certain."

Nuke raised his hands again and made a slowing motion. "OK, OK. Let's think this through. So we can't enter the temple without the Council's consent, and we can't wake the Council unless everyone is sure I'm the prophet of Erabon?"

Halayal nodded.

Nuke sighed. "Well, that's quite the dilemma, isn't it?"

Halayal nodded.

"There's only one way out of this."

"What's that?" Halayal's voice was now low, subdued.

Nuke looked directly into her eyes. "Faith."

SIXTEEN

OBTAINING FAITH

That evening Nuke met with his friends just outside their sleeping quarters. There were hugs and handshakes all around. After everyone settled into the seating area, all looked at him expectantly. He knew they wanted to know all that went on while he was away.

Nuke smiled. "I'm just so happy to be back with all of you."

Michael nodded. "Same here, buddy. Tell us everything that happened."

Nuke sat back, took a deep breath, said "Well . . . " and then went through everything that took place. There were a few interrupting questions through his talk, but most sat wide-eyed as Nuke laid things out. When he came to the end, all remained quiet for several seconds.

Nuke laughed. "That spellbinding, huh?"

Michael shook his head. "No, it's just that you lost me after you said 'Well.'" He cocked his head. "Mind repeating all of that?"

Nuke gave him a smirk and kicked Michael's foot off the leg it was resting on. Michael laughed. "No, it's quite the remarkable story."

Z'zlzck nodded. "I can't believe they still doubt."

Bicca agreed. "I saw the man you call Zael. Knowing he had been a Dark One . . . " He shrugged. "Seems pretty convincing to me."

E'oa shook his head. "I think it's easier to say you doubt than to admit you agree and have to change your opinions about things."

Ti'sulh chuckled. "That's what Nuke and I were discussing the other day."

Nuke nodded. "Change is hard for everyone."

"Yes," E'oa said. "We've all been there."

Everyone nodded.

Michael broke the silence. "So what now?"

Nuke tilted his head slightly with little expression. "Halayal wants us to sleep on it."

Michael chuckled and shook his head. "Yeah, that always works so well for me." He stood. "Well, I'm going to go for my thinking-it-through nap now. I doubt I get any sleep, but it's been a day."

Most of the others left for their rooms as well. Only Nuke and Ti'sulh were left in the main area. She gave a warm smile. "It really is great having you back so I don't have to worry." She held up her hand. "For a little while."

Nuke laughed. "Yeah, depending upon what they say tomorrow, you may have to start worrying about me freezing to death."

Ti'sulh grimaced. "You do feel confident about this, though?" She looked deeper into his eyes. "Don't you?"

"Well, about as confident as I can be, I guess. Not knowing how to react until I'm in the actual situation doesn't exactly instill calmness, but through everything that has happened, I'm more assured."

Ti'sulh patted his knee. "Well, I have confidence in you."

She stood and he followed. "Thanks. I'll see you in the morning."

She nodded and gave him a hug. He felt her tentacles caress the back of his neck, sending tingles down his spine and causing him to feel warm all over. He pulled out of the hug before the emotion of the embrace became too intense. "Good night, Ti'sulh."

She headed for her room, giving a glance back at him before she entered. Nuke stepped into his. Now he had two reasons not to be able to sleep.

Nuke woke the next morning after a somewhat fitful night. He dressed and went to the conference room for the scheduled meeting to decide whether to wake the Qerachian councilmembers in stasis. Most had already gathered. The antsy mannerisms displayed by all showed that putting off the decision until this morning really hadn't helped.

Halayal was the last to arrive. Around the table Nuke counted sixteen: the six of his group, the six of Halayal's group, and Jayahel, Hael, Zael, and Elyahel. Apparently the elders of the Dark Ones had given Jayahel the authority to act on their behalf. Nuke knew Jayahel had met with them the previous evening.

Halayal sat and placed her palms on the table. "I assume everyone has met with their respective people to discuss this matter."

There were nods around the room.

"I'll try and simplify this. First, who has reservations about awakening our councilmembers?"

Zaveh and Elnah raised their hands—as did Jayahel.

Nuke's eyebrows went up. He had not expected this from Jayahel.

Halayal nodded. "Can each of you explain your reasoning?"

Zaveh stood. His eyes, golden in color, didn't reveal anything emotionally. He seemed extraordinarily matter-of-fact regarding his rationale but with a touch of superiority in tone. "Until we have irrefutable proof, I don't think we should risk awakening them."

Zael raised his hand halfway. Halayal, however, nodded toward Zaveh. "And what do you consider irrefutable proof?"

Zaveh cocked his head. "I need to see some type of evidence myself."

Zael's eyes widened. "So you don't consider anyone else's report valid unless you witness an event firsthand?"

Zaveh's expression didn't change, making it difficult to gauge if he was emotionally charged or not. "No offense," he said to Zael, "but you are an outsider."

Zael quickly pointed to Yahel. "He is not, and he witnessed Nuke pacifying a wild arnoclid."

Zaveh glanced at Yahel and then back to Zael. "Yes, but he used to be a Dark One."

Zael's jaw dropped. "Are you even trying to be open-minded?"

Zaveh gave him a hard stare. "This decision is too important for simply giving one the benefit of the doubt."

Howeh gave Zaveh a surprised look. Having his eyes entirely white, including his irises, it was difficult to tell his emotion, but the tone of surprise in his voice came through clearly. "I witnessed that event as well."

Zaveh seemed to ignore Howeh's statement. He sat and remained stoic.

Howeh crossed his arms, giving Zaveh an irritated stare. Zael sat back and shook his head. He looked at Nuke and rolled his eyes. Nuke had to agree with Zael's sentiment.

Halayal then turned to Elnah. Nuke had to admit her bright blue eyes made her somewhat captivating to look at. He thought her face had a delicate nature to it, almost like a porcelain doll. "I feel our instructions from the Council were quite clear," Elnah said. "Under no circumstances were we to awaken them without knowing the certainty of Erabon's return."

E'oa looked at her. "And you are uncertain?"

She nodded.

"And how long would it be before Erabon is to return once his prophet truly returns?" E'oa asked.

Elnah looked at E'oa with a blank stare. After several seconds, she shook her head. "I can't answer that. The prophecy does not say."

"So you would rather wait until Erabon himself returns before you take them out of stasis?"

Elnah's eyes widened. "No, of course not. That . . . that would be ludicrous. The Council would never forgive us for such a thing."

"So what's the answer?" E'oa asked.

She shook her head. "I don't understand the question."

E'oa sighed. "If Nuke is the prophet of Erabon, how long would you wait until you awaken the Council?"

"Oh, immediately."

E'oa cocked his head. "So, you don't believe he is the prophet of Erabon?"

"Oh, I didn't say that."

"So . . . you do believe he is?"

"I didn't say that, either."

E'oa sighed. "Well, either he is or he isn't. Which one is it?"

"Well, I . . . I don't know."

"And what would convince you?"

"Him"—she pointed to Nuke—"entering the temple."

E'oa threw up his hands. "You think *not* making a decision *is* a decision?"

Elnah pressed her lips together but did not respond.

E'oa looked at Halayal and shook his head. "You can't answer a question with the same question trying to be answered."

Halayal didn't acknowledge this statement but now turned to Jayahel. "You raised your hand as well. What is your objection?"

Jayahel gave a small shrug and glanced at Nuke. "I'm speaking for all my people. Some believe Nuke is the prophet of Erabon and others do not. So it's a toss-up in my book. Whatever decision is made will make some people happy and others unhappy."

Elyahel leaned forward slightly. "Would those unhappy with raising the Council be happy if they could enter the temple?"

Jayahel gave a forced smile. "Of course."

Elyahel shook his head. "I hardly count this as a negative vote."

Jayahel shrugged. "Perhaps not, but I have to represent everyone."

Halayal's gaze slowly turned across the room. "Does anyone else have anything to add?"

Z'zlzck pushed back from his chair and stood. "There's a lot of distrust in this room. Actually, there was a lot of distrust on my planet as well when Nuke first arrived." He looked from one of them to another. "Let's take all we know in totality. He proved himself on Myeem, on Eremia, on Sharab, on Ramah, and has done incredible things on this planet already." He shook his head. "You reach a point in which evidence is meaningless. He could do fifty more things that fulfill Erabon's prophecy and we would still be sitting here in this same discussion. At a certain point, you have to pick faith over evidence." Z'zlzck looked down and then back at Halayal. "Use the evidence to bolster your faith, but faith always comes before reality. If you want Erabon to return, then you must allow Nuke to enter the temple." He paused.

Z'zlzck pointed toward Halayal and then looked at Zaveh and Elnah. "You think because you are not one of the Dark Ones you are safe, but your rejection will be considered just as wrong. How do you justify saving yourself and condemning other Qerachians? Is that what Erabon would want?"

Bicca nodded. "Yes, his whole purpose for returning is to unite us all. How can you justify uniting with the other clans if you can't even unite with your own?"

Nuke wasn't sure how Halayal would take all of this, but he was proud of his two friends from Sharab and Eremia. Both spoke truth.

Halayal kept her emotions in check. She looked at everyone and said, "Does anyone have anything else to add or recant?"

Jayahel nodded. "Yes. Despite what I said before, we should definitely go forward. I can't be the one to let my people be separated from Erabon if there is a chance of proving his existence."

"I agree." It was Elnah, and all eyes turned her way. "We need to know the answer. This is the only way."

Now everyone turned to Zaveh. He remained resolute for several seconds.

Howeh looked at him, tilting his head slightly, and said his name in a hushed tone. "Zaveh?"

Zaveh looked at Howeh and then back to Halayal and gave a slight shrug.

Halayal nodded. "Very well. I'm sensing a consensus to awaken the Council." She panned their faces again. "Is there any other objection?"

Silence.

She stood. "We will awaken Wehyahel this afternoon."

Everyone nodded.

"We will come get you all," Halayal said, "when we have prepared his stasis pod for awakening. It will take some time to prepare."

She stood, turned, and stepped from the room. Her colleagues quickly left behind her.

Ti'sulh looked at Nuke. "And so it begins."

Nuke nodded, wondering what Wehyahel would say.

SEVENTEEN

AWAKENING

Almost all of them stood around Wehyahel's stasis pod. Jayahel, Hael, Zael, and Elyahel stayed in the conference room. Halayal pressed a few buttons on the side of the pod causing the device to slowly turn and make Wehyahel stand erect. The pod appeared translucent except for its top part which allowed Wehyahel's face to be seen. He looked asleep and as though he had an immensely content look on his face. The translucency of the rest of the pod allowed a viewer to tell he wore no clothes, but other details were not visible. Nuke could see he had a purple lock of hair, so he knew what eye color to expect once Wehyahel awoke. But, Nuke knew, there was no way of knowing what this councilmember's attitude would be upon being awakened.

Once the pod stood erect, Halayal turned to the others. "Please face away from the pod so we can preserve his dignity until robed." They nodded and turned. From his vantage point, Nuke could see the pod's reflection from the nearest adjacent pod where the side had a mirrored panel. Yet his view was only of the top half of the pod. Yahel was the only one who remained facing the pod. He had some type of garment draped across his arm. After a few seconds of Yahel pressing other buttons on the side of the pod, the fluid began to drain.

Once drained, the top part of the pod tilted outward slightly; this allowed more room for Wehyahel to move. He first began coughing up all the fluid which had filled his lungs, a sound which was very much like he was throwing up, which, in a sense, he was. The sound was distressing, and Nuke noticed the grimace on everyone's faces. Next Nuke saw Wehyahel open his eyes. The brilliant purple color of his irises was mesmerizing. He nodded, and Yahel nodded back. No words were spoken.

Wehyahel reached up and pressed a button above him. The thick liquid dripped from his arms; it had a mucous texture but looked thinner than regular mucous. Water flowed down on Wehyahel and washed all the mucous-like residue from his body. Once that was done, the pod separated somewhat and warm air blew over his body. Nuke could feel some of the warm air that escaped between the pod sections and blew his way. In the reflection he could see Wehyahel's hair blown away from his face; its purple strands glistened reflecting the light. After a few minutes the air stopped and the walls of the pod retracted farther. Nuke could now see Wehyahel's torso and face. He looked fairly muscular and older than Yahel and his friends. After combing his hair, Yahel held out a robe for Wehyahel to don. Wehyahel did so; its fabric constricted and fitted to his build.

"You may now turn around," Yahel said to the others.

All turned. Wehyahel scanned their faces; he had a slightly surprised look. Then a slight smile came across his face. "I am happy to see you all." He first went to Halayal and greeted her with a forearm clasp and put his forehead to hers.

"Rejoice in his return," he said.

Halayal responded, "So shall we all."

Wehyahel did the same to each of the other Qerachians.

Wehyahel—one could tell he was still seeking to steady himself in his new state—looked at the others. "Having members of the other clans here makes me hopeful." He shook each person's hand.

He stopped when he came to Nuke. "You are not one of us."

Nuke shook his head. "No. I come from a distant region of the universe."

Wehyahel's eyes widened. "You are the prophet of Erabon?"

Nuke nodded.

Wehyahel turned to Halayal. "We are on the verge, then?"

Halayal gave a slight nod. "We believe so. But we also need your guidance."

He squinted but did not say more. His focus now turned to Michael. He cocked his head and looked quite puzzled.

Michael smiled as he shook Wehyahel's hand. "I'm the sidekick."

"Side . . . *kick*?" Wehyahel cocked his head in a bit of confusion and looked Nuke's way. "He is . . . with you?"

Nuke nodded.

Wehyahel turned back to Michael. "The prophet of Erabon needs help from another?"

Michael shook his head. "No, he needs no help from me."

"Even prophets need moral support," Nuke said with a small grin.

Wehyahel seemed in deep thought for a couple of seconds. "Ah, I see." He nodded. "Yes, that is important. I'm sure that helps you stay focused in your own reality." His smile turned into a grin. "I'm sure we are different from your world."

Nuke smiled back and nodded. *You have no idea,* he thought to himself.

Wehyahel turned to Halayal. "Am I the first you've awakened?"

She nodded. "Of course, Chancellor."

He turned and looked around. "But you've made no preparation for the other councilmembers?"

She shook her head. "No, we haven't—yet." She looked at the others. "We . . . need your advice first."

His eyebrows raised. His gaze went from Halayal to Nuke and back. "You have doubts?"

Halayal tilted her head slightly and sighed. "We have . . . issues."

He squinted. "Issues?"

"The Dark Ones."

He gave her a puzzled look. "What about them?"

"They're *here.*"

He took a small step backward, his eyes once again wide. "They're here?"

She nodded.

"Why?"

She looked at Nuke and then back to him. He did the same and back to her. He shook his head. "Please explain?"

"They seem to be able to change."

"*Change?*" He shook his head and looked back at Nuke as if he was the one who should explain.

Nuke shrugged. "One born a Dark One has become a White Hair."

Wehyahel's eyes grew wider still. "What? Impossible." His gaze now shot back to Halayal.

She nodded. "It seems to be true. Apparently, our assumptions were wrong. He touts that his encounter with this prophet of Erabon had him experience . . . Erabon. And this changed him."

Wehyahel looked to Nuke.

Nodding, Nuke replied, "It's true. When I first met him, he was indeed a Dark One. After our encounter, he became a White Hair."

"That is why we have wakened you," Halayal said. "Things have not gone per expectations. We want to be sure we are making the right decision before we wake the others."

"Where is this one?" He glanced between the two of them. "Is he the only one?"

Halayal nodded. "Yes, so far." She pointed to the conference room above them in the distance. "He and the leader of the Dark Ones are there."

Wehyahel looked up toward the room. "I must meet him."

Halayal headed in that direction and Wehyahel followed. The rest of them followed these two. Yahel walked behind Wehyahel, watching him carefully as if concerned for his stability after being in stasis for so long.

As the conference room door opened, those inside stood. Each introduced themselves. When he came to Elyahel, Wehyahel smiled. "Elyahel, you haven't changed a day."

Elyahel smiled and gave a slight bow. "Neither have you, Chancellor."

Wehyahel laughed. "We, each, for different reasons." He turned back to the others. "I wish to speak to each of you, but could I first speak to Zael alone?"

Jayahel looked at Zael and back. After a brief moment of staring at Wehyahel, he nodded. "Very well."

Wehyahel turned to Halayal. "Please make everyone comfortable in one of the adjoining conference rooms."

Halayal nodded and opened the door for all to exit. As Nuke headed out, he heard Wehyahel call to him. "Prophet of Erabon. Please stay."

Nuke turned. "If you wish." He went and sat next to Zael. Wehyahel sat across from them.

Wehyahel gestured toward Zael. "Please. Tell me your story."

Zael nodded. He gave a brief description of how he was born a Dark One, what he was taught all his life, how he grew to hate White Hairs, how he hated Nuke when he first arrived, his fight with Nuke, and how he encountered Erabon as the electricity from Nuke went into his temples. He told how the next morning his outward appearance had transformed, as had his inward thought processes. He looked at Nuke and smiled. "Now I consider him a friend."

Wehyahel nodded. "I see. That's quite a story. And why did this not happen before? Or since?"

Zael shrugged. "Watching an event and experiencing an event are two different things."

He paused a moment, then went on to tell of the wild arnoclid experience and how Nuke resolved it.

Wehyahel's eyes widened. "An arnoclid? Really?"

Nuke nodded.

Wehyahel cocked his head. "That's another remarkable story. So you're saying everyone was impressed, but not everyone was convinced?"

Zael nodded.

"And what do you think will convince them?"

"Nuke entering the temple."

He turned to Nuke. "You have agreed to this?"

Nuke nodded. "If doing so will help convince everyone, then I'm willing. Yet I feel everyone needs to experience entering the temple in order to have a change of heart."

"I agree with Nuke," Zael said. "Everyone has been taught the prophet of Erabon is the one who will open the temple. If they see Nuke do so, then they will believe. Only . . . " Zael stopped.

Wehyahel's eyebrows lifted. "Only . . . what?"

"My people are here and will experience it, but your people need to experience it also."

Nuke nodded. "This is more than just turning the Dark Ones. It's getting everyone to believe. I think we need to awaken everyone."

Wehyahel rubbed his chin. "Everyone? I had not considered that. There is no turning back once we do that."

Zael gave a slight shrug. "You either believe Nuke is the prophet of Erabon or not. There is no halfway."

Wehyahel got a faraway look in his eyes.

Nuke looked at Zael, who just shrugged but then decided to speak. "Chancellor."

Wehyahel turned toward Zael.

"It's a matter of faith," Zael said, looking into Wehyahel's eyes. "You're either in or out. We all stand in the balance, but you're the fulcrum." He glanced at Nuke. "The prophet of Erabon can fulfill his duty, but it's up to you to decide if it's for all or only a select few."

Wehyahel gave a slight nod. "Faith sounds simple. But it's never easy."

EIGHTEEN

REUNITING

Nuke looked up and saw Zael approach.

Zael gestured to the seating area. "Mind if I join you?"

Nuke nodded. "Sure. By all means."

Michael moved over on the sofa so that he sat across from Nuke and made room for Zael. "So, what's taking them so long?" Michael asked.

Zael shrugged.

Nuke knew all six councilmembers had been in this meeting for hours. "I can't imagine so much time is needed to make a simple decision."

Zael shook his head. "Not simple from their point of view."

Ti'sulh nodded. "I think you have upset their thought process, Zael, and they have to come to terms with it."

Z'zlzck chuckled. "Nuke, you seem to do that wherever you go as well."

Nuke smiled. Yet Z'zlzck's statement, meant to be humorous, rang truer than perhaps he meant it to be.

E'oa nodded. "But that's why Erabon sent him to us. We have to get past our preconceived ideas and get back to what Erabon intended for us from the beginning."

Bicca patted E'oa's shoulder. "I agree, E'oa. We all still have a lot to learn when it comes to what Erabon requires of us."

Z'zlzck nodded. "True. We are all Erabon's descendants, and it's time we treat all clans, even our own clan members, as such."

Nuke put his hand to his chin. Maybe these Qerachians were more prejudiced against the Dark Ones than he thought. He would have thought they would be happy that those who were considered unredeemable were restorable. "Zael, do you think the length of the meeting is because of the animosity between the two Qerachian factions?"

Zael gave a shrug. "Maybe. But I don't think it is animosity, per se."

Ti'sulh leaned forward. "What do you mean?"

Zael tilted his head slightly. "Well, I think the animosity existed when White Hairs became Dark Ones. But when most of those died out and only their descendants remained, their feelings turned more to apathy toward us than animosity." He raised his eyebrows slightly. "Now they have to recognize the error in their thought process."

"Changing your way of thinking is difficult," E'oa said.

Zael looked at E'oa and nodded. "It definitely is." Zael pointed to himself. "It's hard for me to consider myself a White Hair. It's just . . . strange."

"I get your point," Nuke said with a shrug. "I just hope they can admit to what the evidence is now telling them."

Nuke looked up and saw Halayal approaching. The others followed his gaze and sat up straighter.

Expressionless as she entered the room, Halayal stood before them and, without emotion, said, "The council has made its decision."

Nuke raised his eyebrows. "Bad news?"

Halayal shrugged. "Depends upon your point of view, I guess."

As Nuke stood with the others, he glanced at their faces. They too thought Halayal's statement strange. No one said anything, however.

Without saying more, Halayal gestured for them to follow her to the conference room.

When they entered the room, she walked over and sat next to her council counterpart. All six councilmembers had their younger counterpart next to them: Halayal, Jaeyre, Elnah, Yahel, Howeh, and Zaveh. At the other end of the table sat Jayahel, Hael, and Elyahel. Nuke's group found the remaining empty seats around the table.

Wehyahel spoke for the council. He gave what looked like a forced smile and interlocked his fingers with his hands on the table in front of him. "Sorry for the long deliberation. But we had a lot of things to consider."

Nuke cocked his head. He thought this statement odd since he couldn't see how it was true. The issue seemed pretty black and white to him.

Wehyahel continued. "We had four things to consider. First, we had to be sure what we heard about Zael was true and would be true for all Dark Ones."

Nuke glanced at Zael, but he remained stoic. Jayahel, on the other hand, shifted in his seat. Evidently the statement didn't sit well with him. Nonetheless, he remained silent. Nuke looked back at Wehyahel.

"Second, we had to consider if this was the appropriate time to wake our brothers and sisters from their stasis. That . . . " He glanced at one of the other councilmembers. " . . . took up most of our time of deliberation."

When Nuke looked at the other councilmember, he remained stoic. Evidently he felt justified in his statements, whatever they were.

Wehyahel's gaze turned specifically to Nuke. "Then, that led us to discuss our belief in you being the true prophet of Erabon."

Nuke was definitely curious as to what they said about him. He was listening with rapt attention.

Wehyahel didn't elaborate, however, but simply went on. "And finally, our discussion led us to consider whether you entering the temple would be the best way to confirm all of these things." He took a deep breath and returned to his seat.

"So here is the order of what we have decided."

He nodded toward Halayal.

Her smile looked forced. She gave a slight nod to Wehyahel. "Thank you, sir." Her gaze then panned the rest of them, paused when she looked at Nuke, and then she continued. "The council has decided all Qerachians will be awakened from stasis first."

Jayahel and Hael sat up in their seats. Evidently this decision surprised them. Elyahel just grinned.

Her gaze now turned to Nuke. "After everyone is acclimated, you will attempt to enter the temple."

Nuke's eyes widened a bit. He was surprised she put extra emphasis on the word *attempt*. Did that mean she didn't really think him to be the prophet of Erabon?

Nuke didn't question; he just nodded.

Halayal remained mostly expressionless. "If that is success-ful, the other issues will fall in line. Everyone will accept you as the true prophet of Erabon, likely the Dark Ones will turn, and we will know Erabon's return is near."

Wehyahel patted Halayal's arm with his hand. "Thank you, Halayal, for that summary." His gaze panned the table. "Any questions?"

Elyahel leaned forward still wearing his grin. "I have an important question. Does the council believe in this plan, or are you just *allowing* this plan?"

Wehyahel cocked his head. "And what difference does that make?"

Elyahel was still smiling, just less so. "Your belief will fuel that of all Qerachians. A mere tolerance will only fuel skepticism."

Wehyahel stared at Elyahel for several seconds. "We will promote this plan without any complaints against it."

Elyahel continued to stare. "That's not the same thing."

Wehyahel remained stoic for several seconds. He forced another smile and then looked around the table again. "So, any other questions?"

No one said anything. Wehyahel looked at those at his end of the table. "We will begin the process of taking everyone out of stasis tomorrow."

All nodded.

Ti'sulh caught Yahel's gaze. "How long will that take?" she asked.

Yahel glanced at Wehyahel and then back to Ti'sulh. "Well . . . " It looked like he was doing mental calculations as he seemed deep in thought. "It will likely take most of the week to do this. As we take some out of stasis, they can in turn help us take more out of stasis."

Halayal nodded. "It will start out slow but pick up speed as more come out of stasis."

Ti'sulh nodded. She glanced at Nuke and then back to Halayal. "So, you would expect Nuke to enter the temple . . . when?"

Halayal looked to Wehyahel. He spoke next. "So you can prepare, let's say ten days from now."

Nuke nodded. "Thank you. I look forward to helping your people believe in Erabon and his return again."

Elyahel reached forward and patted Nuke's and Jayahel's arms. "And to bring all Qerachians together again, united under Erabon."

Wehyahel nodded. "So may it be."

All the Qerachians responded, "So may it be."

Nuke gave a slight nod. Maybe they were beginning to think differently already.

NINETEEN

AWAKENINGS

Nuke thought the week went by too slowly. He noticed the facility get more and more busy and crowded with people. Most did not engage him in conversation; many pointed and spoke to others in hushed tones when he walked by. Hardly any adults spoke to him personally.

The children, though, were another story.

As he walked by a seating area, he noticed three children playing together. Two were a White Hair and one a Dark One. Nuke stopped and pointed out the scene to Ti'sulh. As they watched, an adult White Hair came over and pulled her child away from where the children were playing. She said something to the little girl in an animated manner before they left. The little girl looked back with a forlorn type of gaze. Nuke felt sorry for her.

The white-haired boy looked up and pointed at Nuke. The other boy, a Dark One, followed the little boy's gaze and then nodded to the White Hair.

Nuke wondered what they were saying, so he walked up to them with Ti'sulh. "Hi. I'm happy to see the two of you playing together," he said.

The one with the white hair looked at Nuke and then at the other boy and smiled. "We like to play together."

The other boy nodded.

Ti'sulh sat on a nearby chair and leaned forward. "So, your differences don't bother you?"

The boy with white hair just stared at her. "Difference?" He looked at his friend. "What difference? He's a boy. I'm a boy."

Ti'sulh smiled and glanced up at Nuke. "Too bad the adults can't see as these do."

Nuke nodded.

The boy with dark hair looked up at Nuke. "You're the one who will make me have white hair?"

Nuke squatted down and looked at the boy. "Do you want to have white hair?"

He looked over at his friend and then back to Nuke. "Do I get to choose my eye color?"

Nuke shrugged. "I don't know. I guess that would be between you and Erabon. What color would you want?"

He looked back at his friend, who wrapped his arm around the boy's shoulders. "You should ask for red eyes," his friend said. "Then we can be twins."

The dark-haired boy smiled and nodded. He looked back at Nuke. "Yes, red eyes. That is what I want."

Nuke rubbed the boy's head, tousling his hair slightly. "Then just ask Erabon. Yet whatever he chooses for you will be special, and your friendship with each other can still continue."

Both boys nodded. Nuke stood as the boys went back to their table game, which looked something like three-dimensional chess, but the holographic board looked hexagonal, so he wasn't really sure what the game was. Both boys seemed extremely engrossed in the game.

Ti'sulh stood and took Nuke's hand as they walked away. "If everyone was like these two, you wouldn't have to enter the temple."

Nuke nodded and replied, "As we get older, often our head knowledge overwrites our heart knowledge. We need Erabon to rewrite both for us."

Ti'sulh looked at him and smiled. "Well, aren't you the philosophical one this morning?"

"Maybe I'm just becoming who I'm supposed to be."

Ti'sulh tugged his hand a little tighter and leaned into his shoulder. "Perhaps you are."

As they looked up, they saw Jaeyre approaching. She passed by them without saying anything. Both he and Ti'sulh looked at each other with raised eyebrows. Ti'sulh shrugged.

Suddenly, Jaeyre stopped and turned their way. "Oh, hello. I'm sorry. I didn't mean to ignore you."

Both Nuke and Ti'sulh turned. Nuke waved. "Don't worry about it. I know you're extremely busy."

She shook her head. "No, really." She put her hand to her chest. "I truly didn't mean to be rude." She sighed. "It's just . . . " She gave a short laugh. "I thought I knew what busy meant. Yet I have a new appreciation for the word."

Ti'sulh laughed. "I'm sure."

Nuke shrugged. "Anything we can do?"

Jaeyre took a step closer, her tone now more serious. "Just be you. You have won me over." She touched his arm. "I know you will enter the temple and win over the hearts of everyone." She looked at him intently. "We live in a unique time." She nodded slightly. "I am truly blessed to witness it."

Nuke didn't know what to say. He just looked at her.

Jaeyre smiled. "Sorry, but I must go. Believe me. There are more who believe in you than those who do not. It's just that the doubters are more vocal." She shook her head. "Don't worry. Erabon will guide you. Of that, I am certain." She turned and headed off.

Nuke turned to Ti'sulh with raised eyebrows. "Wow. She acted so resistant in the beginning."

Ti'sulh smiled and hugged his arm. "With that attitude she can win over the hearts of many even before you enter the temple." She looked into his eyes. "See? Erabon is going before you to prepare their minds. Then when you enter the temple, the event will push them over the edge in true belief and change their hearts."

Nuke patted her hand. "I'm so glad you're with me on this journey." He shook his head. "I don't think I could do this without you."

A big smile came across her face. "Yes, you could. Yet from how you have described desserts on your planet, that is the cake. I'm the icing on your cake."

At first Nuke just stared at her. That turned into a smile and then a laugh. He wrapped his arm around her shoulders. "That's a good analogy, Ti'sulh. A particularly good analogy." He looked into her eyes. "You are definitely my icing. The journey is definitely sweeter with you on it with me." He gave her a side hug.

Nuke heard a loud "Ahem" behind him.

Nuke turned and saw Michael and Z'zlzck. Michael had a huge grin on his face. Nuke chuckled. "Your jealousy is coming through."

"That obvious, huh?"

"So what are you two doing?" Nuke asked.

Z'zlzck pointed back from the way they had come. "We were just watching them taking more of the populace out of stasis."

Michael nodded. "They're close to finishing."

"Yes," Z'zlzck said. "I think they are right on schedule." His eyes widened a bit. "Are you ready, Nuke?"

Nuke tilted his head back and forth slightly. "As ready as I can be, I suppose." He forced a slight smile. "I'll be honest. I'm a little nervous, but excited at the same time. I look forward to having them all united again."

Ti'sulh told Michael and Z'zlzck of their encounter with the children.

Michael nodded. "If only we all could be like that."

Z'zlzck put his hand on Michael's shoulder. "If we were, there would be no need for Erabon to return, as he would never have had to leave us." He turned to Nuke. "Yet we are getting close to getting back to that state when Erabon will be with us forever. Thanks to you, Nuke."

Nuke felt his face flush slightly. While he knew the truth of Z'zlzck's statement, he felt unworthy of such praise. He certainly hoped what Z'zlzck said would come true in the near future, and he was glad to be part of this process. While none of these clans were related to him, they had become special to him. Creating a special future for them was definitely what he wanted.

"Let's go and look for ourselves," Ti'sulh said as she turned to Nuke.

Michael pointed in the opposite direction. "Bob and I were heading back to find E'oa and Bicca. We'll meet you back outside our sleeping quarters."

Nuke nodded. He watched the two of them head down the corridor. He took Ti'sulh's hand and walked in the direction Michael and Z'zlzck had come.

Ti'sulh looked up at Nuke. "Michael is a good friend."

Nuke looked at her and nodded. "The best. I've known him my entire life. That Erabon allowed him to be here with me is a true blessing." He kissed her hand. "Just like him putting you in my life."

"I agree," she said. "But you have the order backwards."

Nuke furrowed his brow. "What do you mean?"

"Erabon put *you* in *my* life. Not mine in yours."

Nuke laughed. "Technically, I guess that is true. At any rate, he put us together, and I'm grateful."

She smiled. "Me too."

When they reached the large picture window looking over the stasis pod area, they watched in silence. Nuke guessed that more than three-fourths of the pods had already been opened.

It wouldn't be long now, so he needed to mentally prepare himself for what was coming. The thought of being squeezed between two blocks of ice gave him a brain freeze.

TWENTY

ENTERING THE TEMPLE

Nuke swallowed hard. The time had come. He stood next to Wehyahel and faced everyone. To his right he saw a sea of colored dots and streaks throughout the sea of people, their white hair blending in with the surrounding white snow. That contrasted with those on his left, the Dark Ones, who added a swath of black to the white backdrop. Nuke wondered what they thought of him. According to Jaeyre, many believed. He hoped that was true. In a short while their belief would be confirmed. But a tinge of doubt always seemed to accompany his actions—even though he knew, deep inside, that Erabon had appointed him. Still, the doubt he felt inside now was not like the doubt that prevailed when he lived on Myeem.

But it was something like a crack in a sidewalk, which isn't a big deal structurally, but nonetheless mars the beauty of the concrete and can become a distraction. If he failed to enter the temple, everything the Qerachians had done would be in vain, and they would not be able to go back to their previous state, even with how flawed their thinking was. So he worked hard to push all that from his mind. All the evidence, and all he had been through on Myeem, Eremia, Sharab, and Ramah proved Erabon had chosen him. He would not let him down now.

Wehyahel held up his hands to quiet everyone. A hush dropped over the crowd. Nuke could hear a slight wind blowing through the mountains. "My fellow Qerachians, you have been awakened to join us for this momentous occasion. You will get to witness the prophecy left to us by our ancestors. The true prophet of Erabon will give the temple to us once again and lead us to the return of our beloved Erabon."

Nuke heard one of the councilmembers whisper to another, "Hopefully, this is not another Elyahel moment—a complete disaster."

Nuke saw Wehyahel give the councilmember a hard stare, then turn back his way. Evidently, he had heard the man as well. The councilmember swallowed hard and directed his gaze away from Wehyahel.

Wehyahel forced a small smile. "Nuke, prophet of Erabon, our hopes and prayers are with you as you enter the temple. May Erabon be with you."

Nuke turned to face the temple. He had been in this location before, but he hadn't realized the presence of the temple since the Qerachians had let snow accumulate over the structure since the time it was sealed by their ancestors. Now the temple was uncovered and polished, reminding Nuke of an ice sculpture centerpiece he had seen at the Academy formal dance his senior year. In comparison, though, this structure looked massive. The crystal clear ice now reflected the sunlight; this solar system's sun was just now setting behind it. He could feel the temperature drop slightly as the sun descended closer to the horizon. Supposedly, the temple would come to life with color once he entered. Wehyahel had decided having Nuke enter the temple after sunset would help his people believe because not everyone would have to be close to the temple to witness the explosion of color which should take place.

A cool wind hit Nuke's face. Yes, this was a nice plan to demonstrate his entrance, but worse for him in the way he had to enter. The Qerachian ancestors had sealed the opening to the temple with solid ice and he was now supposed to enter without any tools.

He looked over and saw a solid, three-meter-thick slab of ice which the Qerachian ancestors had also built and which had almost killed Elyahel. This slab would somehow move and seal him between it and the temple entrance. Then he would somehow get through the ice sealing the temple to the holy place—all without dying, of course. When Nuke thought about this earlier, the process had somehow seemed simpler. Now that he saw the slab of ice—and knowing he had to stand between the two structures—the feat seemed daunting.

He and the councilmembers turned toward the temple. Nuke looked at Michael and motioned for him to come with him. Michael pointed to himself, looked around, and then back at Nuke's gaze. "Me?" he mouthed. Nuke nodded. Michael looked at Z'zlzck and shrugged. Z'zlzck patted him on his shoulder and gave Michael a slight push forward.

Michael quickly walked to Nuke's side. "Hey, buddy. What's wrong?"

Nuke gave a small smile. "Nothing's wrong. I just need you to do something for me."

Michael gave him a curious look but nodded. "Anything, buddy. Anything."

Nuke walked over to stand at the temple entrance. Michael stood beside him. Half the councilmembers stood close to the temple and the other half near the giant ice slab. Once Nuke stood at the temple entrance, he noticed grooves in the ice where the slab would travel to seal him in.

Wehyahel looked at Nuke. "Ready?"

Nuke nodded. Wehyahel pressed something in his hand and the giant slab of ice moved toward the temple—slowly but steadily. Nuke looked at Michael. "Stand between me and the crowd so they can't get a good look at me."

Michael cocked his head. "OK . . . but why?"

Nuke started to disrobe. Michael's eyes grew big. "Nuke, what are you doing? You'll freeze to death."

Nuke shook his head. "If I don't do this, I'll die."

Michael held out his hands to take Nuke's clothes.

Nuke shook his head again. "No, Michael. I need to keep them for when I enter the temple, but I need my bare skin to help me generate the heat to get through the ice." He patted the air with his hand. "Just be the barrier to protect my modesty a little."

Nuke stood as close to the temple as possible without touching the structure so he didn't freeze too early. The cold breeze wasn't helping. He placed his clothes at his feet hoping they would not get too wet before he had to wear them again. He glanced back and noticed a man-shaped indentation in the slab. For that he was grateful since the slab wouldn't crush him—at least at first. He might freeze to death, but at least he wouldn't be squeezed to death. Nuke had to laugh lightly, for just a second, to himself. *How magnanimous of them.*

As the slab came close to the temple's icy surface, Nuke made his stance match that of the indentation. He looked over at Michael and gave a final smile.

Michael gave a nod. "You've got this, Nuke." As the gap narrowed, he added, "I'll see you shortly."

As the slab drew right next to the temple, all light was shut out. Nuke now stood shrouded in darkness. The indentation, only a few centimeters larger than his own outline, left little room for movement, and the freezing temperature of the ice caused him to jerk every time his bare skin touched its cold surface. His muscles started to shake as the temperature dropped inside his cocoon of ice. He suddenly realized he had little time before his air would run out.

Nuke closed his eyes and tried to slow his heart rate and control his shaking. The air, already getting thin, increased his anxiety level even as he attempted to establish calm within himself. He felt his skin prickle. *Good.* That was what he needed. The shaking of his muscles from the cold inhibited that process, though, so he tried to block the coldness from his mind. He felt his skin prickle more. Then his skin began to feel warm and his muscles slowly stopped shaking. As his body temperature rose, he placed his hands on the ice in front of him. That ice began to melt. Slowly at first, then faster and faster.

In a short time Nuke was able to extend his hands in front of himself. He then pressed his torso into the ice—it was severely cold at first—but that too began to turn warm and he felt the ice melt further. His body now was getting hotter and hotter. Some of the melted ice now turned to steam from the heat of his body. He slowly moved forward as the ice kept melting. As his body kept warming, he became concerned his core body temperature might get too hot. That would not be a good thing. He hoped the ice was not too thick as he needed to get through before his internal body temperature got too high. After a few more minutes, he felt the last of the ice melt away.

He was through to the other side!

Nuke stepped into the temple. It now felt strange to not have anything but air in front of and around him. As he turned and flapped his arms to try and cool down faster, he slowly felt his body temperature return to normal, although the time to do so took longer than the time it took his body to reach the very warm level.

Nuke reached for his clothes. Some of them were damp, but not too much; most of the melted ice went from water to steam quite quickly and this, thankfully, allowed the dampness to not go all the way through the material. After he donned his clothes, he looked around. There seemed to be extremely dim lights outlining six circles equally spaced around the circular structure. He looked upward but couldn't make out how high the ceiling stood above him. He could vaguely make out the walls of the large domed structure.

He realized the lighting on the floor illuminated the base of some large statues. As he examined the lights, he noticed they could tilt, so he tilted several of them upward. Each statue appeared to be an image of a Qerachian who stood facing the center of the building while holding the long strand of his hair upward. Nuke walked to the other statues and saw they were the same. There were six in all. Nuke nodded. That made sense since there were six types of Qerachians.

He stood with his hands on his hips in the center of the six. *Now what?* he wondered as he looked around, not seeing anything else. He knew, however, that didn't really mean anything as he recalled other temples where holograms appeared and things rose from the floor. Nuke turned again, but what was he supposed to do to make any of that happen?

Then a light came on in the center of the ceiling—not bright, but enough illumination for him to see better from floor to ceiling. He could see some type of apparatus near the ceiling, and as Nuke looked around wondering how to reach the device, a stair lit up behind him. He turned and walked to the first stair. Once he stepped on it, the next stair lit up. Each successive stair lit as he took the next step. The stairs slowly ascended, all the way around the domed structure, until they reached the ceiling of the dome where the unknown apparatus was located. He walked slowly to prevent himself from getting dizzy and lightheaded from the circular ascension of the stairs; the ascent had become tighter and tighter the higher he climbed.

The device at the top looked odd—something like a giant clear needle with a golden tip pointing upward. The tip reminded him of the golden pins he had used on the other planets to prick his finger so a drop of his blood could be placed in the center of the talismans. He looked down. This was the center of the six statues. Perhaps this was like the talisman, only larger. Nuke reached over and put his finger on the end of the golden needle, producing a drop of blood on its tip as he removed his finger. As he watched, the drop was pulled into the needle. Looking more closely, he realized the needle had six thin chambers that pulled the blood down, into, and along the tiny chambers, probably utilizing capillary action, which was similar to what he had seen when medics used tubes somewhat like this to collect his blood from a pricked finger.

He watched as the blood slowly descended in the tubes and touched the ends of the upstretched hair of each statue—at this point the temple burst into color. Blue, red, purple, gold, white, and clear light—one for each statue—traveled down the simulated locks of hair creating a rainbow of light that filled the temple. Nuke knew this was visible from the outside since the walls, made of ice, looked like translucent glass. Each statue now glowed pure white. Each statue's eyes glowed in the color of its lock of hair. Then the light from each eye, like lasers, highlighted the opposite wall with the commandments of Erabon. Nuke's gaze turned and he saw the words—the same ones he had seen in every other temple he had entered.

He saw something form in the middle of the statues at their base: a hologram of the planet Myeem. The words for the planet circled the hologram. Above Myeem appeared the planet Eremia with Erabon's words for this planet circling it. This continued with each successive planet until the planet Aphiah appeared in direct line of sight from where Nuke stood. After a couple of minutes the holograms collapsed on themselves and Nuke saw the new planet Erabon form as the holograms combined. The sight was stunningly beautiful. The words for this planet circled it: *Praise be to Erabon anew who will return and make all things new.* Nuke's eyes watered, but he blinked to keep the tears at bay. He whispered, "Praise be to Erabon who makes all things new."

A laser from the light above him then melted the remainder of the ice that blocked the temple doorway, including the slab which had sealed him in. Then everything went dark. The light of each stair went out as he descended. Once he stepped off the last stair, he stood in total darkness except for the dim light coming from the now open doorway. He slowly walked out of the temple. As soon as he exited, a force field sealed the doorway. The *swoosh* sound startled him at first, and he quickly turned. He turned back to all those standing there watching him. How long had he been in the temple? He didn't know.

He took a few more steps toward them and stopped. His eyes met those of Ti'sulh, who was watching him. Her face was wrapped in a parka. He could see admiration in her eyes. As he scanned the crowd, he noticed similar looks.

Suddenly the whole crowd erupted in applause accompanied by shouts and whistles.

Nuke held up his hands to signal for quiet; it took no little time for everything to be still again. A large smile swept his face. He pointed to the temple and said, "Erabon has given his temple back to you. Back to *all* Qerachians."

The crowd erupted in another round of applause, again with shouts and whistles. All the councilmembers rushed to Nuke's side and shook his hand.

TWENTY-ONE

TURNING OF THE DARK ONES

As Nuke talked to Wehyahel, Jayahel approached. Nuke gave a slight bow. "Nuke, I want to ask for your forgiveness." Jayahel gestured toward the temple. "What you did . . . " He stopped and swallowed to prevent his voice from cracking. He shook his head and looked back at Nuke. "I'm sorry."

Nuke put his hand on Jayahel's shoulder. "All has occurred according to Erabon's design."

Jayahel nodded. He turned to Wehyahel. "May my people enter first? He glanced back at them. They are extremely eager to enter."

"Don't you want to wait until morning?" Wehyahel asked. "It's getting late. Let them get some sleep first."

Jayahel stared at him, eyes wide. "Sleep? Are you joking? After what we have seen, sleep is the farthest thing from our minds. We would like to enter now. We have been separated from Erabon for too long. He is now within reach."

Wehyahel nodded. "I agree, but it's getting quite cold. Place your people in the order you wish them to enter. I've sent Yahel to open the observation deck. Your people can wait there and witness what is occurring with those of your people who enter and exit the temple first."

Jayahel nodded. "Thank you." He bowed slightly, looked at Nuke for a couple of seconds, then turned and went back to his people, who crowded around him.

Nuke turned to Wehyahel. "I didn't know you had an observation deck."

Wehyahel smiled. "It's only now that I realize why we have one. It's never been used, to my knowledge, since the temple was sealed."

Nuke heard a noise and turned. The side of the mountain containing the settlement was actually retracting, causing snow to cascade down the mountain below the large picture window now appearing.

Nuke looked at Wehyahel in a stunned fashion. "Everyone will now have a clear view of the temple."

Wehyahel nodded. "It dawned on me as you were inside the temple why the observation deck was created." He gestured for Nuke to walk with him back inside the mountain. "I think this whole area was a complex of some type. I have asked Yahel to find the blueprints of the original construction so we can make this area look the same as before." He glanced at Nuke and nodded. "Our people deserve that."

Seeing Halayal walk by, Wehyahel waved her over.

She gave a slight bow. "Yes sir?"

"Please work with Jayahel to get his people organized to enter the temple."

She smiled. "Heading there now. Howeh and I will take care of it."

He nodded. "Very good."

Halayal's gaze turned to Nuke. She looked down and then back in his eyes. "I'm deeply sorry for my attitude earlier. Please forgive me."

"All was forgiven even before you asked," Nuke said.

"Thank you." She hurried toward the group of Dark Ones.

They will likely not be Dark Ones much longer, Nuke thought.

As he entered the observation deck, many children had gathered at the picture window and were talking excitedly. He saw Ti'sulh behind them talking with Zael. He walked over.

Ti'sulh hugged his arm. "You did it, Nuke." She gave a broad grin. "I knew you would."

Zael nodded. "We had no doubt."

"Well—" Nuke felt someone pulling on the fingers of his other hand. He looked down and saw the Qerachian child he had seen playing with the Dark One's child earlier. He smiled and patted the child's head.

The child's red eyes looked up at him. "Have you seen him? Have you seen him?"

Nuke squatted down to wrap his arm around the child's shoulders. "Seen who?"

"My friend."

"The one you were playing with earlier?"

The child nodded, his eyes bright with expectation. "He will get his red eyes tonight. I want to see him."

"Well," Nuke said, "they might not be red, you know, but he will still be your friend, right?"

The boy nodded, then cocked his head. "Erabon won't give him red eyes?"

Nuke patted the child's shoulder. "Maybe. We'll have to wait and see."

The boy looked at him for a couple of seconds and nodded. "I'll see what color they are when he comes out of the temple," he said.

Zael squatted next to Nuke and the boy. "You may have to wait until morning to see them change." He shrugged. "At least that's how it happened with me."

The boy's eyes grew wide. "You're the changed one?"

Zael looked at Nuke and then back at the boy. "Yes, I guess that's what I am."

The boy nodded. "I heard my father talk about you. He said you were strange, but . . . I like you." He stared into Zael's eyes. "You have nice eyes."

Zael laughed. "Well, thank you. I like yours too."

The boy smiled. "I'm sure my friend will have nice eyes too."

Zael nodded. "I'm sure he will." He patted the boy's head. "Just don't expect to see a change as soon as he exits the temple." He tapped the boy under his chin with his index finger. "Yet by breakfast tomorrow I'm sure your friend will have very nice eyes."

The boy nodded with excitement and ran back to the picture window.

Nuke and Zael stood again. Ti'sulh giggled. "I wish everyone was like him."

Zael nodded. "One day. One day we all will be like him."

Ti'sulh smiled. "Very true," she said.

Zael crossed his arms in front of his chest. "He does bring up a good point."

Nuke turned his head. "What do you mean?"

"Well, many of the Dark Ones may expect an immediate change and be disappointed if they exit the temple and not look different."

Nuke nodded slowly. "I see. The inward change is immediate, but not the outward change."

Zael nodded. "That's how it was for me. I think I'll hang out at the temple entrance and engage those who exit so they don't become discouraged with their expectations."

Ti'sulh looked at Zael and smiled. "Zael, you not only have nice eyes, but a nice heart to go with them."

Zael chuckled. "Well, it's the least I can do." He turned. "If I don't see you later, I'll catch up with you tomorrow."

Nuke nodded and patted his shoulder as Zael headed from the room.

Ti'sulh pointed toward the temple. "It's starting. I just saw a flash of blue from the temple."

Nuke led her to some chairs which gave them a good view. They watched as the temple at times reflected blue, at other times red, sometimes purple, at other times gold, sometimes white, and at still other times just a brilliant light. This went on for hours, but the scene was never boring.

After some time, E'oa and Bicca came over and joined them.

E'oa chuckled. "I just heard many of the White Hairs want to enter the temple tonight as well."

Bicca nodded. "No one wants to wait until morning." He shook his head. "I've never seen such contagious energy to enter a temple of Erabon."

Nuke felt a pat on his shoulders. He looked up and saw Michael behind him. "That's because Nuke has started a cascade of excitement that Erabon can use," Michael said.

Z'zlzck, standing next to Michael, smiled. "I don't think sleep is on anyone's mind tonight."

Both Michael and Z'zlzck also found seats.

"I never tire of seeing the changing colors within the temple," Ti'sulh said. She squeezed Nuke's hand. "All thanks to you, everyone is being unified."

Michael laughed.

"What's so funny?" Nuke asked.

Michael waved a hand as if to dismiss the thought. "Sorry, a thought just came to me."

Nuke wrinkled his brow. "What? You have to tell me now."

Michael looked at him, a grin slowly forming. "I now know why Ti'sulh likes you so much."

Nuke cocked his head and turned the corner of his mouth up. "Oh? And why is that?"

"You have a hot body." Michael pushed on Nuke's shoulder and burst into laughter. So did everyone else.

Nuke jabbed back at Michael. "Oh, please don't quit your day job."

A couple of seconds later, Michael went on. "But seriously, Nuke. Did you ever think the abnormality, as the doctors called it, in your skin would turn out to be such a blessing?"

Nuke shook his head. "Never in a million years." He turned to Michael. "What was abnormal on our world has turned out to be just what I needed on these worlds."

Michael nodded. "You were part of a grander plan even before you were born."

Z'zlzck leaned forward. "Is there anything left to do here?"

Nuke shrugged and tilted his head. "If there are no Dark Ones by morning, I would think our job here is done."

Ti'sulh turned to him. "So it's on to Aphiah?"

He nodded. "I think so."

Ti'sulh paused, in thought. "So, who from here should we have come with us?"

Nuke scanned their faces. "Who do you think we should ask?" He knew who he wanted to bring, but he wanted to get their thoughts as well.

E'oa spoke first. "I think we should bring Zael." He shrugged. "I mean, he was the first Dark One to turn and has a good perspective on Erabon and what he can do."

Everyone else nodded.

Nuke scanned his friends' faces again. "So it's unanimous?"

All nodded.

"Good. I'm glad to hear that. He was the one who came to my mind first as well, but I wanted to get your thoughts before I said anything." Nuke smiled. "I think he'll be excited to go. I'll talk with him and Wehyahel about it tomorrow."

As small talk took over the group, Nuke realized he now had a contented feeling about these people. The activity ebbed and flowed between the time one group entered the observation deck area from the temple and the time until the next group took its place. As the night went on, the time of the lull between activity got longer as sleepiness overcame the enthusiasm of many. Yet Nuke didn't see any of them leave for their sleeping quarters.

Early in the morning the activity picked up with everyone once again wide awake. The Dark Ones who had entered the temple found themselves White Hairs. Their excitement produced a great commotion. They were laughing, crying, and giving everyone around them hugs. Each person looked at the color of their long swath of hair and got emotional again. Ti'sulh and Nuke enjoyed the scene together; they found it extremely rewarding.

Two small boys ran up to Nuke with extreme excitement. "Prophet Nuke! Prophet Nuke! Erabon did it! Erabon did it!"

Nuke recognized the boy as the one who had talked to him earlier while thinking about his friend. He bent down and hugged each of the boys together. "Congratulations. Erabon has made you twins after all."

Both boys nodded enthusiastically. The boy who previously had dark hair kept holding his red swath of hair up to his friend's, and both would giggle. He would then hold his hair up in the air like the statues in the temple and shout, "Erabon!"

Nuke and his friends looked at each other and laughed. The boys ran off in their excitement.

Ti'sulh shook her head. "That is priceless."

Nuke nodded. "Before long I bet we find them both curled up on a sofa somewhere. They've got to be close to worn out."

Over the next few hours, the activity declined again and the number of people in the observation deck dwindled as people slowly left for sleeping quarters. Nuke looked at his friends, who were also starting to nod off. After a bit longer, Nuke knew he needed to make a decision.

"OK, everyone. I think it's time we turned in."

Michael pulled his head off Z'zlzck's shoulder. "Why? We're still good."

Z'zlzck nodded.

Nuke laughed. "Yeah, I can tell." He smirked at Michael. "Come on. Let's all get some rest so we can be helpful tomorrow." He looked at his chronometer. "I mean, later today."

All reluctantly agreed and followed Nuke back to the sleeping quarters.

As they passed a long sofa in another nearby seating area, Ti'sulh pointed and laughed. On one side of the sofa were the two boys with their heads on the same pillow. They looked in extreme peace as they slept.

Ti'sulh laughed again. "Too bad we can't take them with us."

Nuke nodded. "They would definitely be great ambassadors of how Erabon brings unity through diversity."

Ti'sulh found and draped a blanket over the two boys. They stirred slightly, but then returned to restful sleep.

Once Nuke got to his sleeping quarters he stripped and fell into bed. He was asleep almost as soon as his head was resting on the pillow.

TWENTY-TWO

LEAVING QERACH

Nuke woke and stared at the ceiling. He thought back on his time on Qerach: not an easy time, for sure, but certainly a rewarding one. He took his shower, ate his supplements, dressed, and headed to the seating area.

He was taken back when he saw Wehyahel in one of the chairs.

"Wehyahel, is something wrong?"

Wehyahel laughed. "Does my presence always mean something is wrong?"

Nuke sat on the sofa, chuckling. "Well, no, but it often seems that way. So, what can I do for you?"

"I just wanted to thank you for helping us find ourselves again. We focused on our differences and let them divide us— causing us to stop caring for the good of everyone."

Nuke smiled. "I've discovered Erabon wants to unify through diversity."

Wehyahel nodded. "I think we had forgotten that."

"After last night," Nuke said, "I think your people are on a good path in the preparation for Erabon's return. I think it's time for us to now head to Aphiah."

"I think we are," Wehyahel said. "I've never experienced such excitement and unity among our people." He stood. "So, when do you expect to leave?"

"Well, that's one thing I want to talk with you about."

"Oh?" Wehyahel sat down again and looked Nuke's way.

"Yes. I would like to take Zael with us."

Wehyahel put his hand to his chin, then nodded slowly. "Yes, I think he would be an excellent choice. Have you talked to him about it?"

Nuke shook his head. "Not yet. I was going to talk with him today."

"May I do so first?"

Nuke tilted his head and gave a slight shrug. "Sure, that would be great."

Wehyahel stood. "I'll get things prepared to give you a send-off."

As he started to leave the room, Nuke turned and saw Ti'sulh step into the outer area.

She walked over. "Was that Wehyahel?"

Nuke nodded.

"What did he want?"

Nuke smiled and pulled her down gently to take a seat next to him. "He was just thanking us for helping get his people all on the same page."

She leaned into him and chuckled. "You mean, he was thanking *you*."

"It was a team effort."

She poked him in his ribs and Nuke let out an *umph.*

Ti'sulh giggled. "You are a good man, Nuke." She smiled at him and gazed into his eyes. "You really are."

He put his face to hers. "And you are a good woman." He gave her a quick kiss.

She leaned back and snuggled into him. He put his arm around her. She looked up at him and spoke quietly. "Nuke, do you think we have a future after all this is over?"

He quickly turned her way. "Why wouldn't we?"

She shook her head lightly. "I don't know. I sometimes get this feeling our journey together ends when Erabon returns."

"And you think that is soon?"

She gave a slight shrug. "Don't you?"

He gave her a light squeeze. "I'd be lying if I said otherwise." He turned more in her direction. "Is there any prophecy as to how soon he will return once the clans reunite?"

Ti'sulh bit her bottom lip and slowly shook her head. "No, not really. Yet . . . " she shrugged. "It just seems . . . almost wrong for him to wait."

Nuke nodded. He couldn't really say otherwise since he thought the same. While he really liked Ti'sulh, and often envisioned a life with her, he told himself that maybe he should hold off—at least until their mission on Aphiah was complete. After all, they were together and could support each other.

Both sat up a bit more as several doors opened and the others came out to join them. They talked for several hours about what had happened on Qerach, on the other planets, and what they might expect once they reached Aphiah.

Nuke looked at his chronometer. "I'd better go find Zael and be sure he can leave on such short notice."

Ti'sulh stood as he did. "I'll go with you."

He and Ti'sulh left the group to seek out Zael. After checking in several places, they couldn't find him. Then they started checking various rooms. When they entered the conference room that overlooked the sea of stasis pods, it too was empty.

Ti'sulh grabbed Nuke's arm.

He turned. "What's wrong?"

She pointed. "I thought everyone was brought out of stasis. One pod is still horizontal."

"What?" Nuke went over to the large window and looked. Sure enough, all the stasis pods were vertical, the position required to drain the fluid and have the Qerachians exit stasis—except for one. Nuke grabbed Ti'sulh's hand. "Let's go see."

When they reached the stasis pod, Nuke gasped. Ti'sulh did the same.

She looked at Nuke, eyes wide. "Why?"

Nuke shook his head slowly. He could only ask the same question. Was Wehyahel trying to sabotage their mission?

Zael had been placed in the stasis pod! Nuke looked up and saw Wehyahel approaching.

Nuke stiffened the closer Wehyahel came. What explanation could Wehyahel possibly give? He had told Wehyahel he wanted Zael to go with him, and now someone—and Wehyahel was their leader—had put Zael into stasis. Nuke bit his bottom lip to try and prevent saying something which would make things worse. He thought they were all on the same page—but apparently they weren't.

Wehyahel gave a large smile as he approached. Nuke thought that strange.

"When I saw the two of you in here, I thought I should come and explain."

Nuke crossed his arms in front of his chest. "Yes, I think that is a good idea." His words came out much more tersely than he expected.

Wehyahel patted the stasis pod. "Don't worry. Zael isn't in stasis."

Nuke looked from the pod back to Wehyahel. "Well, it certainly looks like it."

Wehyahel tilted his head. "Well, I guess it would to you."

Nuke furrowed his brow; he wasn't following at all.

Wehyahel pointed to the view port of the stasis pod. "Look. You can see Zael's face clearly. He isn't immersed in the stasis fluid."

Nuke's eyes widened. Wehyahel was right. Had he been wrong? He looked back at Wehyahel. "So why is he in the pod then?"

Wehyahel put his hand on Nuke's shoulder. "Zael was extremely excited when I told him you wanted him to go with you to Aphiah." Wehyahel shook his head. "But then he realized he didn't know how to fly a jet. He was so disappointed." The White Hair leader patted the device. "That's when I remembered these stasis chambers and what they can do."

Nuke shook his head. "I don't understand."

"One of the reasons we were able to be in stasis for so long is because our minds were kept occupied." He touched the pod again. "These not only do simulations, they can help one learn new skills in a fraction of the time."

Ti'sulh looked from Zael back to Wehyahel. "Oh, so Zael is taking flying lessons?"

Wehyahel smiled. "Yes, but more than that. He is not only getting trained but undergoing countless hours of experience in only a fraction of the time."

Nuke put his hand to his chin. "Wow. That's . . . that's incredible." He looked at Zael. "So how much longer does he need to be in there?" He wanted Zael with him but had wanted to leave soon. In another sense, however, Nuke knew Zael was worth the wait.

"Oh." Wehyahel looked at the side of the stasis pod. "Actually, he should be waking up in only a few minutes."

Nuke's head jerked back. "Really? That fast?"

Wehyahel nodded. "Yes, experience gained from simulations only takes a few hours."

As they continued talking, Nuke heard the stasis pod make a noise. He turned and saw the pod raise Zael to an erect position. The pod opened and Zael, having just awoken, slowly stepped out.

A smile crept across his face. "Nuke. Ti'sulh. I wasn't expecting an awakening committee."

"How do you feel?" Nuke asked.

Zael's smile grew large. "Like flying."

Nuke chuckled. "Glad to hear it. Will you be ready to go before the day is over?"

Zael nodded. "Yes. There's no real ties for me here."

Wehyahel shook his head. "Not true, Zael. You have made so many friends here by being the example for all of us to follow."

Zael turned to Wehyahel. "Thank you. But I don't really have close family." He shrugged. "So . . . "

Wehyahel patted Zael's shoulder. "Yet, we will still miss you."

Zael produced a smile with a nod and then looked at Nuke. "The only close relationship I have is with Yel and Zel. Want to go say goodbye?"

Nuke nodded. Suddenly he felt guilty because he had almost completely forgotten about Zel. He really did want to say goodbye to the creature who played a significant role in the people of this planet accepting him.

Zael turned to Wehyahel. "Don't forget to watch over them for me."

Wehyahel nodded. "Don't worry. I've made arrangements. They will be well looked after."

The two creatures were where Zael and Nuke left them. Zel walked up to Nuke and put his nose in his new friend's chest. Nuke patted his head and ran his hands over the creature's tentacles. The creature seemed to sense his leaving and looked into his eyes as though Zel also knew this was goodbye.

"Bye, Zel." He rubbed his large friend's forehead once more. "Thanks for everything."

The creature snorted and raised its head up and down as in a final goodbye.

Zael said his goodbyes to both creatures. When he turned, Nuke could see a few tears on his cheeks. Zael quickly wiped them with the back of his hand.

Ti'sulh stayed back while the two of them had this private time. When Nuke stepped away, she took his hand gently to give him assurance. He looked her way and smiled. "Goodbyes are always bittersweet," he said. "The end of one experience, but the beginning of another."

Once back inside, they headed to the location where they had first arrived inside the mountain. The hallways were lined with many people ready to see them off. There were smiles and waves. Nuke saw the two little boys again, now with arms around each other's shoulders.

He knelt beside them. "I'm glad you've become such good friends."

Both nodded. One grabbed Nuke around the neck and gave him a big hug. "Thanks for my red eyes," he said with a big smile.

Nuke returned the hug and chuckled. He pulled the boy back from his shoulder, looked in his eyes, and playfully touched the boy's nose with his index finger. "You tell Erabon 'thank you' for your red eyes. After all, he's the one who changed them for you. OK?"

The boy nodded. Nuke patted him on his head and rose to continue down the hallway. Once they reached the larger reception area, others were waiting. Drinks of some sort were passed out. Nuke had no idea what the concoction was, but its taste had a fruity flavor. Although he had no idea what type of fruit, the taste was like a blend of mango and coconut. *Odd*, he thought. *Yet also very good.*

Jayahel walked over. His eyes and swath of hair were now a golden color. He shook Nuke's hand. "I really can't thank you enough for how you have changed our lives for the better."

Nuke shook his head. "All the credit goes to Erabon."

Jayahel nodded. "Of course—but he used you." He held up his glass, turned to everyone, and called in a loud voice, "Thanks to Nuke, the prophet of Erabon, and his friends!"

Everyone held up their glasses. This turned into applause and a few whistles. Wehyahel walked over and shook Nuke's hand. "Safe journeys," he said.

Nuke nodded, gave his thanks, and turned to his companions. "Shall we get going?" Each stood and headed outside to the large landing bay area. Michael had ensured all jets were still in good condition. Zael's jet was fueled and ready and Zael had been given one of the ear comms for the trip.

Once outside, Ti'sulh went with Nuke to his jet. Z'zlzck went with Michael. Each person checked all systems to be sure everything was working after sitting idle for some time. Once all checklists were finished, they met again briefly and then returned to their jets. Many people had exited into the bay area to see them off. The pilot group waved and climbed into their cockpits.

Nuke helped Ti'sulh in first; as before, she would ride in the tight space behind him. He looked in after she was in position and gave her a smile. "Settled OK?"

She nodded and returned his smile. "All's good."

Nuke climbed in and closed the cockpit canopy. Once all had powered up, Nuke spoke into his comm. "OK, everyone. This is our last mission. I'll see you at the gates."

All acknowledged; they took off one after the other. In only a matter of minutes, Nuke arrived at the gates, which looked exactly as he had left them, and the others arrived shortly after. Seeing the gates always reinstilled a sense of adventure in Nuke—along with an adrenaline surge. While things should be routine, he remembered things could go horribly wrong. He had a much keener sense of protocol now when he used the gates than he did at first.

Nuke opened his comm. "Michael, see if you and Z'zlzck can get the gates programmed. Bicca, you and E'oa help me get the second gate tethered to my jet." They helped Nuke get attached to the gate as they had done before.

Michael spoke next. "Nuke, I have the gates programmed into a stable orbit above Aphiah. Once Bob and I arrive, I'll program our gate to receive traffic from yours."

"OK," Nuke radioed. "You all know what to do. Same as last time. Bicca, you help Michael guide the gate through the activated gate. I'll then have E'oa and Zael come through once you give the word all is a go. I'll come through last."

After a few minutes Nuke saw the gate activate. The silvery shimmering film spread from the corners and met in the center. The ripples produced were mesmerizing as they constantly moved, waxing and waning in brilliance, seemingly in no pattern. Michael tethered himself to the first gate and pulled the large triangle through the activated gate.

Nuke radioed to Bicca. "Just do what you did last time. We don't want to lose you."

"Understood." Bicca laughed. "Don't worry. I won't disconnect until we are safely there."

"OK. OK. I know you know what to do, but better safe than sorry." Nuke knew he'd never forgive himself if something happened to those he now counted as extremely good friends.

"Roger that," Bicca replied as their jets and the other gate went through the activated gate.

After about half an hour, Nuke received word from Michael that everything was set on his end above Aphiah. He let E'oa know to go through the gate followed by Zael a few minutes later. Once Nuke received word both had arrived, he gunned his jet and used the centrifugal force to loop him around and through the gate.

He called to Ti'sulh, "Ready?"

"I'm ready," she called to the front. "Do it."

As his jet went through the gate's horizon, he again felt himself becoming weightless. He knew the gate was now folding in on itself and would follow him through the generated wormhole. Light appeared to stretch and elongate around him, producing a colorful display. Although he knew he was travelling extremely fast, he felt like he wasn't moving at all. Who knew if he was traveling through the wormhole or if space was actually folding around him? The next thing Nuke knew his jet exited the gate above Aphiah, and the gate to which he was tethered came through behind him. Nuke then decelerated, and quickly put his jet into reverse to slow the gate, as three of the others hooked the cable loops of the gate to help the structure decelerate and maintain stability as they came to a stop. Nuke then towed the gate several hundred meters away from the other gate and disengaged.

When Nuke looked at the planet below him, everything looked different—vastly so—from the other planets they had visited. Everywhere looked wispy, like clouds. He wasn't sure what to expect. Because all he could see, for the most part, were clouds, elevation differences here would be hard to detect. He would have to rely on instrument readings to find the ideal place to land. Nuke had his computer initiate a life-form scan of the planet. The greatest concentration this time seemed to be in Aphiah's southern hemisphere. Flying in that direction would likely prove the best strategy. He knew his scan only captured this side of the planet, and different readings could be obtained once they orbited toward the other side.

Nuke spoke into his comm. "I suggest we circle the planet to see where the largest concentration of Aphiahians is located."

As they orbited, Nuke found the other side of the planet looked the same, just with extremely few humanoid life-forms. They headed back to the other side of the planet where he found the largest populated area. While there were a few other groupings, one seemed clearly the largest. With so much cloud cover, Nuke wondered what they would find. Would these people be on the surface with such limited visibility? He also wondered what their thoughts about Erabon and his prophet would be. What would they require him to do? He hoped the requirement would be something simple—for once.

Nuke took a deep breath and headed for the planet. The others followed.

TWENTY-THREE

APHIAH

As Nuke approached Aphiah, he wasn't sure where to land. "Ti'sulh, what do you see on the monitor?"

She didn't answer but seemed to be staring.

"Ti'sulh." No answer. "Ti'sulh!"

"Oh, sorry. This is just so bizarre."

Nuke glanced from her to his other instruments. "What are you seeing? Do you see a place for us to land?"

"Uh, maybe." She shook her head. "It's like the planet is broken up into multiple pieces."

"What?" Nuke glanced back her way. "What is that supposed to mean?"

Ti'sulh shrugged. "Just as I said. Somehow, there are multiple pieces of land separated from each other. Just . . . floating." She glanced up at him. "And this phenomenon seems to be the same around the entire planet." She looked out the cockpit window. "It looks like they are all under cloud cover."

As if on cue, the clouds seemed to be blown away from several of these floating islands of land. One looked quite large.

Nuke pointed to the monitor. "This one is now showing and looks large enough for all of us."

Ti'sulh nodded. "OK. We'd better land first to be sure it's stable."

"Good idea." He touched the comm in his ear. "Ti'sulh and I will land first to be sure the land mass is stable for the jets. Stay airborne until you hear from me."

All gave the affirmative.

As Nuke landed, the cloud cover came back over the island of land, but the air turbulence of the jet caused the clouds to scatter. As his jet touched down, Nuke felt the landing to be quite solid, not different from any other landing. He looked at Ti'sulh. "Felt solid to me." She nodded.

Nuke radioed to the others to land behind him. Michael and Bicca did so, side by side. Then E'oa and Zael sat their jets behind them. After Nuke did a quick atmospheric check, they all stepped from their jets and gathered.

Wind blew the clouds away again. As they looked, someone approached out of the cloud cover. Nuke thought the walk of this one quite feminine. Her clothing, apparently extremely lightweight, billowed around her with the wind, as did her long blondish-brown hair. As she got closer, he noticed something different about her face, arms, and legs. There were what appeared to be small pipes of different lengths along her arms. One also appeared along the bridge of her nose and another across her forehead. Because her clothes were somewhat sheer, he could see the same was true for her legs as well. Yet while they appeared hollow, this piping seemed to be *under* her skin, like it was part of her anatomy.

A broad smile came across her face. "Welcome to Aphiah." Her gaze went across them from one to the other. She gave a slight nod. "Welcome, my fellow clans—" Her voice stopped short as her eyes widened. Nuke noticed her stare had fallen on Michael.

Michael looked from her to Nuke and then back. "Is . . . is something wrong?"

The woman turned, ran, and jumped over the side of the land mass and into the cloud cover below.

They all ran to the edge and looked over. All they could see was more clouds. As Nuke stared, he realized the wind was blowing the clouds, and he saw several more floating land masses below them. He thought he saw a glimpse of the woman farther down but was unsure; his view was again obstructed by new cloud cover.

As Nuke looked up again, Michael was still wide-eyed. "Nuke, what just happened?"

Z'zlzck squeezed Michael's shoulders from behind. "When you told me your looks slay women, this is not what I had in mind."

Michael took a step forward and turned. "Very funny, Bob." He looked back at Nuke. "Seriously. What's going on?"

Nuke shrugged. He hadn't the slightest idea why the woman did what she did. Ti'sulh followed him to the other side of the island. As they looked down, more of these floating islands were visible as the cloud cover began to dissipate. He looked at Ti'sulh. "Any idea why this planet is like this?"

She shook her head. "No idea. Actually, we know the least about those on this planet." She looked around, lifting her arms and letting them flop to her side. "I haven't a clue as to what this is all about."

Nuke was disappointed to hear that. He had so many questions, but the first was this: how were these land masses floating in the air? Maybe they were composed of magnetized rock of some type. He looked over the side again. There appeared to be many of these islands. Why? How were they supposed to travel from one to the other?

Then, another thought hit him. He had understood the woman's words perfectly. It seemed their dialect was not too different from those on Myeem or Qerach; his comm apparently already had enough key words of their dialect to translate efficiently.

"Nuke."

Nuke turned, coming out of his thoughts. He saw E'oa motioning for him to come back to where the others were.

"What's happening, E'oa?"

E'oa pointed over the edge. "It looks like there are dwellings on some of the islands."

Nuke's eyebrows went up. "Really?" He looked over the edge again. More of the cloud cover had dissipated, and this now provided a much clearer view. Sure enough, he could see dwellings on some of the islands below. "Oh wow. And these island land masses are connected by some type of large vine. I don't know why I didn't see that before."

Michael touched Nuke's shoulder to get his attention. He pointed back and forth. "These islands remind me of . . . almost like leaves as part of some gigantic tree."

Nuke nodded slowly. "Yeah, I can kind of see that. Is that how they go from island to island?"

Zael shrugged. "Maybe. But that doesn't explain why the lady just jumped."

Nuke put his hand to his chin. "Yeah. Good point." As he continued to stare, he thought he saw movement. "Did anyone see that?"

"See what?" Ti'sulh looked from Nuke to the islands below. "What did you see?"

Nuke shook his head. "I don't know. I just saw movement. Then it was gone."

Bicca pointed. "Wait. I see it. The . . . creature . . . thing . . . seems to be circling."

Nuke looked. Sure enough, some type of creature flew in circles below them and seemed to be rising. Nuke turned his head as he began to hear something. *Is that some type of melody?* A tune seemed to be coming on the breeze. "Did anyone hear that?"

Zael nodded. "I do. Very melodic."

Nuke nodded. The tone became clearer as the creature got closer.

"It's a beautiful sound," Michael said. "Is that coming from this bird . . . thing . . . coming toward us?"

Nuke continued to watch the creature. "I think so." As the creature got closer, Nuke realized its wingspan was much wider than any bird he had ever seen. Once the creature reached their level, it flew under their island and then came over the opposite edge from where they stood and landed several meters from them.

Everyone stepped back, startled by something so large landing so close. The bird—Nuke didn't know what else to call it—tilted its head back to produce the same melodic sound they had been hearing: three trills in a row. Nuke found the melody calming. He just thought it odd this beautiful sound came from such a large creature. Yet this massive bird appeared just as beautiful as the sound it produced. The most dominant feature was the yellow crest atop its head. Its feathers—if that was what they were—looked waxy and were variegated, from yellow to orange to red with a tinge of purple on some.

The creature fluffed its feathers and looked at them like it expected them to do something.

Ti'sulh was the first to speak. "What do you think this creature wants?"

Nuke shrugged. "I just hope it isn't hungry." He took a step toward the creature.

Ti'sulh grabbed his arm. "What are you doing?"

He looked back. "We have to do something. I need to see if it's friendly."

Yet the closer he got, the more agitated the creature became. Michael ran up to him and grabbed his shoulder. "Nuke, this isn't going to work."

The creature immediately calmed and did its trill once more. Nuke and Michael just looked at each other.

Z'zlzck laughed. "Michael, you have a better effect on birds than women."

Michael looked back, giving him an exasperated stare and a deadpan retort. "You're a riot, Bob."

Nuke shrugged. "Wait. He may have a point."

Michael gave Nuke a smirk. "Don't you start too."

Nuke patted Michael's shoulder. "No, no. I mean this creature seems to like you more than the rest of us."

"You think so?"

"Seems pretty obvious to me."

Michael nodded and took a step closer to the bird, which then produced yet another trill. Michael held out his hand. "Aren't you the pretty bird?" The creature gave a nod, as if understanding Michael. He chuckled lightly. "Yes, you're pretty—and modest, aren't you?" The creature extended its neck to have its head touch Michael's hand. As Michael took another step closer, the creature curled around him with its neck as if giving him a hug. Michael laughed lightly. "Well, aren't you the chummy one?" He petted the creature's neck.

Michael turned back to Nuke. "Now what?"

Nuke shrugged. "I'm not sure."

"Well, I can't just pet him all day."

The creature suddenly let go of Michael, extended its head upward, and did the three trills once more. Then, in one swoop, and without warning, the creature grabbed Michael with its beak . . . and flew off.

Everyone was in shock. Z'zlzck was the first to respond. He ran forward. "Michael! Michael!"

Z'zlzck looked at Nuke, stunned. All Nuke could do was stare back.

TWENTY-FOUR

ZYHOV

When their wits came back to them, all gathered at the edge of the island and looked over the side to see if they could spot the creature and Michael. They saw the two, but they now appeared to be about the size of a penny as the creature continued to descend.

Z'zlzck looked at Nuke. "What do we do?"

"I—" Nuke's thought was interrupted as he saw two other creatures—these looked like people—descend to the middle of their island. Nuke had no idea how these two were able to fly—or seemed to fly. With their clothes so sheer, Nuke saw, as they landed, what looked like a flap of skin . . . fabric . . . something . . . that went from their elbow to armpit and extended to their side, and also from one thigh to another, although this was hardly noticeable once they landed. One of them appeared to be the same woman they had seen earlier. The other figure was evidently male. He looked similar to the woman but was more muscular and had a different number of raised pipe-like structures on his body than she did. His clothing, however, looked like that worn by the woman. While secured to their wrists and ankles, there appeared to be long slits in the sheer fabric allowing their arms and legs to become exposed as the breeze blew through the fabric. Evidently, exposing their limbs with the pipe structures was important, or at least the norm.

The two of them approached; the male spoke first. "Greetings, fellow clansmen. My name is Kubim, and this is my wife, Seraphia." He approached Nuke and extended his hand.

Nuke was in no mood to greet someone who had let a creature take off with his best friend in its beak. He remained stoic.

Kubim smiled. "You're worried about your friend?"

Nuke nodded.

Kubim chuckled. "Oh, do not worry. If he is with Zyhov, then you have no fear."

Nuke furrowed his brow. "Zyhov? That's the name of the creature who took off with him?"

Kubim nodded.

"Why?"

Seraphia brushed her long hair over her shoulder and onto her back as she gave a broad smile. "Because Erabon's prophecy has just been fulfilled." She glanced at Kubim. "And in our lifetime." Kubim smiled and nodded. She turned back to them. "Praise be Erabon."

All of them, in respect, repeated the phrase. "Praise be Erabon."

Nuke shook his head. "But I don't understand. What prophecy?"

Seraphia's eyes widened. "Oh, you do not know the prophecy Erabon left our people?"

Each shook their head. Ti'sulh stepped forward and stood next to Nuke. "Each planet had a specific prophecy Erabon left to our people. Nuke, here, has fulfilled them all." All the others nodded in agreement. She gestured toward Seraphia. "Your prophecy doesn't include the prophet of Erabon?"

"Oh yes, of course," she said. She looked from Ti'sulh to Nuke. Her hand went to her chest. "Please don't think I meant any disrespect to the prophet of Erabon."

Nuke held up his hand. "No, that's OK. But what about Michael? How is he tied to your prophecy?"

She looked at Kubim and then back to Nuke. "I'm sorry. I'm just surprised the prophet of Erabon doesn't understand what just happened."

Nuke gave a slight shrug. "That's OK. I get that a lot. Please explain."

She paused for a moment, then went on. "Well, the prophecy goes:

My time is near

When clansmen, prophet, and Zyhov appear.

Seven in number to signal my domain,

The sky will resound with triple melodic refrain."

Nuke looked from Seraphia to the others. They had the same blank stare as his. "Uh, sorry. That's a little cryptic. Could you elaborate?"

Seraphia looked stunned. "Explain?"

Kubim put his hand on her arm. "They have not been taught this as long as we have."

She pointed to Nuke. "But this is the prophet of Erabon. Surely we don't have to explain such things to him."

Nuke forced a smile. "Please do, though."

Kubim nodded. "Our understanding of this prophecy is that just before Erabon returns to us, a group of seven will come to Aphiah—one clansman from each planet of the

Erabon system with the prophet of Erabon . . . " Kubim gestured to Nuke. "And with Zyhov by his side."

Nuke scrunched his brow. "I thought you said Zyhov was the creature we just saw."

Kubim nodded. "It is, but its name refers to its color."

"And to its purpose," Seraphia added.

Nuke tried to understand their reference but failed. He glanced at Ti'sulh. She also looked in thought but suddenly stood straighter. Kubim again nodded.

Nuke's eyes widened. "And the color of Michael's hair," Nuke said, the meaning to their words finally dawning.

Kubim gave a slight bow. "That is correct."

Ti'sulh squinted. "But what did you mean by 'its purpose'?"

"Zyhov soars on the breeze of Erabon, being one of a kind," Seraphia said as she smiled. "No other creature on this planet compares to it."

Ti'sulh cocked her head. "This animal doesn't propagate?"

Seraphia shook her head. "No. It's unique."

Nuke looked from Seraphia to Ti'sulh and back. "So, how old is this creature?"

Seraphia shrugged and looked at Kubim, who also shrugged but then replied, "It has been here ever since our ancestors first arrived. Zyhov started out small and has grown in size every year."

Seraphia nodded. "And its melody has always reminded us of the sweetness of the Spirit of Erabon." She smiled. "But today . . . today was the best of all. We finally heard the triple melody of Zyhov."

Ti'sulh's head jerked back. "This was the first time you've heard it?"

Seraphia nodded. "It has never made that sound before. Not until today. Its melody has always been beautiful, but never like that."

"So, you see," Kubim said, "we had to be sure before we invited you in to meet our people. We knew Zyhov would know." He nodded toward his wife. "When she came to me telling of your arrival, we waited for Zyhov to come and test you." He grinned. "Your friend passed with flying colors."

"No one has ever been allowed to approach Zyhov," Seraphia said.

Nuke looked from one to the other. "Why?"

Seraphia's eyes widened. "Oh, Zyhov would never permit it."

"Yes, Zyhov has waited all this time for the prophet of Erabon," Kubim said. "But especially for his companion who would arrive with him."

Nuke put his hand to his chin. Although cryptic, this expla-nation of the words of Erabon's prophecy for Aphiah did make sense and fit what had taken place. "So, where did the creature take Michael?"

Seraphia cocked her head as if that too was a strange question.

"To the temple, of course."

TWENTY-FIVE

HASHEM CELEBRATION

Before Nuke could ask if they could see Michael and question how they would get there, several more Aphiahians arrived.

Kubim gestured toward the new arrivals. "These will take you all to the temple and to see your friend. Tonight we will celebrate HaShem, the Name of Erabon."

"Then, tomorrow," Seraphia said, "we'll teach you all how to fly on the wind of Erabon."

Nuke's eyes widened. "Really?"

Seraphia smiled and nodded.

This was exciting news to Nuke. He couldn't wait for such an experience. He also made a mental note to talk with Michael to see if today was the day he had predicted would be The Name Celebration. If so, that would verify their prediction of how far away from Earth they were. Yet, if true, such information would also verify that they had no hope of getting back to Earth. Home was just too far away.

Two muscular Aphiahians approached Nuke while other Aphiahians approached his friends. They introduced themselves.

"My name is Gavrek," one said.

"And my name is Jerim," added the other.

Nuke shook each of their hands. "You can call me Nuke."

"All right, Nuke," Gavrek said. "We are going to tether you between us and fly you down to the temple."

Nuke cocked his head. "OK. I'm trusting you."

Jerim chuckled. "Don't worry. We can't afford to lose the prophet of Erabon."

Nuke laughed. "Glad to hear it."

He stood still while they wrapped some type of material around him and connected the ends to themselves. The material felt stretchy and spongy and Nuke realized that should allow it to give a little yet still be supportive.

As Nuke looked around, he saw his friends being connected to Aphiahians in the same manner. Gavrek and Jerim led Nuke to the edge. Nuke took a deep breath as his pulse quickened.

Jerim pointed. "If you count three layers down, you can see a white building on the land mass which looks almost hexagonal." He looked at Nuke. "Do you see it?"

Nuke squinted. The distance looked a long way down, but the building was definitely identifiable. He nodded. "Yes, I see it."

"Good," Jerim said with a nod. "Knowing where you're going is half the battle."

Gavrek smiled. "Just let Jerim and me do all the work." He patted Nuke's shoulder. "You just have fun."

Nuke forced a grin. "Fun. Yeah, that's just what I was thinking." He reminded himself he had flown in jets doing all sorts of maneuvers and had parachuted in all sorts of conditions. Yet he was always the one in control in those situations. Now he was relying on two people he didn't know. For some reason, that unnerved him. He could feel his heart beating hard in his chest.

Gavrek and Jerim backed up with Nuke. Gavrek explained what was about to take place. "We're going to do a running leap, so stay in step with us. OK?"

Nuke nodded.

Gavrek and Jerim each put an arm around his shoulders. Gavrek spoke next: "Ready, set . . . run."

Nuke timed his running speed with theirs and basically ran off the edge of the island. Both Gavrek and Jerim let go of him and spread their hands and legs. Since they now had less drag, they rose slightly above him, their winglike structures catching the wind and providing lift. Nuke's body rode a little lower than theirs since he was dead weight, so to speak, at this point.

"How are you doing, Nuke?" Jerim called his way.

He looked up at Jerim and gave two thumbs up. Actually, he found this more fun than he expected it to be. The feeling wasn't that different from skydiving after all—as long as he didn't think about not being in control of his dive. He could also now see that the flap between his pilots' arms and side, and between their legs, was their skin and not something they wore, as they wore no shirt or vest. He glanced up and saw his friends not far behind. Gavrek and Jerim flew him around several of the islands. He noticed the islands were connected with some type of thick vine that looked a couple of meters in diameter. As they flew around the temple, Nuke's eyes widened as he saw something like a large stream of water flowing alongside the temple and over the edge of the island, creating a mist as the water descended to whatever was below. Out of the water, and evidently through the island, grew the large vine, and here it produced large green leaves that seemed to come to a point at the bottom of each leaf.

Once around the temple structure, Gavrek and Jerim made nearly a perfect landing several meters from the temple entrance.

Jerim began unhooking Nuke. "How was it?"

Nuke laughed. "I'm ready to do it again."

Jerim grinned. "Well, from what I hear, you'll be doing this all by yourself after tomorrow."

After being unbound, Nuke patted the shoulders of both men. "Thanks to both of you."

Both waved and ran off the edge of the island. Nuke had no idea where they were heading.

His other friends landed in swift succession. As Nuke turned to the temple, he saw Michael approach, a large smile on his face. "That looked like fun," Michael said.

After his initial shock at seeing Michael again, Nuke responded. "Actually, it was. How was yours?"

Michael's eyes widened. "I wouldn't call my experience fun. For a few minutes I thought I had become dinner."

Nuke chuckled. "So did we." Then, with sarcasm, Nuke said, "But now I know you're special."

Michael laughed. "Told ya."

Nuke turned serious. "Really, though, Michael. This means both of us were destined to be here."

Michael stopped and seemed to be in thought. "I guess that's true. Strange, though. I thought I was just here to support you. I never thought I was part of this whole Erabon returning thing."

Nuke laughed. "Looks like you're the star of the show this time." Seeing others approach, he turned somber. "Michael, when did you calculate this planet's HaShem celebration would occur?"

"Today, actually. Why? What have you heard?"

"That it's today." He sighed. "So I guess we were right after all. We're so far from Earth the hope of getting back seems next to impossible."

Michael nodded. "Seems that way." He got a silly grin on his face, though, and gave Nuke a jab to his shoulder. "But cheer up. You've got a good thing going with Ti'sulh, right?"

Before Nuke could respond, Kubim and Seraphia arrived. On their heels came their friends.

Kubim nodded. "I hope you had a pleasant experience."

Nuke chuckled. "I told Jerim I was ready to do it all over again."

A smile came across Kubim's face. "Soon, you will." He gestured for all of them to follow him. "As you can see, we are preparing for the HaShem celebration. You all will be our honored guests." He turned to Michael. "You will sit in a seat of special honor: next to Zyhov."

"I don't get to sit with my friends?"

Nuke could tell all this special honor business wasn't sitting so well with Michael.

"Zyhov always attends," Seraphia said, "but always alone. You sitting next to Zyhov will send a message to our people that Erabon's prophecy is being fulfilled right before their eyes."

Michael gave a shrug. "OK. I guess." He looked at Nuke— with his head turned from the others—and rolled his eyes. Nuke gave him a quick pat on the shoulder.

There were several long tables with cushions for sitting. A hubbub of activity went on around them as food and drinks were brought to the tables. Many were already gathering and sitting. As the sun was setting, antigravity orb lighting was placed all around, creating a nice ambience; there was enough light to see, but not too bright. Kubim had them all sit in the center of a long table facing the temple. Michael's table sat a couple of meters behind theirs and was raised higher than the others. The other tables went back from this first long table on both sides, forming a V-shaped opening with Michael in its center.

Uplighting highlighted the temple in the distance. The building appeared pure white and reflected the light, making the temple nearly glow. After several minutes, Nuke saw the color of the temple change. The lighting would slowly change from blue to gold to red to purple to white. One color would slowly morph into the next, going from a weak color intensity to a deep color, and then fade and transition to the next. The morphing of color was almost mesmerizing and provided an excellent backdrop for the festivities.

As the other Aphiahians flew in, all seemed in a celebratory mood, greeting and laughing with each other as they found their seats. All looked similar to Kubim and Seraphia in appearance and dress with one notable difference: each had different numbers and sizes of the pipe-like structures on their bodies. Some stopped abruptly and pointed at Michael as if they were surprised, and then seemed to discuss his presence among themselves with nods, shrugs, and animated gestures before they took their seats.

Once everyone arrived, Kubim and Seraphia stood. All became quiet. Kubim raised his hands and looked upward. "Erabon, we give you special thanks on this Day of HaShem. After all this time you have brought to us our fellow clansmen, your prophet, and his Zyhov. We are truly blessed to have your prophecy fulfilled before us today on the day we celebrate your Name."

Nuke heard a fluttering noise above and behind them. He turned and saw Zyhov land beside Michael. Those closest looked a little nervous at first but settled back unworried as Zyhov did its triple trill once more. Nuke heard gasps from the people. Evidently they too understood this as a fulfillment of Erabon's prophecy to them. Nuke glanced back and saw Michael petting the giant bird and the creature looking quite content.

The wind, which had been constantly blowing, suddenly stopped. A complete silence came across the crowd. Zyhov did its trill again. Then, amazingly, but in sync with one another, the people began to sway and chant in a rhythmic manner:

HaShem, our praise is to you whom we seek.
This one day of each cycle we gather to pray.
Zyhov represents your Spirit, being unique.
May your coming be soon and without further delay.

The people must have repeated this chant more than a dozen times. Their arms were constantly raised toward the sky as they knelt, but each time they did the chant they leaned farther and farther back until they were almost flat on their backs looking up.

As suddenly as it stopped, the wind blew again, and the people ended the chant and sat upright again. Seraphia clapped her hands three times and everyone began to eat bowls of food which were set before them. Nuke heard music again. He looked back at Michael, but Zyhov wasn't producing the music this time. He saw movement in his periphery and looked back to his front.

Several Aphiahians were moving in a choreographed manner to their front and side. The music, beautiful and melodic, came from them. Nuke realized why the people had the pipe-like structures on their body; the structures produced the music! Each person would move and turn in agile but determined movement to make the wind pass through the different pipe-like structures on their arms, legs, and faces. Now he understood why some had longer structures than others and some had more of the structures and some less. When they did their movements in synchronous ways, they produced various melodies and harmonies. Nuke found the experience mesmerizing.

This went on for several hours as everyone ate and talked. No one talked loudly as the music was the main show of the evening. Nuke noticed the people had unbound their clothes attached to their wrists and ankles so their arms and legs could be exposed to catch the breeze. Nuke's eyes widened when they combined all of this with various acrobatic movements. He found the show awe-inspiring.

He looked over at Seraphia. "This is so incredible. I'm extremely glad we didn't miss this."

She smiled. "We always expected you to come on HaShem. We just couldn't conceive of a better day for something like this to occur."

Nuke looked back at Michael. Although alone, he seemed to be enjoying himself with Zyhov. Michael would hand feed the creature from his plate and pet Zyhov as it ate. Periodically, Zyhov would mimic or repeat some of the tones the Aphiahians produced. Michael would laugh and pet the creature again.

Nuke looked at his friends. Everyone seemed to be enjoying themselves. He turned to Ti'sulh. "What do you think of all of this?"

"I think it's incredible." Ti'sulh said. "I've never witnessed anything like this. The experience really makes one feel Erabon's Spirit is present."

Nuke nodded. He felt the same way.

"However . . . "

Nuke turned back to her with a questioning look. He whispered: "However?"

She nodded and leaned toward him, also whispering. "It just seems they're honoring the wrong thing."

Nuke glanced back at Michael. "You mean having Michael as the focus?"

Ti'sulh tilted her head back and forth slightly. "Sort of."

"Aw. I think it's nice he gets his day in the sun."

She smiled. "I do too. But it's not that. It's just . . . "

Nuke cocked his head. "What is it?"

She let out a sigh. "Well, the emphasis just feels a little backward."

He glanced around at everyone and then back to her, unsure what she was intending. He shook his head just a bit.

"I know the Spirit of Erabon is important and we should treat it so." She looked down and then back into his gaze. "I just think the Spirit would want the praise to be focused on Erabon himself. The Spirit would honor Erabon and not Erabon the Spirit." She shrugged. "Maybe I'm making too much of it." She gave a weak smile. "Don't get me wrong. I am having a good time."

Nuke smiled back at her. "I'm glad." Giving a slight shrug, he said, "Let's see how things go over the next few days and we can make a better judgment on the matter."

She nodded.

He held up his glass in a quiet toast to her and she did the same. They both returned their focus to the dancers and the fabulous music.

TWENTY-SIX

FLYING LESSONS

Nuke sat up as he awoke. His sleeping quarters reminded him somewhat of those he had used on Qerach, just more spacious. They were located somewhere behind the temple in a building that evidently housed some of the temple caretakers—if he had heard the explanation correctly the night before. He had arrived after dark, and was quite tired after the festivities, so Nuke simply followed his guide here without any questions. He couldn't wait to take a look outside now that it was light. He was heading to the shower when he heard a knock on his door.

"Yes. Come in."

The door opened with a soft *swoosh* and Jerim entered. "Good morning, prophet of Erabon."

"Please, call me Nuke. Doing so just makes things easier."

Jerim smiled. "Very well, Nuke. Here are your clothes." He held up two pieces. He draped one over his arm and held up the other. "This is your flying vest. Just strap it on. How should be self-evident. If not, just let me know and I'll help you." He threw that one on the bed then held up the second. "I think you already know about this piece as everyone else is wearing them. They have attachments at the end of the sleeves and ankles." He gave a broad smile. "Let me know if I can help you with anything."

Nuke nodded. "I think I'm fine. I'll take a shower and be right out."

Jerim gave a slight nod. "Very good. I'll have breakfast ready for you then."

Nuke nodded and Jerim left his room.

Nuke took his shower and then came back to the bed to examine the clothes. He held up the sheer material and chuckled to himself. Good thing he would have a vest underneath. He placed that back on the bed and picked up the vest, which felt quite lightweight, like some type of fine mesh material. *Simple enough.* He stepped into the bottom part, which was like wearing a pair of boxer briefs, though the flap between the legs felt weird; still, he assumed he would quickly get used to the feeling. He then put his arms through the vest and secured the straps over his shoulder, noticing the flaps underneath his arms. He lifted his arms up and down several times to see how the flaps worked. He noticed a button near the top of the vest and pressed it. All parts of the suit automatically adjusted to his physique. He rubbed his hands over his chest and sides and nodded. It felt amazingly comfortable.

He picked up the sheer body suit. He found himself wondering the point of such a thing. He shrugged. *When in Rome* . . . He strapped the sleeves at the wrist and the legs at the ankle. He chuckled again. At least he was more covered than he had been on Myeem. Here, there were just more social mores to get accustomed to.

Once he stepped from his room, he found several of his friends seated at a table at an outside portico. Some were already eating, and others were being served. Jerim looked up. "I see you found all in order?" He gestured for Nuke to sit.

"Yes. Thank you, Jerim." Jerim set a plate of food in front of him. "Are you one of the temple caretakers Kubim spoke of last night?"

Jerim nodded. "Yes. Me, Gavrek, who you also met yesterday, and a few others."

"Well, the garden area looks magnificent." He could see topiaries and colorful flowers around the temple complex. He looked back at Jerim. "Thanks for letting us see all this up close."

"Our pleasure," Jerim said as he gave a slight bow. "I'll leave you to your meal. Just come to the front of the temple when you're done, and I'll get Gavrek and some others to give you your flying lessons."

Nuke gave him a thumbs-up.

Jerim chuckled and left them to their meal.

As Nuke looked around the table, he saw everyone except Michael. He turned to Z'zlzck. "Where's Michael?" He laughed. "Is he being a sleepyhead?"

Z'zlzck took a drink and shook his head. "I don't think so. I saw him earlier headed toward the temple."

"Any idea why?"

Z'zlzck shrugged. "No idea." He looked up and pointed. "Well, you can ask him. He's coming back now."

Nuke turned and saw Michael approaching. He looked deep in thought. Michael came to the table, sat, and took the cover off his food plate, but he seemed to have a confused look on his face as he slowly began eating. He didn't even say anything to his friends.

Nuke watched Michael for several minutes. "You OK, Michael?"

Michael looked up from his plate and shook his head. "Kubim and Seraphia met me earlier. They . . . " Michael paused and shook his head again. He set his utensils down and held up his hands. "Nuke, this is not my idea."

Nuke cocked his head. "What? What's not your idea?"

Michael sighed. "They want *me* to enter the temple."

Nuke gave a dismissive gesture. "Sure. I thought I'd ask for all of us to enter the temple."

Michael shook his head. "No, Nuke. They want me to be the one to open the talisman."

Nuke stopped chewing. Was that possible? He had never considered whether Michael could do that. But Michael was a red-blood like him, so maybe it was possible.

Before he could say anything, Ti'sulh responded. "This is what I tried to tell you last night, Nuke. Something's off here."

The others nodded.

Michael held up his hands. "Nuke, I didn't encourage this at all. I would prefer you do it. They seemed pretty adamant, though."

E'oa set his utensil down and gestured. "Actually, this would be the opportunity for all the clansmen to open the talisman without you, Nuke."

Michael looked at E'oa. "What do you mean?"

"Well, this is the first time we have a clansman from each planet together. I would think they would want us all to be there for such an occasion—an occasion that hasn't been possible in more than a thousand cycles."

Michael's eyes went slightly wide. "Oh, I never thought about that." He glanced at Nuke. "What do you think?"

Nuke shrugged. "I think that would be a great gesture on their part, to allow that." He put his hand to his chin. "No offense, Michael, but why do they want you to do it?"

Michael shook his head. "They just kept talking about the Spirit of Erabon and how wonderful it would be to have the prophet's Zyhov open the talisman to reveal all six revelations of Erabon."

Ti'sulh huffed.

Nuke turned to her. "Are you OK?"

"No, she is not," Bicca answered. "And neither am I. Ti'sulh's right. They are thinking themselves superior to all of us."

Nuke sat up straighter. "You think that's what they're doing?" He scanned the faces of his friends. They each nodded. "Why, though?"

E'oa leaned forward and looked at Nuke. "What is the revelation from Erabon for this planet according to the talisman?"

Nuke thought a second. "Let the music of the Spirit of Erabon become your gavel."

E'oa raised his eyebrows with a slight nod as if to imply that was self-evident.

Nuke put his hand to his chin. Just when he thought all would go well on this last of the planets. He shook his head. "Because the wind here represents the Spirit of Erabon and they make music from it, they can judge everyone else."

E'oa nodded.

"Another misapplication," Ti'sulh said.

Nuke rubbed his forehead in thought. He did this for several seconds. "That's why they want Michael to do this—to show their superiority to the other clans." He looked up and sighed. "Well, the least I can do is insist we all enter the temple with Michael."

Several of his friends started to speak, but Nuke held up his hands. "It is their temple, after all. We can't force them to do things our way."

Each nodded slowly as realization seemed to sink in. Ti'sulh put her hand on his arm. "You're right, Nuke." She looked at the others. "We'll follow your lead."

The others nodded.

"Nuke . . . everyone, I'm really sorry," Michael said, looking crestfallen.

Z'zlzck put his hand on Michael's shoulder. "It's not your fault, Michael. You can't help being special."

Michael gave him a smirk.

Z'zlzck laughed and everyone joined in. That seemed to make Michael feel a little better.

Nuke stood. "All right, let's all go get our flying lessons. We'll deal with this later when we see Kubim and Seraphia."

Nuke was proud of his friends. As they walked toward the temple, each of them gave Michael's shoulder a pat or squeeze to let him know they had no hard feelings. By the time they reached the temple, Michael's spirits seemed back to normal.

Those who had helped them get from their jets to the temple yesterday were waiting for them when Nuke and his group arrived.

Gavrek stepped forward and gestured to his fellow Aphiahians. "Each of us who helped you yesterday will assist you today." He smiled. "The only difference is you will not be tethered to us today." He held up his hands. "Yet we will be right beside you to assist and offer instruction."

He then went through several instructions on how to take off, maneuver left and right, and finally how to land. Gavrek first had them practice while still on land. Nuke felt somewhat silly doing the maneuvers on foot but acting as though he was in the air. Yet he reminded himself that doing so seemed no sillier than many of the things the Academy had him do during his basic training days.

After a while Nuke and his friends got into the exercise and began making fun of one another; this acted as an icebreaker and a way to get to know their fellow Aphiahians. By the end, all were laughing and joking with each other.

After about an hour, Gavrek held up his hands. "OK, everyone. Now it's time for the real thing. Get with your partners. And please, do whatever we tell you to do. Please."

Everyone nodded and paired up with their instructors.

Gavrek and Jerim came alongside Nuke. This time Jerim spoke. "OK, Nuke. You just received the basics. Now you only have to put them into practice."

Nuke nodded. The exercise seemed simple enough—it was akin to skydiving without a parachute. The hard part was acting like a bird on landing. He would have to pull himself upright once he neared the ground so he could then let gravity take over. The trick was to not be too far off the ground when he did that.

Jerim pointed to an island not far from where they stood. "This should be an easy test run to practice. It's not too far, and the island is pretty wide in case you roll."

Nuke nodded. He was excited to do this, but he could feel his heart pounding both from the excitement and the adrenaline surge.

Jerim and Gavrek put their hands on his shoulder. "Now, just sort of lean off the edge," Jerim said. "Spread your hands and legs, feel the lift, and just let the wind take you there. Once you're over the land, pull up hard and gravity will do the rest."

"OK. Let's do it," Nuke said.

Nuke felt the slight push both of them gave his shoulders as he let himself fall over the edge. Although a little disorienting at first—likely what base jumpers on Earth must feel the first couple of times they jump, he surmised—he spread his arms and legs and yielded to the experience. He felt the wind rush over him and the pull on the fabric between his arms and chest, and between his legs, which produced an exhilarating feeling. He reminded himself he had to concentrate. If he missed his landing, he wasn't sure where the next island was and where he would end up. The land mass came up more quickly than he expected.

He heard Jerim yell, "Pull up! Pull up hard!"

Nuke did so but found the ability to pull up harder than he thought; he had to use his abdominal muscles more than he realized. Both Jerim and Gavrek pulled up with ease and landed effortlessly. Nuke pulled up later and higher than they did. His drop proved harder than he expected, and he fell to the ground, rolling, because he had come down at an odd angle.

Both Jerim and Gavrek came over and helped him up. Jerim laughed. "Not too bad for a first try."

Nuke smiled. He knew they were being kind. He was sure his landing had looked pitiful. He could hear his sergeant from the Academy yelling at him: "Concentrate on what you're doing, ladies! Get it right or go home!" Nuke watched his friends come behind him. Most did what he did. Some a little better. Some a little worse. Poor E'oa. With his larger and rounder body, he almost rolled off the land mass. His Aphiahian guides were able to catch him in time. The error didn't seem to bother E'oa in the least; he just laughed about his poor job of landing. Nuke was glad E'oa could laugh at himself.

Gavrek pointed back to the temple. "OK, now we go back."

Nuke's eyes widened. "Go back? How do we fly up?"

Gavrek laughed. "It's called air currents."

"There is a science behind it," Jerim said. "But there's also an art to it. We can tell you the science, but you have to find the art."

Nuke nodded. Although unsuccessful with his first attempt to land back on the island housing the temple, he came back to the lower island and landed again.

After a brief time, he became an expert at landing. Soon he was able to land almost as effortlessly as Gavrek and Jerim. Still, he knew he had a lot of work to do on this "art."

On his fifth attempt to fly back up to the temple, Nuke made it. By lunchtime he had successfully flown back and forth between the two islands without much trouble.

They all headed to the table, where they ate a midday meal. This time their fellow Aphiahians ate with them. Everyone seemed to enjoy each other's company, and lunch became a series of tales of failure and laughter.

"Seriously, though," Jerim said. "It's now just a matter of putting what you learned into practice."

Nuke sat back in his chair. "Mind if I change the subject and ask a few questions about your planet?"

Jerim gave a slight shrug. "Sure. What's on your mind?"

"Well, first of all, how are all of these land masses floating in the air?" Nuke shrugged. "It's not like your planet doesn't have gravity."

"I guess we've stopped thinking about that," Jerim said with a slight tilt of his head as if pondering the question. "We were taught the core of these masses is composed of magnetized rock and is of opposite polarity to the planet's core."

Z'zlzck leaned forward. "So what keeps them from bumping into each other and destroying themselves?" He sat back again. "I mean, I can feel them moving, even if ever so slightly."

Gavrek nodded. "Yes, they do move over time. But our ancestors took care of that problem long ago."

Z'zlzck cocked his head. "What do you mean?"

"Today," Gavrek said, "there are no two land masses on the same plane, so they may pass over or under one another, but never into each other."

"Oh," Ti'sulh said, sounding surprised. "How did they manage that?"

Gavrek shrugged. "I'm not sure. Maybe they destroyed those on equal planes."

"Or maybe they moved each to another plane," Jerim said.

Gavrek nodded. "Could be." He shook his head. "I don't know how the land masses were arranged in the beginning, but there's no concern about them crashing together now."

Jerim stood and all the Aphiahians followed suit. Nuke turned and looked where their gaze was focused. He saw Kubim and Seraphia approaching. When they arrived, the other Aphiahians gave a slight bow.

Kubim looked at Michael. "I trust you had a good morning."

Michael smiled and nodded. "Yes. Very much. Thank you."

Kubim then turned to Jerim. "Mind if I steal them away for a while?"

Jerim nodded. All the Aphiahians who helped them that morning said their goodbyes and headed toward the temple complex.

Seraphia stepped forward. "Now, let's talk about our temple."

TWENTY-SEVEN

ENTERING THE TEMPLE

"What's this?" Michael looked from what Seraphia had just handed him back to her.

She smiled. "Just something for you to remember how you're tied to Zyhov."

Z'zlzck held his hand toward Michael. "You've got to pass it around and show us."

Michael chuckled as he passed the memento to Z'zlzck. "As long as it comes back."

Z'zlzck laughed. "Don't worry." He looked at the piece and passed it on. "That's pretty special."

When Nuke held the piece, he was amazed at the craftsmanship. The replica looked like Zyhov in every detail—just in miniature. Although the item was flat for fitting easily around Michael's neck and resting flat against his chest, the Zyhov replica looked three-dimensional. He was glad that Michael had this special memento. He handed the necklace back to his friend. "Very nice."

Seraphia intercepted the necklace and turned to Michael. "Let me put this around your neck."

Once around him, Michael raised the piece to eye level. "Seraphia, this is so special, and I appreciate it. But . . . "

Her eyebrows went up.

"I'm not sure I'm the one to enter the temple."

Seraphia put her hand on his shoulder. "Well, of course you are." She turned to Nuke. "No offense intended. But you saw how Zyhov accepted Michael. He is special."

Nuke tilted his head slightly. "I can't argue with you there. Yet I feel inviting all the clansmen leaders into the temple would be appropriate as they represent Erabon as well. After all, each planet represents the path to Erabon. No one planet is the total answer."

Seraphia gave a small squint, as though she didn't believe everything Nuke said. "Well . . . "

Kubim touched her arm. She turned to him, somewhat startled.

Kubim smiled. "I think we can accommodate." He gestured toward them. "After all, they've come all this way." He gave a slight shrug. "I mean, it's only right for them to see the prophet's Zyhov open the talisman."

Seraphia gave a concessionary nod. Still, Nuke found her air of superiority palpable. From the faces of his friends, he knew they felt the same.

Nuke knew he needed to diffuse things. "Thank you, Kubim. I think this is truly an all-clansmen moment. Everyone being there will be special."

Seraphia gave a hard nod. "OK. I agree. Let's make this special event happen."

Nuke gestured toward her. "Lead the way."

She and Kubim turned and put Michael between them. The rest followed the three to the temple entrance.

Ti'sulh came up next to Nuke and took his arm. "Can we say 'condescending'?" she whispered.

Nuke patted her arm. "Now, now. I know it's irritating. But I'm hoping once they see the full message of Erabon, they will change their attitude."

"I certainly hope so."

"Just remember we've had to help every clan understand what Erabon is really teaching. Let's not judge them too harshly, too quickly."

Ti'sulh shook her head. "I've seen some reject your claims, but never totally ignore you before."

Nuke chuckled. "Yeah, it's kind of weird. This is a totally different experience."

"Do you think Michael can open the talisman?"

Nuke gave a slight shrug. "I would assume. His blood is as red as mine."

Ti'sulh shook her head. "Yes. But that will just make them even more insufferable."

Nuke chuckled. "You always told me to trust Erabon. Let's not stop now."

She looked into his eyes and smiled. "You really have become his prophet, you know?"

He patted her hand, which lay on his arm. "Only because you finally drilled the message into me."

She chuckled. "And now you need to drill the same back into me."

He smiled in appreciation for her once more.

Once all had gathered at the temple entrance, Seraphia said, "The music of Zyhov becomes our gavel." Nuke thought that an offbeat interpretation, although still accurate. Apparently, Erabon agreed because the temple door opened. All entered. Michael, of course, was told to enter first.

While this temple was cubical, like the last couple they had been in, this one was as unique as the others. As they entered, Nuke found himself surrounded with color. Purple, red, blue, white, and gold holographic streaks appeared to move at random, as if blown by a breeze. Everyone's movements made the colors change course, as if their motion created eddies of air. All this seemed normal to Kubim and Seraphia. Everyone else was mesmerized by the effect.

The colors surrounding them then morphed into words. As Nuke read them as they went by, he realized these were the commandments Erabon had given them which had been posted in each previous temple. Here they appeared to travel on the breeze. Suddenly the meaning hit him, and he gasped just a bit.

Ti'sulh turned his way. "What is it?"

"The words. They are on the breeze, which represents the Spirit and breath of Erabon. They are truly the words of Erabon. This symbolism makes his words more powerfully stated."

Ti'sulh nodded. "Yes, there is much symbolism here."

The whirling words then grouped together and formed the outline of a table. As the words dissipated, a table with the talisman remained. Everyone, except for Kubim and Seraphia, watched in stunned amazement.

Seraphia opened a drawer to the table and pulled out a small box containing gold pins. She handed one to Michael. "We would like you to have the honor to open each component of the talisman."

Michael looked from her to Nuke. "I . . . I'm not sure this is for me to do."

She put her hand on his shoulder. "You are a red-blood, as well as is the prophet of Erabon. Being a pure red-blood is what will open each section of the talisman in order. As his Zyhov, it is fitting for you to be the one to open these on Aphiah, the planet of the Spirit of Erabon."

"Uh, excuse me."

Everyone turned Nuke's way.

He gave a forced smile but tried to make it as genuine as he could. "If you want Michael to open the talisman, that is fine. However, I want to be sure you understand each planet plays a role in the path to Erabon. Yet each planet does not have the exclusivity to that role but represents that particular step. All people of each planet can, and should, take each step to return to Erabon."

Both Kubim and Seraphia gave Nuke a blank stare. Kubim finally responded. "It's clear Erabon's Spirit abides here with us."

Nuke continued to smile. "His Spirit abides with all who believe and trust in him."

They simply turned back to Michael without acknowledging his statement.

Michael looked at Nuke as though unsure what to do. Nuke nodded. Michael closed his eyes briefly and shook his head slightly. He pricked his finger. Both Kubim and Seraphia gasped when they saw a drop of red blood appear on his finger.

Seraphia, now in a hushed tone, said, "Now place your blood in the center of the talisman."

Michael dipped his finger into the black depression in the center of the talisman and brought his finger back. All waited . . . but nothing happened.

Michael looked at Nuke. "Does it take a while for something to happen?"

He shook his head. "It normally happens instantaneously."

Seraphia looked at Michael, then Kubim, then Nuke. "I . . . I don't understand. He is a red-blood." She scanned the room. "You saw it. He is a red-blood and the Zyhov of the prophet of Erabon."

Ti'sulh nodded. "Yes, but he is not *the* prophet of Erabon. Only the prophet of Erabon can open the talisman."

Seraphia looked at Ti'sulh with her mouth open; it was as though she was unable to comprehend Ti'sulh's words. "But how is his blood any different?" She turned to Nuke. "Explain."

Nuke shook his head. "I can't explain."

Ti'sulh interjected. "While it may not be logical, we can't thwart Erabon's plans. Let Nuke open the talisman."

Seraphia stepped back. "You can open the talisman when Michael, here, cannot?"

Nuke stepped to the table. "It would seem so." He picked up another gold pin. "I would have rather had each clansman in turn open their part of the talisman so we all could have been a part of this to welcome back Erabon in unity. Perhaps my efforts here will restore the unity among the clansmen, which has been broken for all these years."

This time, Nuke instinctively knew Erabon would come through. He didn't know how or why, but Nuke had faith he would. He had done this five times before. Why would he fail now?

Nuke took the pin and pricked his finger. His bright red blood appeared. Everyone leaned in, waiting expectantly for something to happen. Nuke put his finger in the center depression of the talisman.

The first section of the talisman opened immediately. Everyone gasped. Nuke smiled. Erabon had come through. He always did.

Out of the talisman came blue light, and it seemed to absorb the blue wisps flowing on air eddies around them, and went to one of the walls, which also turned blue. A relief of Myeem appeared along with a relief of a Myeemian. As they watched, the Myeemian turned into a three-dimensional hologram and raised his hand upward, toward the center of the room. Then, under the relief of the planet, these words appeared: *To reach Erabon, the step of purification must first come.*

Kubim and Seraphia looked dumbfounded. Seraphia whispered, "Amazing."

Before anything else could be said, the second section of the talisman opened, and gold light, also absorbing the golden air eddies, went to another wall, which also turned a golden color. A relief of Eremia appeared along with a relief of an Eremian. This relief turned into a three-dimensional hologram as well, and this one also raised his hand toward the center—now touching the hand of the Myeemian. Under the relief of the planet these words appeared: *Through gates of sanctification to Erabon you must travel.*

Next the third section opened. Red light went out from the talisman, absorbing the red air eddies from around them, and then went to another wall, which also turned red. A relief of Sharab appeared along with a relief of a Sharabian. Once again, this relief turned into a three-dimensional hologram raising his hand to touch that of the other two. Under the relief of this planet these words were shown: *Trust in Erabon; tribulations of more than one will be their sum.*

Purple light shot from the next section, absorbing the purple air eddies, and went to the fourth wall, which also turned purple. A relief of Ramah appeared along with a relief of a Ramahian. E'oa, watching intently, now appeared to glow purple as well. Nuke knew he was attuned to Erabon in this moment. His other friends were not startled, but Kubim and Seraphia stood wide-eyed in a new state of amazement. The relief on the wall turned into a three-dimensional hologram raising his hand to touch those of the others. Below the relief of Ramah appeared these words: *Through struggles come great rewards which Erabon will never allow to unravel.*

The next section of the talisman opened. White light came forth capturing the white air eddies and went to the ceiling, which turned white. No colored eddies were around them any longer. A relief of Qerach, and a Qerachian, appeared. When this relief turned into a three-dimensional hologram, the figure rotated to have the Qerachian's feet on the floor and the figure raising its hand, along with a lock of hair that touched the hands of the other holographic clansmen. The eyes and lock of hair of the Qerachian representation contained all six colors rather than just one. Below the relief of Qerach these words appeared: *Hesitation to unite through Erabon will make the hope of your soul go numb.*

The last section of the talisman opened, and a bright light came out and went into the floor, causing the floor to seem to disappear and, at first, this disoriented and startled everyone. Then a relief of the planet Aphiah appeared as well as an Aphiahian, which then morphed into a three-dimensional hologram that rotated to stand on the floor with hand raised to touch the hands of the other five holograms. Below the relief of the planet Aphiah appeared the following words: *Let the music of the Spirit of Erabon become your gavel.*

Before anyone could say anything, all five colors of light came out of the center of the talisman and spread throughout all walls, floor, and ceiling, making it appear as if all the walls disappeared and were suspended in space with the five colors moving throughout. After a couple of minutes the five colors came together in the center of the room under the upstretched arms of the clansmen. Each planet relief turned into a hologram and floated into the center with the swirling mass of color. What formed was a planet from the combined planets, just as Nuke had observed in the other temples.

"It's beautiful," Seraphia said in a whisper. Kubim nodded.

Under the planet appeared the words: *Praise be to Erabon anew who will return and make all things new.*

Even without having to ask, or be led, everyone said, "Praise be to Erabon who makes all things new."

Nuke assumed that ended the presentation since this was all he had observed in the other temples. He started to seek everyone's attention to go over the need for unity, but before he could do that, the hologram morphed into the picture of a face.

Everyone gasped—including Nuke. This had not occurred in any previous temple. The face looked extremely tranquil and peaceful, and the image rotated through the various colors. The face began to speak.

"My friends, thank you all for coming and joining me and representing each of your planets and clansmen." The image gave a broad smile. "This is the first time all members of each clan have been together for over one thousand cycles. Your presence here pleases me greatly."

Nuke wondered if this was a prerecorded message. Since all the sections of the talisman couldn't be opened without all the clans present, this could be. Nuke thought this quite clever. He was abruptly brought out of his thoughts when he heard his name.

"Yohanan, thank you for being willing to be my prophet to my fellow clansmen." The image smiled once more. "And

Michael, thank you for being willing to be my prophet's Zyhov to help everyone understand the purpose of my Spirit."

Nuke's mouth fell open. He looked at Michael, who looked stunned as well. So did everyone else.

Nuke's mind went into a chaos of thought. *How is this possible? Could this have been prerecorded?* Did Erabon know of his coming more than a thousand cycles ago? He put his hand to his chin. Well, he supposed that could be true. If Erabon was indeed God and knew everything, he certainly could. After all, didn't Old Testament Scripture predict the role of Cyrus nearly five hundred years before Cyrus was born? Was that what was happening here? His destiny determined long before his birth? Did that still happen?

The image continued. "Ti'sulh, Bicca, Z'zlzck, E'oa, Zael, Kubim, and Seraphia, look at each other." They all did so, and in an equally dazed manner. "You have each made history today. For the first time in over a thousand cycles, all clansmen representatives are in my temple together. Do not think this insignificant. My purpose is to bring unity through diversity. I delight in diversity in my universe but also delight in unity of heart. You are the new generation of bringing this back to all your people. I trust you do not squander this opportunity. I hope to see you soon. Do not neglect your duty."

The image dissipated. All walls went back to white. They were standing in an empty room once more. Everyone looked stunned and left the temple without a word.

This time, Seraphia gestured for Nuke to exit first.

TWENTY-EIGHT

DECIPHERING INFORMATION

Seraphia seemed completely disoriented after she stepped from the temple. She turned several times, as though she didn't know what she wanted to do or where to go. She looked at Nuke. "I . . . I need to do some thinking." She took a few steps and then turned back. "I'll come see you later." She and Kubim walked away. Although Kubim tried to comfort her, she kept shaking her head and acted upset.

Ti'sulh came up to Nuke. She rubbed his arm. "There's several benches behind the temple in the garden. Let's all go there and talk."

He nodded and turned to everyone. "Follow us, guys. Let's regroup."

Once they reached the garden area, some sat on benches, some on planters, and a couple on the ground.

Nuke stood. "I thought we should talk through what happened in the temple."

"Yeah," Michael said. "What *did* happen?" He shook his head. "I mean, I know I'm not the prophet of Erabon, but my blood is just as red as yours, so the reason has to be something else."

Nuke shook his head. "I . . . I don't know." He looked at Ti'sulh.

Ti'sulh looked to Bicca. He shook his head. "I always thought the reason was Nuke's red blood, which Erabon also had," Bicca said.

"No, it's more than that," Zael said, speaking up. All eyes turned his way.

"Nuke, think about the arnoclids. Both you and Zel had an electrical conductance connection."

Ti'sulh's eyes went wide. "That's it. That's one thing you and Michael don't have in common."

Michael laughed. "Nuke, I knew you were nuclear for a special reason. Turns out, you're more special than either of us realized. Erabon chose you because you're as unique as he is."

Nuke shook his head. "That's a big stretch."

"I said 'as unique,' not 'as powerful.'" Michael gave Nuke a smirk. "Don't get a big head."

Z'zlzck chimed in. "Like you, Zyhov boy?"

Michael turned to Z'zlzck. "What was that supposed to mean?"

Z'zlzck laughed. "Just that, around here, both of you are unique, and it's up to us to keep your egos in check."

Michael laughed. "Thanks, Bob. I appreciate your sacrifice."

Z'zlzck shrugged. "One does what one has to do." This brought a few more laughs.

Bicca spoke up. "So what do we do now?"

Nuke tilted his head with a shrug. "I guess the next step depends upon Seraphia."

"You don't think she'll ignore what she witnessed in the temple, do you?" Ti'sulh asked, a concerned look on her face.

Nuke shrugged. "I know she's trying to process it. She looked pretty confused."

Z'zlzck pushed on Michael's shoulder. "You disappointed your worshipper."

Michael's hand went to his chest. "Me? You can blame Erabon for that." He paused, then shook his head. "That didn't come out right. Blame is not the right word."

Z'zlzck patted Michael's shoulder. "We know what you meant. Interesting that you were part of the prophecy, though."

"Yeah," E'oa said. "We all were."

Zael nodded. "Amazing that he mentioned each of us by name. And I thought my coming here was my decision."

"Well, it was, wasn't it?" Nuke asked.

Zael turned to Nuke. "Yeah . . . I suppose so." He gestured. "But you were the one who suggested it."

"True, but you're the one who agreed. So the decision really was yours after all."

"So how did Erabon know?"

Ti'sulh chuckled. "You don't expect him to know everything?"

"Well, yes," Zael said. "But . . . if my coming here was my decision, how did he know, millennia ago, I would actually come?"

E'oa squeezed Zael's shoulder. "Proves how unique he is, don't you think?"

Zael paused and nodded. "Yes, it really does."

In the next few moments Jerim walked up to join them. "Anyone hungry? We have dinner ready." He gestured toward the portico where they had eaten that morning.

All nodded and stood to follow him back. Nuke realized they had gone from morning to afternoon without eating. They had been so wrapped up in what occurred at the temple that the thought of eating had escaped all of them.

Jerim looked at Nuke. "I hear you had an interesting day."

Nuke's eyebrows went up. "Really? How did you hear about it?" He knew his friends had been with him the entire day and had not talked to anyone.

"Gavrek overheard Seraphia and Kubim talking."

"And what do you think about what you heard?"

Jerim glanced at Nuke and shook his head. "Didn't hear all of it, but Gavrek said Seraphia was upset Erabon didn't consider Aphiahians superior to the other clans."

Ti'sulh furrowed her brow. "But why did she think that in the first place?"

"Oh, not only her," Jerim said, "but most of our clan." He shrugged. "But that's probably because that's what we've been taught."

E'oa cocked his head. "But not you?"

Jerim tilted his head and gave a slight shrug. "I've had my doubts. I guess because of us taking care of the temple, we think more about these things. I always wondered about the rest of Erabon's message since we only get one part of it. I could never understand why Erabon would have one part of his creation more special than another."

Nuke patted Jerim on a shoulder. "Nice to hear not everyone took the perceived interpretation as the only legitimate interpretation. When you put Erabon's entire message together, the meaning reveals he wants everyone to follow him and that everyone plays a special role in his plan."

"That sounds more like the Erabon we would expect him to be," Jerim said.

Bicca turned to Jerim. "So how do you let all of your people know this?"

Jerim pressed his lips together as though in thought, then said, "I think that is really up to Seraphia and Kubim."

"Well," Nuke said with a slight raise of his eyebrows, "I certainly hope she comes around."

All found seats, and others set plates of food in front of them. Nuke invited Jerim and Gavrek to sit with them. They were happy to do so. He invited the others, but they said they had other obligations to take care of first.

"Gavrek, Jerim told us about some of the things you overheard. What's your take on what you heard?" Nuke was curious what others were thinking.

Gavrek gave a slight grimace and shot a look to Jerim, who returned a sheepish smile.

"Please do not spread that news. I . . . I don't want Seraphia or Kubim to think I spied on them. I was pruning in the garden near where they talked, so I overheard some of what they said."

Nuke held up his hands. "Don't worry. Your discovery is safe with us." Nuke looked at the others and they nodded. "But I am curious as to what you think."

Gavrek glanced at Jerim. "Well, what I overheard confirms what some of us had been discussing."

Jerim nodded.

"Which was?" Nuke asked.

Gavrek shrugged. "Well, probably what Jerim already told you. The message we were taught didn't seem to fit what Erabon was supposed to be about."

E'oa leaned in. "Can you explain that a bit more?"

Gavrek looked at E'oa. "Just because you are different from me doesn't mean Erabon would think less of you than of me."

He shrugged. "Why would he? I mean, after all, he created both our clans."

Jerim nodded. "It seems Erabon loves diversity but wants unity. Our history seems to confirm this."

Ti'sulh nodded. "Absolutely. It's good to hear thinking like that. But what about others?"

Jerim shook his head. "Most take what they are told without really thinking through the implication of the message."

Gavrek nodded. "Unless Seraphia changes her thinking, I don't know that others will."

Nuke put his hand to his chin. "Well, I certainly hope she and Kubim come around. Without their acceptance of unity and equality among clansmen, I'm not sure we can expect Erabon to return."

Gavrek scrunched his brow—as much as he could since the pipe-like structures on his forehead didn't allow his brow to move much. "Why is that?"

"Well, the prophecy states Erabon wants all the clans to reunite before his return. As you just said, he loves diversity but demands unity. He is not going to force it. He didn't force obedience the first time he came, and he will not again. He wants all to come to him on their own decision."

"And if they don't?" Gavrek asked.

Nuke shrugged. "I'm not sure, but I don't think the outcome would be good."

Jerim put his hands on the table and produced a small smile. "Well, I'm certain Erabon has everything under control, and what he wants to happen will happen."

"Hey, who's the prophet around here?" Nuke asked, mock seriousness on his face.

Jerim looked at Nuke with concern but then broke into a broad grin after Nuke did.

Nuke nodded. "I just hope others see things the way you do, Jerim."

"So do I," Jerim said as he stood. He turned to Gavrek. "We have to get back to our work."

Gavrek nodded and stood. He looked at Nuke. "Maybe we can go flying again tomorrow."

Nuke nodded and smiled. "Absolutely. If my muscles don't rebel."

Gavrek laughed. "Oh, they most assuredly will. But that's the best time to work them again."

Nuke cocked his head. "OK, then. I'll see you tomorrow."

Both Gavrek and Jerim nodded, turned, and left.

Nuke looked at his friends. "Everyone else game?"

All nodded. Michael laughed. "Can't let the prophet of Erabon outdo his Zyhov."

Nuke laughed and raised his glass to Michael.

While they were still talking under the portico after dinner, Nuke saw Seraphia and Kubim approach the table. He stood.

She motioned for Nuke to be seated. "May the two of us join you for a short while?"

Nuke gestured toward the empty seats. "Please do. What's on your mind?"

Seraphia chuckled. "I think you already know." She glanced at Kubim. "Both Kubim and I have been talking all afternoon after leaving the temple."

Nuke nodded. "You did seem upset as you left."

Kubim shook his head. "Upset? No."

Seraphia interjected. "More like confused."

Kubim nodded.

Ti'sulh leaned forward. "So, what about Erabon's message surprised you?"

Seraphia shook her head slowly and slightly, looking upward for a second before returning her gaze to them.

"Everything," she said.

Ti'sulh turned her head.

Seraphia sighed. "I know that likely sounds silly to you, but please understand. We only had the message for our planet to go on. I think . . . " She paused and looked at Kubim.

He put his hand on Seraphia's arm and picked up where she left off. "The message evidently got misinterpreted a long time ago, and we never thought about correcting it." He shrugged. "I'm afraid that message fed our ego, so we didn't really try to challenge it."

E'oa nodded. "Believe me, we all can identify with that."

Seraphia's eyebrows went up. "Really?" She scanned their faces. "Why?"

Ti'sulh laughed. "Because we all did the same thing. We never really considered Erabon's message to us was only part of the puzzle. We capitalized on that part and elevated Erabon's message to us as the most important message he could give."

Bicca nodded. "We all did. Once we heard the full message of Erabon, it humbled us and made us understand we are all his children and need to be united to look forward to his return."

Seraphia's gaze scanned their faces again. "So . . . you're not furious with us . . . me?"

Nuke shook his head. "Not if you take Erabon's message to heart."

"And," added Ti'sulh, "if you teach your people the full message of Erabon. They all need to unite under his full message."

Seraphia nodded. She glanced at Kubim and then back. "We've already scheduled a meeting with everyone in a couple of evenings."

"That's great," Nuke said.

Zael leaned in. "Why don't we turn the meeting into another celebration?"

Seraphia looked at him quizzically. "Why?"

Zael shrugged. "This is really an important message, and one your people should take to heart and celebrate."

Kubim's eyebrows shot up. "Yes, that is an excellent idea." He pointed to each of them. "And each of you should be part of it."

Nuke sat up straighter. "What?"

Seraphia smiled. "Yes, you all should participate to signify our unity."

Nuke's eyes widened. "You want us to . . . to dance?"

Seraphia nodded. "I'll talk to Gavrek. You have just enough time to practice." She looked excited and turned back to Zael. "Thank you, Zael."

Nuke looked at Zael and replied, in deadpan, "Yeah, thanks Zael."

"My pleasure," Zael said as he gave a nod to Seraphia and then an exaggerated smile to Nuke.

Nuke laughed and shook his head.

Ti'sulh patted his hand. "Oh, it'll be fun."

Seraphia smiled and stood. "Thank you all for your understanding. I feel we are starting a new journey which will be most pleasing to Erabon."

As Seraphia and Kubim left, Michael stood and held out his hands to Nuke, one slightly higher than the other.

Nuke scrunched his brow. "*What* are you doing?"

Michael grinned. "Asking you to dance."

TWENTY-NINE

EXPLORING

Luke groaned and rubbed his abdomen as he woke the next morning. His abdominal muscles were extremely sore. Evidently, being physically fit was not enough when new techniques were learned. Anything new required using muscles in a different way, and this led to soreness. He didn't realize how much he had used his abs the day before. He shook his head. His first landing of this day would be difficult.

After getting dressed and eating breakfast, he and his friends went to the front of the temple. Gavrek and Jerim were waiting for them.

"Ready to do some flying?" Gavrek asked.

Michael looked around. "Only the two of you for all of us?"

"We're here just to rescue and help you get started. Not to do the flying for you," Jerim said, chuckling.

"Besides," Gavrek said, "just put into practice what you already know." He smiled, likely seeing the worried looks on all the faces. "We'll repeat what we learned last time and go from there."

Nuke saw everyone's muscles relax a bit after hearing those words.

After everyone came to the edge of the land mass, Jerim pointed to the nearest mass below them. "OK, everyone. Just fly to the land mass below and then fly back here."

Everyone jumped. Nuke got an adrenaline surge—not from worry, from the thrill. He felt confident in what he had learned, and he had done this a dozen times the day before. All went according to plan, and he pulled up for his landing as scheduled. Of course, he had to force his mind to overcome the pain from the soreness of his abdominal muscles to land properly.

They flew back to the temple, then repeated this flight path a couple more times. The more Nuke did this, the less sore his muscles became; he hoped it was the same for the others. He paid special attention to E'oa and smiled when he saw him land just as well as the others. It was a relief to know he didn't have to worry about his friend rolling off the edge as he had feared. Once Jerim suggested everyone go free flight—flying over or under several land masses before landing—he felt ready.

Just before they started to free fly, Zyhov flew past and did his triple trill. Michael jumped over the edge and flew after the creature. Nuke followed fast on Michael's heels. He looked back; the others were following. Zyhov flew under the land mass holding the temple and through the spray from the spring flowing over the side. All followed. The spray felt cool and refreshing, but because of the mesh material and constant breeze, Nuke was dry again in a matter of minutes.

Following Zyhov, they flew over several floating land masses. This allowed Nuke to see there were dwellings on many of them. Most had gardens. Those under the mist from the temple had some type of structure for catching the water droplets falling from the temple.

Zyhov turned and went deeper toward the cloud cover. Nuke wasn't sure if they should follow him. While this creature may know how to maneuver with zero visibility, Nuke thought, they certainly didn't. Yet Michael was on its heels and showed no signs of pulling back. Nuke cocked his head. *OK, buddy. I'm trusting you.*

Right before Zyhov reached the cloud cover, the creature began to rotate, creating eddies which caused the clouds to dissipate, thus creating a line of visibility. The next thing Nuke knew, Michael was doing the same. *How is he doing that?* He kept observing Michael's technique and then attempted the feat. Nuke didn't turn fast enough, lost his stability, and dropped some in altitude. Although he managed to right himself and use the breeze to rise back to his position behind Michael, his bad technique unnerved him—yet also gave him the adrenaline rush he loved. He did the maneuver again and was able to maintain his altitude. After a few minutes, Zyhov, Michael, and Nuke were flying, twisting, and turning. He couldn't remember having so much fun. This was almost better than flying jets.

Zyhov caught an updraft. He and Michael copied whatever the creature did. Nuke looked back. So far, everyone was still with them—only much farther back. Zyhov flew past the temple again but kept going upward, then turned and flew to a series of small land masses that were positioned very near each other. Zyhov went to the top one and landed. Nuke and Michael flew around and landed on the one just below Zyhov. The others landed on nearby land masses. All were close together and attached by the huge vines that seemed to hold everything together.

Michael flew up to where Zyhov was and began petting him. The others flew to Michael and Zyhov's land mass. There wasn't room for everyone on the mass, but because the vines were so thick, some of them sat on the vine and dangled their feet over its edge.

Jerim held up his backpack. "Anyone hungry?"

Everyone nodded. He passed out some type of sandwich—or what looked like a sandwich. Nuke wasn't sure what he was eating, but the taste was wonderful. Jerim passed around a canteen of water as well.

Gavrek handed the canteen to Nuke. "You and Michael seem to be mastering the technique really well."

Nuke chuckled. "Michael copied Zyhov, and I copied him."

"Well, Zyhov is the master of flying, for sure," Gavrek said.

Nuke nodded. "Easy to tell. I can't remember when I've had such fun."

E'oa laughed. "What you call fun, I call work. I likely won't be able to move tomorrow after all this fun."

After eating and a few more laughs, Jerim asked, "Are you all ready to head back?"

E'oa nodded. "I really am." He chuckled. "I think I need a nap, but you may have to pull me out of bed when I wake up. I may be too sore to move."

Jerim laughed. "I'm sure you'll be fine. Anyone else want to go back now?"

All but Nuke and Michael said they were ready to return to home base.

Jerim stood. "OK. Follow me back." He turned to Gavrek. "You'll stay with these two?"

Gavrek nodded. "Although they seem to be doing just fine on their own."

Zael stood. "We'll see you back at dinner."

Nuke nodded. "You all get some rest, and we'll talk when we get back."

They dove and followed Jerim back toward the temple.

Gavrek looked at Nuke and Michael. "Well, what do you want to do from here?"

Nuke shrugged. "I don't know. Anything unusual to see?"

Gavrek's eyebrows went up. "There is something. I didn't say anything before, but from what I've seen, your flying skills are up to it."

That piqued Nuke's interest. "What is it?"

"It's called the Heart of Erabon," Gavrek said.

"Sounds interesting. Lead the way."

Gavrek dove. Nuke followed. When he looked back, Michael was riding on the back of Zyhov! Nuke shook his head. *Now he's just showing off.*

They flew for several minutes before Nuke saw anything. Then he noticed a land mass coming closer, but this one looked different. Initially shrouded in cloud cover, the floating island kept coming in and out of view as clouds swirled around it. Above the land mass, the vine reminded him of the vine behind the temple, one yielding large green leaves that somehow captured the moisture. Although difficult to see due to the mist, there seemed to be a waterfall coming out of the bottom of the structure rather than over the side.

Gavrek flew around the floating island and then dropped lower to where the water turned to mist. He then flew upward toward the waterfall. As Nuke followed, he realized the water surrounded him, but he wasn't getting wet. He looked up and saw another land mass. This one had a hole in its center. He looked back. Michael jumped off Zyhov and followed them. Jerim seemed to fly straight for the hole, which looked not much wider than their bodies. Nuke's eyes grew very wide.

They had better get this right or they'd crash into the land mass itself.

Directly under this land mass blew an extraordinarily strong updraft. Gavrek caught the current, and this propelled him upward. Nuke followed, and he noticed Michael flying directly on his heels. When Jerim got close, he brought his hands together in front of him, just like a diver—only he was diving up, not down. Jerim shot through the hole. Nuke mimicked what Jerim had done. All went black for a couple of seconds as he went through the hole. Because he no longer flew in the updraft, he could feel gravity begin to overtake his upward momentum. He emerged about the time the upward momentum and the pull of gravity equaled each other. His body paused in midair for a brief second and he felt Jerim pull him to the side just before Michael came through. Jerim did the same for Michael.

Nuke felt his body nearly shaking from the adrenaline surge. "Wow. That was a rush." He looked around. "This is incredible." All around him was water, but it was completely dry where he stood.

Michael went over and put his hand in the water. He turned and chuckled. "We're *inside* the waterfall."

Gavrek nodded. "Yes, this land mass is directly under, and the same size as, the inverted land mass above us. The vine from the top structure collects water from the clouds and stores it. Some of the water flows out its center opening onto the inverted structure. Because this one is the same size, the water flows around this one."

Nuke looked up. He could almost touch the mass of land above him. He realized the physics of the entire thing allowed this. Any additional upward momentum and he would have crashed into this upper land mass above him. Any less upward momentum and gravity would have overtaken him; he would have fallen back before entering this inner sanctum.

Nuke turned to Gavrek. "I assume because water is equated to Erabon's Spirit, this is called the Heart of Erabon because we are metaphorically in the center of his Spirit."

Gavrek smiled and nodded. "Special, no?"

Nuke nodded.

Michael's voice sounded almost in awe. "More than special." He turned full circle again. "Gavrek, I feel honored you would bring us here."

Gavrek continued to smile. "I thought this apropos for the prophet of Erabon and his Zyhov."

Michael laughed. "Absolutely."

"I think it's time we get back," Gavrek said. "We can eat and talk about what to do for the celebration." He grinned. "After seeing what you two have done today, I have some ideas."

Nuke looked at Michael with raised eyebrows. "Looks like we've painted ourselves into a corner."

Michael chuckled. "Well, let's get back to the others." He looked at Gavrek. "So, how do we get out?"

Gavrek pointed to the opening. "The same way we came in. Just jump. Gravity will handle the rest. Once through, spread your arms and legs."

Gavrek gestured for Nuke to go first. "I'll go last to be sure you don't have problems."

Nuke stood at the hole and viewed the light below. He raised his arms over his head and jumped. In only a few seconds he was through. He spread his arms and legs, caught the air current, and circled around the waterfall to wait for Michael and Gavrek to exit.

Once Michael exited, Zyhov came under him and flew away with Michael.

Gavrek came out shortly after, and Nuke came up beside him. Nuke pointed to Zyhov and yelled, "Michael's there!"

Gavrek nodded. They headed back to the temple—this flight was amazingly peaceful—and arrived a short time later.

Once they arrived at the portico, the others were already seated and ready to eat. Nuke and Michael went for a shower and then joined them.

When they returned, Nuke sat next to Ti'sulh, but noticed everyone staring at him. He looked down at his chest and then back. "Is something wrong?"

Zael leaned forward propping his chin on his hand. "Gavrek tells us you have made some plans for us for the celebration."

Nuke's eyes widened. "Me?" He shook his head. "I haven't talked to anyone about any plans."

Zael gave a sly grin. "Well, it seems your antics have given Gavrek some interesting ideas."

Nuke quickly pointed to Michael, who put his hand to his chest. "Hey, what did *I* do?"

Nuke gestured to him. "Oh, I don't know. Maybe rode on the back of Zyhov and twirled around like Zyhov himself?"

Michael took a drink and gestured back. "Well, I seem to recall you doing the same." He tilted his head back and forth slightly. "Well, except for riding on Zyhov. But you get the picture."

Zael laughed. "Yes. I think we all get the picture."

Now Gavrek laughed. "We can assign blame later. Let me tell you what I'm thinking while you eat. I think Seraphia and the crowd will love it."

Bicca's eyes scanned everyone's gaze; each eye seemed to keep moving to look at someone different. "But the real question is," he said, "will *we* love it?"

Gavrek just grinned.

THIRTY

WOWING THE CROWD

Nuke felt nervous. Should he have let Gavrek and Jerim talk him and his friends into this? While they had practiced all day yesterday, that didn't really compare to performing in front of hundreds of people. There was no room for error now.

Gavrek came by and looked into Nuke's eyes. "You OK?"

Nuke shrugged. "I'm not sure. I'm nervous and excited at the same time. How's everyone else?"

Gavrek nodded. "I think they're fine." He moved his head side to side a few times. "They too are nervous and excited. But you all did extremely well yesterday during practice." He smiled. "I'm sure all will go as planned."

Nuke tilted his head and shrugged. "I sure hope so."

Gavrek tapped Nuke on the shoulder. "Let's head that way for the opening ceremony." He gave Nuke a quick pat on the back. "That part is easy. You just stand there."

Nuke chuckled. "Yeah, that part I think I've mastered."

Nuke and his friends came along beside him, and they all stood behind Seraphia and Kubim. She turned and smiled at them. Kubim gave a slight nod. They both turned toward the crowd, which was seated in a similar arrangement to the HaShem celebration. This time, though, there was no V-type opening in the back as there had been previously. The ambience and lighting looked similar to the celebration before.

When they reached the front, Seraphia held up her hands. The crowd quieted.

"My friends, we are back together to reveal our discovery when we entered the temple with the prophet of Erabon, his Zyhov, and our fellow clansmen. Erabon proved both awe-inspiring and enlightening, as you would expect. His entire message, revealed to us through his prophet, shed further light on his prophecy which he had left for all Aphiahians. While we are given the privilege to represent his Spirit, this does not mean we are the judge of others based upon our prophecy, but that we are to judge in the light of his Spirit which he has given to all clansmen. So that makes us equals with the other clans and not superior to them."

Murmuring rumbled through the crowd.

Kubim held up his hands. "My fellow Aphiahians. Don't let this revelation disturb you. Erabon still sees us as special—just as special as the rest of his creation now residing on different planets."

Seraphia went on. "As we tell you Erabon's full message, you will see how this is true." She smiled. "And I know you will come to embrace this message joyously, just as Kubim and I have done. Before we begin with Erabon's revelation, I have asked E'oa, our fellow clansman from Ramah, to ask Erabon's blessing on our time and celebration this evening."

E'oa stepped forward, held up his hands, and began to pray. "Our great and mighty Erabon, we ask for your blessing on our gathering."

E'oa's body turned a brilliant purple. The crowd's reaction was one of awe; Nuke could hear gasps from every section.

"Thank you for your message of unity," E'oa continued. "And we pray we obtain a better understanding of your prophecy to us. Give us wisdom how to follow through with your expectations of us."

E'oa stepped back. His purple brilliance began to fade.

Nuke could hear murmuring through the crowd. Neither Seraphia nor Kubim asked for quiet. Seraphia simply motioned for Ti'sulh to step forward. The crowd quieted as soon as she did. If nothing else, E'oa had captured their attention.

Seraphia put her hand on Ti'sulh's shoulder. "Ti'sulh is our fellow clansman from Myeem. Myeem is the water planet which Erabon gave to Ti'sulh's people. As you well know, water is a representation of Erabon's Spirit and of purification. Thereby, her planet and the prophecy given by Erabon to Ti'sulh's people is one of purification. Erabon's Spirit purifies us and makes us suitable for our journey with him. Purification is, therefore, the first step on our path. The path that is available to all clans."

Kubim next asked for Bicca to step forward. He gave a pat on Bicca's shoulder and let his hand rest there. "Bicca is our fellow clansman from Eremia, the desert planet. Desert represents the path of sanctification we must all be on. As we live our lives, we work with Erabon's Spirit to help us become more like the characteristics of Erabon. Sanctification is, therefore, the second step on our path."

Next Z'zlzck stepped forward. Seraphia looked at him and smiled. "This is our friend and fellow clansman Z'zlzck from Sharab, the fire planet. Fire is a metaphor for tribulation. As we live our life with the help of Erabon's Spirit, we will undergo many tribulations. These will be different for each person, and could be fear, lust, hardships, or even pride, which blinds us to our true destiny." She glanced at Nuke. He smiled and nodded ever so slightly; they both knew this had been Seraphia's blind spot, which she had now overcome. "It is only by yielding to the leadership of Erabon's Spirit that we overcome."

E'oa stepped forward. Kubim smiled at him and placed his hand on E'oa's shoulder. "As you have just seen, this is E'oa from the planet Ramah, the mountainous planet. Mountains represent hardship but also triumph. This could be tied to tribulation, and likely the reason Erabon placed Sharab and Ramah closer to each other than any other two planets in our system. Yet struggles may also occur separately from tribulation. Erabon helps us overcome struggles and helps us soar to great heights as we yield to the guidance of his Spirit."

Zael stepped forward next. Seraphia stood beside him. She placed her hand on the back of his shoulder. "Our new friend Zael is from Qerach, the ice planet—our neighbor." She pointed upward. "The planet that gives us light at night. As ice is formed by decreasing temperature, causing the movement of water to slow and turn to a solid, we can sometimes, through our hesitation to act, make it difficult for Erabon's Spirit to work through us. We must become pliable to his Spirit to help us act in the way he desires for us."

Jerim now stepped forward and stood next to Ti'sulh while Gavrek stood next to Zael. Seraphia took a couple of steps toward the crowd and smiled. "Now we come to us. As we have already said, we represent Erabon's Spirit. Yet we have seen how Erabon's Spirit is involved in each clan represented with us tonight. This shows Erabon's Spirit is involved in the beginning of our journey with him and throughout our growth by us yielding to his leading. Only by his Spirit are we drawn to Erabon himself."

The crowd erupted in applause. This shocked Seraphia and she took an involuntary step back. A huge grin came across her face. Her people had understood the message and embraced it! She looked at Nuke and Michael and motioned for them to step forward.

She held up her hands and the noise of the crowd slowly died. "My friends and fellow Aphiahians. Erabon has brought us this message to help us realize we all need to unite. He brings unity through our diversity, and he has sent us these two, specially chosen by him, to help us find our way." She took a step back and gestured toward them. "I think we also owe them a show of gratitude." The crowd stood and applauded. Nuke turned and saw all his friends clapping as well. He didn't know what to say or do. He was willing to endure the awkward moment, though, as he knew this meant everyone had accepted the message Erabon had brought him here to deliver.

Kubim stepped forward. "In honor of the complete message Nuke and Michael have brought us from Erabon himself, and to show how we are equal in his sight, those here have put together a show, if you will, of how diversity can be celebrated and still bring unity of purpose."

At that moment, Zyhov flew by just above everyone's heads and gave his triple melodic trill. Michael then ran after the creature and dove off the edge of the land mass. The crowd gasped and stood to watch. Nuke and his friends then split, half running to one side of the land mass and the other half running in the opposite direction. They also ran off the land mass, dove into the air, spread their arms and legs, and began soaring upward.

Before the celebration, Jerim and Gavrek had placed colored smoke cannisters on the heels of his friends. As Nuke circled above, this gave him a splendid view of what occurred below. Ti'sulh, Z'zlzck, and Zael came, flying from one direction, and Bicca and E'oa were flying from the other. They crossed in front of the crowd at the same time, one layered above the other. The cannister on Ti'sulh's heels gave off blue-colored smoke, the one on Bicca a golden color, Z'zlzck red, E'oa purple, and Zael a white-colored smoke.

The crowd erupted in applause and whistles. Many stood. As the colored smoke lingered in the air, Michael, riding Zyhov, flew in a turning motion, and this made all the colors mix. Zyhov then went almost straight up and came down, farther back toward the temple, and came in for a landing with Michael on its back. After Zyhov landed, the creature raised to its full height and allowed Michael to stand with one foot on its head and one at the base of its neck.

The crowd at first ducked, then erupted in new applause.

Nuke's friends then flew in front of the crowd again, producing the five streaks of color. This time Nuke, Jerim, and Gavrek came across in a turning fashion, similar to what Zyhov had just done earlier, and this caused the colors to mingle. They each then turned and flew nearly straight up. As they pulled upright, they let gravity begin to pull them down. They allowed their arms to open slightly to decrease the rate of their descent and then turned like a corkscrew until they landed, producing a flurry of mixed colored smoke around them.

The crowd whistled and applauded even more. Everyone, now on their feet, rushed forward. They put each of the performers on their shoulders and paraded them. After a short while, Kubim managed to get everyone back in their seats, and the performers who had danced at the HaShem celebration returned to the front to perform their melodic, agile, and lithe movements.

Food was served. A wonderful celebration, reminiscent of the previous one, was held.

Nuke looked around. He couldn't be happier. This was the best demonstration of unity through diversity he had observed since arriving on this side of the universe.

THIRTY-ONE

WHAT NEXT?

Nuke showered, dressed, and went to the portico; the morning sun was already high in the sky. The festivities the night before had gone on until the wee hours of the morning. He saw no one else around. Either they were still sleeping or had gone on with their day without him. There was a bowl of fruit of some kind on the table, so Nuke took a piece and ate it while he walked through the garden area behind the temple.

He looked up and saw the giant vine growing through the land mass and on to another one above the one he was on. Walking to where the vine exited from a small lake, he admired the large green leaves. He examined one which had fallen on the grass next to the water's edge and found its texture thick and stiff. As he rubbed his finger over its surface, he expected a prickly feel. Nuke had noticed some type of small projections on the surface of the leaf; yet the tiny projections were soft, giving an almost velvety kind of feel. As he looked up, he saw water droplets forming and dropping into the lake from the many leaves this part of the vine produced. For some reason—he wasn't sure why—these leaves only formed near water sources. He cocked his head slightly and shrugged. Likely, the water was only to be found at these places because the leaves allowed their collection. Somehow, these leaves were extremely efficient at drawing water out of the light, foggy mist which frequently passed by, and, maybe, out of the atmosphere itself. There was a constant *drip, drip, drip* which produced a slight, almost imperceptible cadence of sound; it was somewhat hypnotic. Nuke closed his eyes listening to it. *This place is so peaceful.*

As he rounded the edge of the lake, he saw Ti'sulh sitting on one of the benches nestled within beautifully colored flowers and overlooking the water. What looked like a type of iridescent butterfly, going from flower to flower, attracted his attention. As he looked more closely, the tiny creature hovered using three wings. Underneath the wings was what looked almost like a tiny cuttlefish. The creature seemed to puff air from the middle of its tiny tentacles, propelling the small creature from flower to flower and then using its wings to hover to obtain the nectar—or at least he assumed these flowers produced nectar. Once the tiny creature realized Nuke stood close, its tentacles squeezed together in a flash, creating an iridescent blur as it zoomed off into the distance. Nuke laughed. *Efficient little thing.*

Ti'sulh must have heard his chuckle. As he righted himself, she was smiling at him. "Enjoying the scenery?" she asked.

He nodded, came over, and sat next to her. "This is the first time I've taken the time to just take in all the beauty that is here. It's quite peaceful. The steady breeze seems to keep the air from getting too hot even when the sun is bright."

Ti'sulh nodded and took his hand. "I've just been sitting here enjoying the view. I assumed I was the only one up since

I haven't seen anyone else. You're the first one I've seen up and about this morning."

Nuke grinned. "Everyone is probably recovering from their late night. I know Zael and Bicca were still up when I turned in. I lost track of Michael and Z'zlzck."

"I know E'oa turned in early, but I also know he was extremely sore." Ti'sulh laughed. "I think our performance pushed his endurance over the edge. He's likely still sleeping."

"It couldn't have been easy for him," Nuke said. "His body type and size are not really designed for these kinds of maneuvers. I'll check in on him if we don't see him before lunch."

"He really was key last night, though. I think his prayer and connection to Erabon set the tone and left everyone really paying attention. I think he prepared everyone's heart to truly hear the message Seraphia and Kubim told their people."

"I agree," Nuke said. "His body turning a brilliant purple definitely got their attention. I heard gasps throughout the crowd."

Ti'sulh nodded. It was clear she had too.

She leaned her head onto his shoulder. Nuke let go of her hand and put his arm around her. She then put her hand back into his. They sat in silence for several minutes.

Ti'sulh was the first to speak. "So, what do we do now?"

"What do you mean?"

She sat up and gazed into his eyes. "I assume our mission is accomplished. Where do we go from here? And what do you and I do?"

Nuke widened his eyes for a second and then shrugged. "Actually, I've never really thought past this point—about what Erabon wants us to do, I mean." He smiled. "I have thought about us, but . . . "

She put her hand to his cheek and said, in a low tone, "But what?"

He took her hand, kissed it, and then held it in his lap. "I've thought about us having a life together back on Myeem. I've wondered if there is more to do to unite the clans before Erabon return. I've wondered, when my mission here is done: would Erabon send me back as mysteriously as I arrived? I've thought how impossible getting back to my world really is. I've considered staying here no matter what. And I've considered . . . I'm in a coma and all of this has been a dream my mind has conjured up."

Ti'sulh locked her gaze with his for several seconds. "How real can a dream be?"

Nuke shook his head slightly. "I don't know. I've never experienced anything like this before."

She leaned into him. He didn't budge. "How real does *this* feel?" Her lips touched his, and her tentacles wrapped around his neck, lightly touching his skin, with one caressing his head and another moving slightly down his spine underneath his vest. The feeling was intoxicating. He kissed her harder; everything else seemed to melt away. He felt his consciousness seem to meld into hers, creating a blissful feeling. She slowly ended the kiss. He wasn't sure how long the kiss lasted. It felt like an eternity, and at the same time it felt too short.

Her hand went to his cheek. "Did that feel like a dream?"

He shook his head. "No. That kiss felt like a piece of heaven."

She smiled and put her forehead to his. "That's how I hoped you would feel." She put her head back onto his shoulder and he wrapped his arm around her again. They sat and admired the nature in front of them and enjoyed the closeness with one another.

Nuke could now indeed picture a life with Ti'sulh. Yet there was something deep within him that made him doubt they would have such a life. Did he have that feeling because his mission was not yet complete? But what else would Erabon have him do? Almost everyone on each planet had accepted Erabon's true message. Not everyone had, of course, but wasn't expecting every single person to accept and believe a little too idealistic? Nuke was convinced Erabon would want that, but each individual, no matter the clan, had to want that as well. The ancient adage "it takes two to tango" came to Nuke's mind. Although cliché, the saying was certainly true. He just couldn't shake the feeling something more was in store for him. What he couldn't tell was whether Ti'sulh was part of his future.

He looked down at her and kissed her on her head. She glanced up and gave him a side hug. Until he knew for sure, he wasn't going to waste his opportunities with her. If they were to go different paths, getting emotionally closer to her now would certainly make things harder later. But for now, he really wanted to enjoy her company. If Erabon's path for him was for them to be together, all the better.

If not? He paused in his thinking. Would he willingly put the relationship with Ti'sulh aside if Erabon asked him to do that? If he was honest with himself, he wasn't sure about that. He desperately wanted to fulfill the mission Erabon had entrusted to him. Yet he also wasn't sure if he was strong enough to fulfill that mission if Ti'sulh wasn't part of it.

He said a short prayer asking for Erabon's wisdom and guidance. He still was certain he was going to need it.

THIRTY-TWO

PREPARING FOR ERABON

Once Nuke and Ti'sulh got back to the portico, they still didn't see anyone.

Nuke laughed. "It appears our party animals are still recovering."

Ti'sulh chuckled. "Apparently so."

Just then Jerim walked by. Nuke got his attention. "Jerim, excuse me. Have you seen any of our friends today?"

He shook his head. "No, I haven't. I thought we would give them time to recover and perhaps have an early dinner. I didn't realize the two of you were already up. Would you like something before then to hold you over?"

Nuke nodded. "If not too much trouble."

Jerim held up his hands. "Oh, no bother at all. What about something similar to what I prepared for our flight trip the other day?"

"Oh, that's perfect," Ti'sulh said. "That was really good."

Jerim gave her a wink. "I'll be right back."

As they waited for Jerim to return, Nuke looked at Ti'sulh. "Want to go flying again after we eat?"

She nodded and smiled. "That's a great idea. I'd like to see more of this planet."

After eating they took to the air. They went farther down than they had the time before, but when the clouds got too thick, they headed back up. They again rested where they had on their previous trip.

Ti'sulh sat back propping herself with her hands behind her. "I'm going to miss this place. This has been quite the experience."

Nuke leaned closer. "I want to show you what Gavrek showed Michael and me the other day. It's in some cloud cover, but not too much. Want to see it?"

Ti'sulh nodded. "Must be pretty amazing if you want to see it again."

"It is," Nuke said. He thought he'd take her to see the waterfall but not go through the hole. He wasn't sure he could explain how to enter through the land mass and didn't want to stun her with a surprise she wouldn't be ready for.

"Lead the way," Ti'sulh said.

Both leaned over the edge and let their bodies fall off the small land mass. Nuke headed in the direction Gavrek had taken them previously. In a brief period of time the waterfall came into view. He looked over at Ti'sulh and pointed.

She looked at him and grinned. Because of the wind, he couldn't hear her, but he read her lips as she said, "It's beautiful."

As they rounded this amazing view, they saw Zyhov approach. Nuke wondered what the creature was doing here this time. As it entered the cloud cover, rather than the clouds dissipating as had happened before, the cloud cover just disappeared, as though the creature had somehow absorbed it.

Nuke's eyes widened and he looked at Ti'sulh. Her expression seemed to match his. He pointed and indicated for them to follow Zyhov. She nodded. Wherever Zyhov flew, the cloud cover simply disappeared. Nuke knew that didn't make any sense. *Is Zyhov really absorbing that cloud?*

After some time Nuke turned and motioned for Ti'sulh to follow. He headed back to the land mass housing the temple. After they landed, Ti'sulh still looked wide-eyed.

"Did you see what I think I saw?" she asked.

Nuke nodded. "It looked like Zyhov was absorbing the clouds."

Ti'sulh wrinkled her brow. "But how is that even possible?"

Nuke shrugged. "Looks like we have some dinner conversation."

As they approached the portico, everyone was there and seemed engaged in conversation.

Nuke gestured their way as he and Ti'sulh approached. "Well, finally the dead have arisen."

E'oa chuckled. "Well, I certainly felt like I was dead last night."

Nuke patted him on his shoulder. "How are you now, my friend? I appreciate you being such a trouper last night."

E'oa nodded. "I feel much better now. I think I just overdid things and needed the extra rest."

Nuke nodded and took a seat. Ti'sulh sat next to him.

Nuke looked at Michael. "And Michael, I lost track of you and Z'zlzck. What time did the two of you get to bed?"

Michael laughed. "Late. Extremely late."

Z'zlzck grinned. "Or, you could say, extremely early."

Michael nodded. "Yes, we retired before sunrise, but not too much before."

"Really? What were the two of you doing?"

Michael glanced at Z'zlzck and back to Nuke. "I gave Bob, here, a ride on Zyhov."

Nuke's eyes got big. "I thought the creature only responded to you."

Michael shrugged. "That's what I thought. But after the celebration he seemed more mellow than normal. Qerach was bright, so we just went exploring."

"It was incredibly beautiful to see everything at night," Z'zlzck said. "Since we were on Zyhov, we didn't have to worry about running into anything."

Michael laughed. "Yeah, we just had to be sure we hung onto Zyhov. He did some tricky maneuvers. Right, Bob?"

Z'zlzck nodded.

Ti'sulh leaned in. "Well, speaking of changes with Zyhov, Nuke and I saw something strange today."

Michael's eyebrows went up. "What sort of thing?"

"I took Ti'sulh to see the waterfall Gavrek showed us the other day," Nuke said, "and we saw Zyhov flying around."

Michael nodded. "That doesn't sound unusual."

Ti'sulh shook her head. "No, but what the creature did certainly was."

Michael squinted. "And what was that?"

"This is going to sound strange," Nuke said, "but when Zyhov went through the cloud cover, the cloud cover just disappeared."

Michael tilted his head a bit. "You mean, it sort of faded away? Like we've seen? It dissipated?"

Nuke shook his head. "No. I mean it just disappeared."

Ti'sulh nodded. "It was as if Zyhov just absorbed the cloud."

Nuke heard a gasp behind him. He turned and saw Seraphia standing there with hand over her mouth.

Nuke realized she knew something. He gestured for her to have a seat. Gently, he asked her, "What does that fact mean to you?"

Seraphia shook her head. "It's not something bad. It's actually something good—something wonderful." She smiled. "It means Erabon's return is quite near."

Everyone at the table sat up straighter. Nuke looked from her to his friends and back. "What? How do you know?"

"It is prophesied Zyhov will prepare the way for Erabon's return." She shook her head. "I don't really know how or where this particular prophecy originated, but we have always been told that just before Erabon returns, Zyhov will be filled with the breath of Erabon."

Ti'sulh cocked her head. "And you believe this act of Zyhov is . . . proof of that?"

Seraphia nodded.

"Why?"

"The breeze is symbolic of the Spirit of Erabon, as is Zyhov itself. The movement of the cloud cover is evidence of the breeze and, thereby, evidence of Erabon's Spirit as well."

Michael leaned in. "So this means what, exactly?"

She turned to Michael. "Erabon will return once all the cloud cover is removed from our planet."

Michael's eyes grew wide. "You mean Erabon will come in person . . . " He pointed his index finger and tapped it on the table in front of him. "Here?"

Seraphia nodded. "That's what we believe." She shook her head. "I just never thought such a thing would happen in my lifetime."

THIRTY-THREE

ERABON RETURNS

The next couple of days were ordinary and extraordinary at the same time. Everyone went about their normal routine, but everyone kept an eye on Zyhov. The creature was in constant movement now, and each day more and more of the cloud cover was gone.

Nuke stood looking over the edge of the temple land mass. He could now clearly see so many of the land masses he could not see well before. He realized there were so many more of these than he had thought.

Ti'sulh came and took his arm. He looked at her and smiled.

"You've been standing here a long time. What are you doing?"

Nuke gestured with his head toward Zyhov, who was circling a great distance below them. "Just watching Zyhov removing the cloud cover."

Both stood looking for several minutes.

Nuke glanced at Ti'sulh and then back at Zyhov. "Does he look bigger to you? I mean, look how far below us he is, yet his body doesn't look as small as I would expect."

Ti'sulh cocked her head. "I see what you mean." She turned to Nuke. "So absorbing the cloud cover makes him grow?"

Nuke shrugged. "Seems to be."

"You think that's significant?"

"I'm sure it is. I'm just not sure in what way." Nuke noticed E'oa coming their way. As he arrived, Nuke said, "Ready for some more flying maneuvers?"

E'oa held up his hands. "Please, no. My body is just now recovering."

Nuke laughed. "I hear you. Anything on your mind?"

E'oa nodded. "I feel we're on the verge of something."

Nuke nodded. "Yes. And that's what Seraphia said."

E'oa shook his head. "No, Nuke. Don't you feel it? Each day I get a stronger and stronger feeling of Erabon being closer."

Nuke wasn't sure if this was just E'oa getting caught up in Seraphia's emotion, or if his feelings were real. After all, his was the only body that glowed when he prayed. Maybe he was more attuned to Erabon than any of them. So Nuke really couldn't discount what E'oa was saying.

Ti'sulh touched E'oa's arm. "So what exactly are you feeling?"

"It's hard to describe," E'oa said as he shook his head. "It certainly isn't negative, but . . . ominous. Something good filled with something unknown." He sighed. "Does that make any sense?"

Ti'sulh smiled. "Sort of."

"Can you tell how much time will pass before Erabon's return?" Nuke asked E'oa.

E'oa looked at Nuke and shook his head. "No, but I just know it's not too far from now."

"How many cycles or rotations of Aphiah are you talking?"

E'oa shook his head. "Definitely not cycles. Rotations—and not that many. Maybe . . . maybe not even one."

Nuke's eyes widened. "That soon?"

E'oa nodded. "I think so."

"And then what?"

E'oa shrugged. "Your guess is as good as mine."

Ti'sulh hooked her arms into both Nuke's and E'oa's. "I think we then get a new beginning."

E'oa raised his eyebrows. "You mean . . . "

Ti'sulh nodded. "I think he will rebuild the planet Erabon of old."

"And how will he do that?" Nuke asked.

"I don't know," Ti'sulh said, shaking her head. "But I was talking to Seraphia last night. I asked her about the surface of this planet. She said that as far as she knew, there is no surface."

Nuke's eyes now got very large. "How is that possible? Something has to be making these land masses float."

Ti'sulh nodded. "Yes, that's true. Something has to be there, but it doesn't have to be a planet surface."

E'oa scrunched his face. "What do you think is there?"

"I'm not entirely sure," Ti'sulh said, "but she said her ancestors kept talking about this planet being key in bringing all of the clans back together."

E'oa shook his head. "I don't understand. So what do you think is there?"

"There is a myth. And Seraphia said she had heard the same as well."

E'oa gasped. "Oh, yes. I had forgotten about that."

Nuke looked from one to the other. "Forgotten what? What did this myth say?"

Ti'sulh looked at him. "It states that when Erabon returns, he will take each planet and use them to make a new one—a new Erabon."

Nuke's eyes grew large. "Just like in the temple. So it's not metaphorical, but actual?"

"Seems to be," Ti'sulh said.

"Wow." Nuke shook his head. "That's hard to take in." He paused. "But if he does that, what does he do with all of the people while he does that?"

Ti'sulh pointed to the scene below. "I think that is what Zyhov will reveal to us. From some of the things Seraphia said, I think the center of this planet is the key to how Erabon will accomplish that feat."

At that moment Zyhov made another pass and something new became visible. Nuke squinted to try and make out what was revealed. "What is that?" he asked his two friends.

Ti'sulh shook her head. "I don't know. But something other than land masses is being revealed."

Nuke looked at E'oa and his head jerked back. "E'oa! Your . . . your body."

Ti'sulh gasped. "E'oa, it's starting to glow."

While not bright, E'oa's body did have a faint, but noticeable, purplish glow.

E'oa lifted his arms and looked at them. "It's happening. We won't have to wait long now."

As they turned, they observed other Aphiahians arriving at the temple. Many genuflected, some bowed, some laid prostate facing the temple. Evidently, they too realized something was happening.

Nuke saw Seraphia, Kubim, and the rest of his friends approaching. Seraphia had a quicker, more determined stride to her step than she had before.

As they arrived, Nuke looked at Seraphia. "Any idea what's going on?"

She looked down and pointed. "Zyhov has exposed the roots of our planet."

"Roots?" Nuke looked from her down to where Zyhov was still flying. Again, he felt certain the creature was getting larger. He slowly nodded. Yes, what was revealed really did look like roots. They seemed to be surrounding something, which he assumed to be the very core of this planet, which evidently gave life to the vine and to the planet as a whole, and likely kept all the land masses suspended in the air. Nuke's skin prickled. He wasn't sure if the reason was because of what was happening or just from the excitement of the anticipation of what would be occurring.

All watched as the last remaining cloud cover disappeared. E'oa's skin became brighter. Not as bright as when he prayed, but brighter than he had been only moments before.

Bicca had been standing next to him and took a step back. "E'oa, what are you feeling? What's happening?"

E'oa shook his head. "I don't know, but Erabon is near. He's extremely near."

Nuke looked down again. Zyhov was now taking the same upward path as the vine, circulating around the vine as the creature rose. Nuke found he couldn't take his eyes off the creature. The closer Zyhov got, the larger the creature appeared. Nuke pointed. "Look!"

All locked their gazes in that direction. Several of them gasped. Michael's eyes widened, and he said in an awed whisper, "Zyhov!"

As the creature got closer, Nuke could tell Zyhov was indeed massive. Its wingspan now looked wider than any of the land masses the creature flew around. They stared, mesmerized by this amazing creature flying closer and closer.

Zyhov then flew past them and above them. Several seconds passed as its body cleared the land mass, almost as if a skyscraper had just flown by them. Zyhov gave out its melodic triple trill, now sounding louder than usual, but still just as pleasing to the ear.

The creature flew upward and hovered over the land mass they and the temple were on. Zyhov then gently settled downward, straddling the temple, with one foot gripping the side of the land mass on one side of the temple and the other foot planted in the same way on the other side. Zyhov was now so tall its body stood higher than the temple. It towered above them like a gigantic colorful mountain. As Zyhov lifted its head skyward, they heard the melodic triple trill repeated several times.

Everyone rose and stepped back as far as they could. As the creature sang, its body and coloring began to fade. But not in brilliance—it somehow just seemed to dematerialize and turn into a circling wind. After a few minutes the body of the creature was gone and all that remained was the wind, now blowing so hard that people had to hold tight to each other to keep from being blown about.

The wind then began to visibly shrink into a type of cyclone, becoming tighter and tighter in diameter. The slimmer the cyclone became, the more elongated it grew, and it climbed higher and higher into the sky.

After a few minutes the wind could no longer be felt. Everyone rose and stared at the spectacle before them. The wind had now formed into an extremely thin cyclone above the temple, continuing to shrink in diameter and extending farther and farther into the sky, becoming so thin that any visibility of it became difficult.

Suddenly, the cyclone burst into a flash of bright white light. Everyone shielded their eyes, yet the light grew so bright Nuke could still see its brilliance with his eyes closed.

The cyclone dissipated as quickly as it had formed. As Nuke and the others opened their eyes, taking quite some time for their vision to adjust, everything looked fairly normal. Yet Nuke noticed E'oa's body now glowed a brilliant purple. Clearly, this was not normal.

Someone gasped and pointed. Nuke looked up. There, floating above the temple, was a man, about his height, Nuke reasoned, and semimuscular in build. His hair, dark in color and about shoulder length, blew in the breeze, and his face . . . Nuke didn't know how to describe it, even to himself. The countenance of this one produced a look of total peace. A look of complete love and acceptance. Nuke noticed he wore a type of kittel, or tunic, all white, that went to his knees with deep slits in the side that allowed free range of motion. It and his trousers underneath, also white, seemed to flutter in the breeze giving him an ethereal look. Around his waist was a type of belt mottled in the colors Nuke had seen in the various temples: blue, gold, crimson, purple, and white. In its center was something like a belt buckle made out of some type of clear crystalline material.

The man slowly descended to the ground in front of the temple.

"Erabon." The name escaped E'oa's lips with a tone of awe.

Almost as if in unison, everyone bowed and gave deference to this one whom they had longed for, waited for, and dreamed about for so long.

THIRTY-FOUR

MEETING WITH ERABON

Erabon was more special than Nuke had ever imagined. When he first arrived, he greeted all the people who had gathered at the temple, giving hugs and handshakes to anyone who stepped forward to receive one.

Nuke and his friends stayed in the back with Seraphia and Kubim, waiting until all the people had been greeted. Nuke saw Erabon glance their way several times and give a smile that looked pleasing and supportive. This was the only way he could think to describe it.

When Erabon finally arrived where they stood, he simply looked at them, one at a time. "Well, my children, we have finally arrived."

All nodded and bowed.

"I have so much to say to each of you. May we go somewhere and talk?"

Seraphia nodded. "Of course, my Lord. Behind the temple is a portico."

He smiled. "That would be perfect."

She gestured for him to walk with her. Both she and Kubim flanked Erabon on the trail that wound through the garden toward the portico and living quarters. The rest of them followed. Since this was their planet, Nuke thought it appropriate for Seraphia and Kubim to be the first to talk with Erabon. Yet Nuke was extremely anxious to talk with him as well.

Along the way they saw Jerim and Gavrek walking together seemingly in deep discussion. Erabon stopped and motioned for them to join him.

Jerim and Gavrek hurried over and bowed. "My Lord, we are so happy you are here. May we do something for you?"

Erabon shook his head. "No. I just wanted to thank you for your service to me and to your fellow Aphiahians. Having such a place of solace and reflection is especially important." He turned and gazed at the garden and lake and then turned back to them. "And you have succeeded admirably."

Both bowed again. "Thank you, my Lord," Gavrek said.

"It has been our pleasure," Jerim added.

Erabon, Seraphia, and Kubim continued walking. Jerim and Gavrek looked at each other, beaming with pride. Nuke patted both their shoulders as they walked by. "That was pretty special, huh?"

Both nodded and smiled.

At the portico, they sat. Others came and sat some drink and small foods in front of them. Erabon ate something, and this encouraged the others to join him in eating as well.

"My friends, a unique time is upon us," Erabon said. "Soon all will be as it was before."

Seraphia looked at everyone and then to Erabon. "So, what do you wish that we do next?"

"There's a lot to do. I think I should first talk to each of you individually." He turned to Seraphia and Kubim. "Care to take a walk with me through the garden?"

Both nodded and stood. "It would be our pleasure," Kubim said with a bow.

As they walked down the garden, the rest of them sat quietly for several minutes.

Ti'sulh broke the silence. "This is so surreal. I had thought of this time for so long, and it's finally here."

Everyone nodded.

"I almost cried when I saw the radiation burn scars on his arms. What our ancestors did . . . " Ti'sulh shook her head and her eyes moistened.

The others nodded. Nuke looked from one to the other. He glanced at Michael, who just shrugged.

"Uh, Ti'sulh, what radiation burn scars are you talking about?" Nuke asked.

Ti'sulh looked at him with surprise. She looked from him to everyone else. "What? You mean you didn't notice them? They're quite prominent."

"I didn't see burns, but I did see scars in his hands," Nuke said. He looked at Michael, who nodded.

Ti'sulh had a bewildered look on her face. She turned to the others. "What did you see, Bicca?"

"I saw the radiation burn scars," the Eremian said.

She looked at the others. All nodded.

Nuke's eyes widened. "Really?"

They nodded again.

"Interesting." He put his hand to his chin. *How is that possible?* He and Michael saw scars in Erabon's hands, but the others saw radiation burn scars on his arms.

Nuke looked up and saw Erabon approaching. He didn't see Seraphia and Kubim with him.

Erabon looked at E'oa. "E'oa, may we walk together?"

E'oa smiled and nodded. He stood and walked off with Erabon.

This pattern continued as Erabon next came back for Z'zlzck, then Zael, then Bicca, and then Ti'sulh. When he returned, Erabon asked Michael to join him.

Nuke was now alone in the portico. He had so many questions to ask. Did Erabon have the time to answer all of them? *Would* he answer all of them? He got lost in his own thoughts. Time seemed to go by quickly, and before he knew it, Erabon was back at the portico.

"Walk with me, Yohanan Chaikin."

It had been a long time since he had heard his full name used. Nuke gave a slight chuckle.

"I sound like your mother, do I?" Erabon grinned.

Nuke chuckled louder. "Somewhat. She's about the only one who calls me that anymore."

Erabon smiled. "I'm sure you have a lot of questions."

Nuke nodded. "Why me?"

Erabon cocked his head, stopped walking, and turned his way. "Why *not* you?"

Nuke shrugged. "I'm not anyone special."

"What makes you say that? You were special on Earth, on Triton, and now here."

"But why did you need me, or someone from my solar system, to be here in this galaxy, this part of the universe, to prepare these people for your return?"

"Sometimes," Erabon said, "a message given by one perceived as different helps others understand the true meaning of what they think they know."

Nuke thought about that. "So you needed someone different enough who could challenge their thinking without them thinking they were traitors to their own people?"

"Something like that."

"I think E'oa felt that should have been him."

Erabon nodded. "I know. We talked about that. He is also special and unique and will be used greatly as we move forward into what is coming. But I needed you to get everyone to this point."

Nuke nodded. He still didn't fully understand why, but the logic Erabon used did make sense.

"And you needed to be here for yourself."

Nuke's head jerked back. "I had to be here . . . for me?" He shook his head. "I don't understand."

"You had doubts."

Nuke could feel heat rush to his face; he knew he had blushed. Yet it seemed foolish to try and hide anything from Erabon. He nodded. "I did."

"And now?"

Nuke chuckled. "No, I couldn't possibly doubt now." He paused. "So, I couldn't have gained the perspective I needed in my own galaxy?"

"The familiar sometimes breeds lack of perspective. What you have learned here, your father had tried to teach you all of your life."

Nuke stopped in his tracks. These words stunned him. *Did he?* He had disagreements with his father nearly his entire life. His father was so old-fashioned. He probably would faint being aware of what Nuke had seen in this part of the universe.

Nuke looked at Erabon and gazed into his eyes. He saw *something.* Those eyes also seemed to smile at him. He knew he was missing something.

"I . . . don't understand."

"What has your father always wanted from you?"

"To study the Scriptures and help him teach them to others."

Erabon nodded. "Why?"

"Well, he believes the message is true for all, regardless of where they are from." Nuke shook his head. "But, forgive me. He is so old-fashioned. He doesn't want to change. He wants all to be the same as it always has been."

"He doesn't want people to forget their history," Erabon said. "Isn't that what has happened here?"

Nuke thought about that. That was what he and Ti'sulh had been trying to get the people on each planet to remember: their history. Not to make them go back to how things were before, but to move forward to the time Erabon had now brought them.

Erabon put his hand on Nuke's shoulder. "Do you believe you have better perspective now?"

Nuke nodded slowly. "I think so. I was so focused on what my father was saying and not on what he was implying."

Erabon nodded. "He too wants people to remember their history so they can be ready for my return. Not to go back to previous times, but to understand what the previous times were pointing toward."

Nuke suddenly felt foolish. All this time he had been resistant to what his father had been trying to get him to see. In doing so, he had lost sight of the message itself.

As Erabon removed his hand from Nuke's shoulder, Nuke saw the scars in his hands. "May I ask you a question about the scars in your hands?"

Erabon smiled. "I thought you already knew why they are there."

Nuke nodded. "Yes, but the others see radiation burn scars on your arms. They don't see the scars in your hands."

"My sacrifice was different for them than for those on Earth," Erabon said. "The scars in my hands remind you of my sacrifice for you. The scars on my arms remind them of my sacrifice for them."

Nuke saw Erabon as more unique than he realized. Erabon was all about love, and with that, benefiting others and helping them maintain perspective.

THIRTY-FIVE

MAKING PREPARATIONS

Nuke didn't see his friends until the next morning at breakfast under the portico. As they ate, each shared about their talk with Erabon. Most told about how Erabon described the new world he would create for everyone, and how their current world would be part of the new world. Everyone was abuzz with excitement.

Nuke listened, but everything that was said made him wonder. Erabon had not talked about the new world with *him*. He had talked about his own world and his own family. Did that mean he would not be part of this new world? If not, how would he get back to his own world? He and Michael had already estimated how far away they were from their own solar system. It would take millennia for them to get back, even if they stretched the capability of their interstellar gates to their maximum range. On the inside, he shrugged. Perhaps Erabon would speak to him further about what his future would hold.

In the middle of E'oa's explanation of how he was going to be a leading part in the worship of Erabon on the new world,

Seraphia approached the table. All conversation stopped; everyone turned her way.

She smiled. "I'm sorry. I did not mean to halt your conversation."

E'oa held up his hands. "No, no. That's all right. We were just relaying what Erabon said to each of us."

Seraphia nodded. "That's what I wanted to talk with you about."

Everyone's attention turned her way. "How would you like to see what's at the core of our planet?" she asked.

Everyone sat up straighter. Nuke nodded. "Absolutely."

"I knew about some of the things Erabon told me, but not all," Seraphia said. "We had been told our people would be part of reuniting the clans." She smiled sheepishly. "That is part of why we felt a little superior to everyone—until Erabon made us see things through his eyes." She shook her head lightly. "Anyway, one of the ways we will be helping to fulfill Erabon's vision is at the center of our planet—something forged by our ancestors not long after they arrived here. Over the centuries, what they accomplished was forgotten and became lost in folklore and myth." She paused as if for emphasis. "What Erabon told me is simply incredible. I'm not sure I can do it justice by telling it." She motioned to them to follow her. "Come see what Erabon has planned."

They stood and looked at each other. Nuke wondered what this could possibly mean. They followed her to the front of the temple. Kubim, Jerim, and Gavrek were waiting for them.

"Everyone ready to follow me down?" Gavrek asked.

All nodded. Nuke stood next to Jerim. "What are we going to see?"

Jerim smiled. "Something wonderful."

As soon as Gavrek let his body fall over the edge, Jerim did the same and followed Gavrek down.

Everyone did likewise. There was no longer any cloud cover to hide anything from view. Nuke estimated the time to reach the center core to be nearly an hour. As they descended lower and lower, Nuke saw the vine become thicker and thicker. Once they got to the roots of the vine, the thickness amazed him. Yet as they continued to descend, the roots branched into thousands of smaller sections that later branched into more. Once they reached the core, the root system looked to be fine filaments entering small holes through some type of hard metal core. Nuke had no idea what type of metal composed the core of this planet.

Yet the core itself was massive; it looked as big as a small asteroid. Gavrek had them land next to what looked to be a type of opening with something like a keypad to one side. He selected the icons displayed on the pad in a specific sequence, and the door turned clear and then began to dissipate. They entered. Nuke felt pulled to the wall of the interior by some type of artificial gravity. Lights came on. Nuke's eyes widened. In the center area were six large ships. They were more than large, however. They were *massive*—even larger than the transport vessels he had seen in his solar system that were used to transport people from Earth to the moon, to Mars, or to Triton.

Seraphia's eyesbrows raised. "Didn't I say words would not be able to describe this?"

Nuke shook his head, went closer to a protective railing, and stared at the vessels for several seconds. "Seraphia, this is . . . incredible."

She nodded. "I knew we were to be part of something big, but I never guessed anything like this."

Nuke turned his head. "You mean your people will be piloting these?"

She smiled and nodded. "Jerim and Gavrek have already volunteered. We're looking for four more. Several others have already applied."

Zael stepped forward. "I volunteer my services as well."

"I have other plans for you, Zael."

They all turned and saw Erabon standing behind them. Nuke had not seen him come in. Maybe he just simply appeared; Nuke wasn't sure.

Zael turned, eyebrows raised. "My Lord. What do you wish me to do?"

"Seraphia and her people will handle the transport. I want the eight of you to come with me back to each planet and get the people there ready for when the transport arrives on their planet."

Nuke felt confused. There had been seven of them who arrived here, but Erabon was speaking of eight.

Likely understanding his confusion, Erabon replied, "You have been my ambassadors until this point. I hope you, as well as Kubim, don't mind being such a little while longer."

Zael shook his head. "I'm willing to be whatever you need me to be, my Lord."

Erabon looked at the others, who also nodded. "Splendid," he said. "After Seraphia gets all things ready, we'll head out first, and she and her people will follow."

Erabon disappeared from their sight.

They gasped. Nuke actually had to laugh. "Well, I guess we shouldn't have been surprised with that."

Seraphia turned to Jerim and Gavrek. "You two go ahead and board a vessel."

Nuke looked from Seraphia to Jerim and Gavrek, then back. "Seraphia, how will they know how to fly these large vessels? Have they had training?"

She shook her head. "No, but there is a neuro-feed which will teach them, downloading needed information in only a short time. The device will provide them with knowledge of various flight experience scenarios."

Nuke's eyes widened. He turned to Zael. "Similar to what you went through, I guess."

Zael nodded. "Likely."

Seraphia gestured toward the sphere's opening. "Shall we head back? I have three more pilots to choose."

"Mind if I stay and tour one of the ships first?" Nuke asked.

She looked at Nuke and turned to Jerim. "Are you all right with that?"

Jerim nodded. "Sure."

"Just be sure he swabs the deck before he comes back," Michael said dryly.

Jerim furrowed his brow in confusion.

Nuke turned to Michael and replied, in a condescending tone, "I think you're confusing a space vessel with a water vessel."

Michael shrugged and grinned. "Just be sure he does something—useful or not."

Nuke rolled his eyes. Jerim smiled. "We'll see."

Seraphia had the others follow her. Nuke followed Jerim.

Nuke was amazed at how large the vessel appeared; he felt like a shrimp adjacent a giant whale. The silhouette of the ship actually reminded him somewhat of a whale. Although without fins, there was a structure which jutted out from the ship all the way around its middle and the place where people would enter.

The inside felt extremely spacious, had lots of windows, several observation decks, and numerous sleeping quarters. Nuke guessed the vessel could house many thousands with ease.

Jerim took Nuke to the bridge. Nuke stood in awe as he looked around. Once again their technology astounded him; that these planets used such marvelous technology so sparingly befuddled him. There was a captain's chair which looked somewhat like a giant cup with a cut-out opposite from where a cup's handle might be where a person could sit. The "handle" was a pivot that allowed the chair to maneuver in any position. Around the bridge were several consoles and many buttons and lights.

"Don't you need more crew to help you with running this ship?" Nuke asked.

Jerim shrugged. "I'll know more after I've received the download. Seraphia tells me the vessel is largely self-sustaining."

Nuke cocked his head. "It's certainly impressive, that's for sure."

Jerim sat in the captain's chair and pressed a button on the side. A message from the computer displayed on the console and via audio: "Captain training module activated."

Several wires came out of the chair and attached to Jerim in various places on his body: forehead, base of skull, neck level, on his arm, on his chest. A type of cap descended and went over his head.

"See you in a few," Jerim said as he pressed another button.

Nuke heard: "Captain training module commencing."

Jerim closed his eyes and seemed to go into a type of REM sleep.

Nuke stayed a few more minutes to see how things progressed. Jerim appeared comfortable and had a pleasant look on his face. The only movement came from his eyes underneath his closed eyelids, and from the various colored blinking lights.

Amazed from all he had seen, Nuke stepped from the ship and the sphere. He jumped into the air and caught a strong updraft that allowed him to follow the vine all the way back to the temple.

THIRTY-SIX

REVISITING QERACH

A great deal of activity took place over the next few days. People packed and got things ready for their journey. All the Aphiahians would be on one vessel. Nuke and his friends had extremely little to do during this time except simply watch everyone else prepare. Most seemed excited about their future. Some were sad to leave behind all they knew and had grown up with, but as far as Nuke could tell, everyone was willing to go.

As Nuke and his friends were sitting at the table under the portico one afternoon, Jerim brought refreshments.

Nuke looked at the Aphiahian. "Jerim, what are you doing?" Nuke realized three days had passed since he had been with Jerim on the ship.

Jerim gave him a quizzical look.

"I mean, you shouldn't be serving us when you have important work to do to get ready for your voyage," Nuke said. "After all, you're the captain now."

Jerim continued to fill glasses. "I'm not a captain until this afternoon. I'm happy to fulfill my role until then."

Nuke shook his head. Such a responsibility would give someone else a big head about their increase in status and responsibility, but such a thought didn't seem to occur with Jerim. Nuke gestured his way. "So how did the download go?"

"Oh, quite well," Jerim said enthusiastically. "The download was fascinating. Most everything in the ship is self-sustaining, just as Seraphia said. But learning all the ins and outs of the ship was thrilling." He smiled. "I don't expect anything to go wrong, though, since Erabon will be guiding us."

Nuke nodded. "I'm sure you're right about that."

Jerim bowed and Nuke's gaze followed him back to the house. He would miss Jerim and Gavrek. They had been such good hosts while he and his friends were here. Yet surely he would see them again once they reached their final destination, wouldn't he?

Seraphia approached the table, breaking Nuke's chain of thought. "I think we're almost ready. Erabon is waiting for all of you in front of the temple."

They looked at each other briefly, rose, and followed Seraphia back to the temple. Nuke looked at the garden and lake a final time. He would miss all the serenity here. The view reminded him of his previous conversation with Ti'sulh. Did they have a future together? He hoped he would be able to broach this subject with Erabon—maybe after their final mission was accomplished.

Erabon, standing with Kubim, smiled broadly as they approached. "Are you ready to return and prepare each clan?"

All nodded.

Erabon looked at Seraphia. "At the core of each planet is something similar to what is at your core. Each ship is equipped with a device that can attract the core and cause the planet to leave orbit and follow the ship. Have each ship follow the course to each successive planet so each retracted planet is observed from each previous planet, but do not have the ship with a retracted planet stop until you reach orbit above Myeem. I need the people of each planet to see the other planets in their sky to help them realize my authority."

Seraphia bowed. "As you wish, my Lord. It will be done. Jerim is piloting the Aphiahian vessel. From here we will travel to Qerach, but will not stop, just as you have said."

Erabon nodded. "Very good."

Kubim put his hand on Seraphia's shoulder. "I'll see you soon." He then turned back to the others. They formed a circle with each person holding the arm of the person adjacent to them.

Erabon looked at each one in succession. "Are you ready?"

All nodded. Nuke felt his body prickle, he went weightless, and his vision blurred. The experience felt remarkably similar to him going through the body displacement device. In only a matter of seconds he found himself, and his friends, on Qerach. He was surprised to find each of them, except for Erabon, now wearing heavy parkas.

Nuke took a deep breath. The cold air nearly gave him a brain freeze. He turned and saw they were next to where he and Zael kept the arnoclids. Both he and Zael walked over and greeted Yel and Zel. Erabon came to where they stood. Both Yel and Zel went to greet Erabon first. They nestled up to his extended arm.

Zael laughed. "Easy to see who ranks first."

Erabon laughed with him. "They are precious creatures." He put his face to their foreheads. The creatures seemed to act in a nearly giddy fashion just being in this One's presence.

Who can blame them? Nuke thought. Once Erabon stepped back, Zel came over to Nuke and Yel to Zael. Zel rubbed

Nuke's arm with his golden tentacle, producing a feeling like meeting an old friend. Nuke buried his head in Zel's soft fur, and this warmed his nose. He had almost forgotten this wonderful sensation.

After a couple of minutes, Zael released Yel and gestured toward the entrance. "This way, my Lord."

As they entered the observation deck, Halayal was the first person they met.

She stopped short. "Zael! Nuke! You've returned with your friends. And even more." Her gazed scanned their faces. When she came to Erabon, she froze. She quickly bowed. "My Lord. You . . . you've come!"

Erabon stepped forward and lifted her to her feet. "Arise, my child."

She looked up; tears ran down her cheeks. Erabon gently wiped them away. "No need for tears now, my child."

Halayal shook her head. "They are happy tears, my Lord. We've been waiting for you for so long."

Erabon nodded. "I know. Where are the others?"

She pressed something on her wrist to summon the others. In only a few minutes, her compatriots and the other leaders were rushing her way. Wehyahel led the group. "What's the matter, Halayal? You should only summon like that if it's an emer—"

Wehyahel's voice stopped the instant he saw Erabon. He fell to his knees. "My Lord!"

After seeing Wehyahel fall to his knees, the others at first looked confused, but as each one saw Erabon they fell to their knees as well.

Erabon went over to Wehyahel, lifted him to his feet, and wrapped his arms around him. Wehyahel wept. "My Lord, my Lord. I can't believe you are here."

Erabon pulled him from his shoulder and looked into his eyes. "Of course I'm here. I said I would return, didn't I?"

Wehyahel nodded. "You did, my Lord. You did. Please forgive my doubt."

Erabon looked at the others and then back to Wehyahel. "I see you have helped set the Dark Ones free." He patted Wehyahel's shoulder. "Well done, my son. Well done."

Wehyahel motioned for the others to come forward. Erabon took his time and welcomed each one. As word spread, more and more people came to the area. Erabon never seemed to tire of hugging, speaking, and wiping away tears.

The little boy Nuke had seen earlier wound his way through the crowd. He had his friend in tow. The little boy tugged on Erabon's pants leg. Erabon looked down and a huge smile came across his face. He knelt and looked in the little boy's eyes.

"I like your eyes," the boy said. "They're not colored like mine, but I still like them." He reached up and touched Erabon's face near the eyes. Erabon smiled back. "Your eyes are dark, but you're not a Dark One. I think I like you."

Erabon hugged the boy. "And I like you. Very much." He then hugged the other boy, who just giggled.

Erabon stood. The little boy still held his hand. "My friends, it is time to prepare for your new home. To know this is true, Aphiah will pass by tonight in your night sky, closer than it ever has before."

Halayal, who stood next to Nuke, looked at him and whispered. "We saw Aphiah fade almost completely away from our night sky just a short time ago."

Nuke nodded. "That was part of the preparation for his return. Tonight, the planet will look different than you have ever seen Aphiah before."

She gave Nuke a confused look but didn't ask any more questions.

Over the next several hours Erabon introduced Kubim to the Qerachian leaders, and Kubim told them about the ship coming to take their people to their new home and how their planet would be towed the entire distance to Myeem. Erabon told the people what to expect about their coming new world.

Excitement grew as the night went on.

When night came, Erabon took everyone out to look at the night sky. Once all were outside, someone pointed and yelled, "Look!"

Nuke heard gasps as they looked up and saw Aphiah move across their sky. Because the planet was now traveling so close to Qerach, Aphiah looked like a patchy ball with light and dark portions. Nuke found the view one of the most amazing things he had ever observed.

As they stood gazing into the night sky, what at first looked like a star grew larger and larger. The large ship landed and an Aphiahian, whom Nuke did not know, stepped out.

Kubim went to greet the man and introduced him to Wehyahel, Jayahel, and some of the others.

The excitement around the room could be felt. The Qerachians went to pack in earnest. Some finished packing that night. Others required more time, but by the middle of the next day, all were ready.

By the end of the next day, everyone had boarded and the ship was ready to be on its way.

Nuke said his goodbyes to all those he had met his first time on Qerach. The ship took off and soon became a star in the sky once more. Erabon gathered the eight of them to him, and they again joined in a circle.

Erabon teleported them to Ramah.

THIRTY-SEVEN

REVISITING RAMAH AND SHARAB

Nuke appeared with Erabon and his seven friends in the large atrium of the Ramahian palace in the late afternoon. Za'avan happened to be passing by at that time. He stopped in his tracks, stunned.

"Nuke! Ti'sulh! E'oa! Welcome back." He rushed to greet them.

Nuke shook his hand and gave him a hug. "Za'avan, I want you to meet—"

Before he could finish his sentence, Za'avan was already in a deep bow. "Erabon! My Lord, it is such an honor."

"Stand, my child," Erabon said as he gave Za'avan a hug. "My dear Za'avan, you have endured much to bring unity to my diverse creation. I applaud your sacrifice."

Za'avan shook his head. "Oh no, my Lord. I don't consider this a sacrifice."

Erabon smiled. "You have a kind heart as well, I see."

Za'avan bowed slightly. "Thank you, my Lord." He gestured toward a doorway. "Shall I introduce you to your servants I'ya and Ya'ea?"

Erabon turned and motioned for E'oa to come forward. He put his arm around him and nodded to Za'avan. "Yes, please announce us."

Za'avan knocked and open the doors to the king and queen's throne room. "Your Highnesses, you have visitors." He opened the doors wide.

Ya'ea stood. "E'oa!" She took quick strides toward him, but when her eyes diverted to the One next to him, she stopped, gasped, and dropped to her knees. "Erabon, my Lord."

Nuke noticed I'ya had dropped to his knees as well.

Erabon approached. "Ya'ea, I'ya. My children, arise."

Ya'ea rose. Her cheeks were tear-stained. "My Lord, you're here. At long last, you are here."

Erabon wrapped her in a warm embrace. "Yes, my daughter, I am here."

I'ya approached. Erabon lifted his arm and I'ya walked into Erabon's embrace, wrapping his arm around him, hugging him firmly.

After the embrace, Erabon motioned for E'oa to step forward. He placed his arm around E'oa's shoulders. "You have a remarkable son. He will be used mightily in my kingdom."

Both bowed. "Thank you, my Lord," I'ya said. "We have always known him to be special. We are pleased you agree."

Erabon chuckled. "I do, indeed." He placed his hands on their shoulders. "My children, prepare your subjects. We leave for our new world soon. Gather them, and I will speak to them later this evening. I will first go to Sharab and then return."

Both bowed again. "Very good, my Lord." I'ya smiled. "Our people will be ready—and ecstatic."

Erabon turned to E'oa. "Spend this time with your parents, and we'll reconnect later today."

E'oa bowed. "Thank you, my Lord."

Erabon patted his shoulder and stepped away. As Nuke looked back, E'oa was in a double embrace with I'ya and Ya'ea. Nuke smiled. It was very clear Erabon valued his subjects and their happiness.

Erabon had Nuke and his friends go to the large balcony off the atrium. He motioned for Za'avan to join them.

Za'avan's eyes widened. "Really?"

With a smile, Erabon motioned him over once more.

Za'avan came to their circle and stood between Nuke and Bicca. They embraced arms and, in a matter of seconds . . .

. . . all were standing in the courtyard outside the Sharabian palace.

Nuke looked up at the obelisk, and this brought back many memories. Most of them were not pleasant.

They walked into the palace. Ch'kxl and Ch'kxl'x were nearby. They first saw Nuke and stopped, startled. Their gaze scanned the others. They froze at the same time seeing Erabon's face. Both went to their knees simultaneously. "Erabon, my Lord!"

Erabon stepped forward. "Rise, my children." He first hugged Ch'kxl'x. "My daughter, you have grown so much in my character, and I am pleased with you."

Tears trickled down her cheeks. "Thank you, my Lord." She hung her head. "I have made so many mistakes."

Erabon lifted her head and gazed into her eyes. "Yet you have learned from them." He gently wiped tears from her cheeks. "And I love you for it."

More tears came. Erabon smiled and kissed her on the forehead.

He turned to Ch'kxl and hugged him. "And I am proud to see you have become the leader I always knew you to be. The time has come. Prepare your subjects."

Ch'kxl nodded. "Yes, my Lord."

"Gather everyone. I will return tonight to show everyone my authority."

Ch'kxl bowed. He and Ch'kxl'x hurried down the hallway. Nuke assumed they would gather the council together and announce the good news.

As Erabon turned, Za'avan stood with Qoftic, whose eyes widened. Both of them, for a change, were fixed on the same person: Erabon. Qoftic immediately genuflected. "My Lord. I am so happy you are here. For this to occur in my lifetime is, indeed, a great honor."

Erabon came over and helped him to his feet. "My dear Qoftic, you have such a servant's heart. Thank you for serving away from your own clan." He wrapped his arms around the Eremian.

"I am happy to serve you in whatever way you wish."

"My Lord!"

Erabon turned. Ch'tsk was falling to his knees. "You're here!"

Erabon chuckled. "Yes, Ch'tsk, I'm here. Stand and give me a hug."

"Willingly, my Lord." They embraced, and Nuke saw the joy in Ch'tsk's face.

Erabon patted his shoulder. "Now, go help your parents get your people ready. Good times are ahead of us."

Ch'tsk bowed. "Yes, my Lord."

Nuke chuckled. Ch'tsk almost skipped his way from the room.

Erabon turned back with a broad grin on his face. "Nuke, you and Za'avan come with me back to Ramah." He looked at the others. "I want the rest of you to help Ch'tsk prepare for my meeting with his people. We will be back when Aphiah and Qerach pass across the sky."

All bowed and headed in the direction Ch'tsk had gone earlier. Nuke and Za'avan stood next to Erabon. Still, Nuke felt confused. How quickly did these spacecraft travel? For them to be here by this evening was remarkable. Could they really travel that far in one day?

"My Lord," Nuke said. "How can the spacecraft arrive after only a single day? Were they built with special capabilities?"

Erabon chuckled. "My dear prophet, they are indeed specially designed. But it takes them a week to arrive here."

Nuke cocked his head. "Then . . . how?"

Erabon smiled brightly and said, in a hushed tone, "I cheated. I had us arrive a week later than when we left Qerach."

Nuke's head jerked back. Erabon gave a hearty laugh. "I love your expression, Yohanan." He held out his arms, and he and Za'avan interlocked theirs with his.

In a matter of seconds . . . they once again stood on the large palace balcony on Ramah.

Many had already gathered. Nuke heard several gasps. Erabon immediately went into his mode of hugging and greeting. As he stepped back into the palace, Nuke observed a domino effect of bowing as each successive group of people saw him and knelt. Erabon went to each one, lifted that person to their feet, and embraced them.

Word spread quickly, and more and more gathered. Soon there was hardly any room to move. Nuke and Za'avan tried to find E'oa to see how they could assist, but they eventually gave up and just stood in a corner area watching how Erabon gently loved his people.

Za'avan shook his head. "Nuke, my friend, I am simply amazed I get to witness this."

Nuke nodded. He felt the same way. He put his hand on Za'avan's shoulder and gave a slight squeeze.

As night fell, the palace balcony became highlighted with various illuminating points. Erabon went to the balcony and addressed all Ramahians. Everyone was spellbound by his words. He spoke of all that was to come and how they would dwell with their fellow clansmen on the same planet he would create for them.

Once he finished, he pointed to the sky. "Behold. This is a testimony to my authority as you see not only Sharab in your night sky, but also Qerach and Aphiah."

Nuke noticed everyone staring upward in amazement. As the people had lined not only this balcony, but all the ones up the sides of each tower, their gasps played out in a nearly stereo-like effect. He couldn't help but smile. As he looked up, both Qerach and Aphiah appeared almost as big as Sharab in the sky. The white of Qerach and the redness of Sharab provided a beautiful contrast. The reflection of light off Qerach made Aphiah even brighter.

Once again, as they looked at the sky, there was one star that appeared to grow brighter and brighter. Erabon spoke again. "A vessel comes for you to take you to your new home. Prepare. We leave as quickly as you can board." He gestured to I'ya and Ya'ea to step forward. "Your king and queen will assist you in your preparations."

While I'ya spoke to his people, Erabon came back to where Nuke and Za'avan stood.

"Za'avan, help E'oa get everyone ready."

Za'avan bowed. "Certainly, my Lord."

"Yohanan, let us return to Sharab."

The two of them locked arms and, in a matter of seconds, Nuke found himself standing with the royal family on their floating balcony. Before he could even turn, he heard hundreds of gasps. He turned, sat next to Ch'tsk, and saw all the people had already gathered as the courtyard was packed with people. Because the balcony was raised, all could see and hear Erabon as he spoke.

He held up his hands. "My children." His voice was soft and loving, but clear in tone. "I have waited so long to be with you here at last. This is a great day, and I give you a great future." He delivered essentially the same speech as he had on Ramah. All the people stood spellbound. He pointed to the sky. "See not only Ramah, but Qerach and Aphiah in your night sky. No one else could do this for you. I am Erabon, and I have returned to be with you always."

All the people clapped and cheered. The floating balcony lowered, and all the people approached. Erabon stepped down and, again, there was a wave of bows and genuflection. Erabon greeted each person as he had done on Ramah earlier. He took his time and did not rush. He never made a single person feel less important than the next.

Nuke looked up and saw another ship approach and land just past the courtyard. Because of the terrain, the ship could not land completely, so the craft hovered, and, to the ridge surrounding the vessel, extended a ramp for easy access to the vessel. Nuke saw someone step from the ship and come toward the courtyard. It was Gavrek.

Nuke weaved his way through the crowd and met Gavrek at the courtyard's edge.

"Gavrek, it is good to see you." Nuke gave him a hug. "This is quite the experience, isn't it?"

Gavrek nodded. "It is indeed."

Over the next several days Nuke introduced Gavrek to Za'avan, Qoftic, and the Sharabian royal family. There was much to do to get everyone ready and settled on their ship. Seeing representatives from each planet gave the people further evidence the prophecy they had been taught all their lives was now coming true—and in their lifetime.

Nuke and his friends, as well as Erabon, traveled back and forth between Sharab and Ramah to ensure all was going according to plan.

E'oa said goodbye to his parents as he was going to continue the trip with Erabon to Eremia and Myeem. Since they knew they would see him again shortly, this goodbye was filled with pride for their son—no sadness, just pride. Soon all those of both planets were ready, and each ship left with their inhabitants.

Za'avan left in the Ramahian ship and Qoftic in the Sharabian ship since they had befriended these fellow clansmen for so long.

Erabon stood with Nuke and his friends: Ti'sulh, Bicca, Z'zlzck, E'oa, Zael, Kubim, and Michael.

They interlocked arms and, in a matter of seconds, stood outside the Eremian encampment . . . now dressed in desert attire.

THIRTY-EIGHT

REVISITING EREMIA AND MYEEM

Bicca rushed into the Eremian settlement to have his people come meet Erabon. Just as he did, Y'din and O'em rounded the dune, appearing to be in a deep discussion. As they glanced up, they stopped in their tracks, eyes wide.

O'em rushed over. "Nuke! Ti'sulh! Why are you—"

Y'din put his hand on O'em's shoulder and immediately bowed. O'em looked at Y'din with a wrinkled brow and then looked back at the group with Nuke. His eyes widened and he too now bowed. "My Lord! Forgive me. I did not see you."

Erabon smiled and walked to the two of them. "O'em. Y'din. Arise, my children." He gave both a warm embrace and looked into their faces, cupping their cheeks with his hands. "You both went from water to desert to help your fellow clansmen. Your servant attitude is greatly appreciated."

"We are just happy to have you with us at last, my Lord," Y'din said.

Nuke couldn't help but smile seeing Y'din smile. *Such a rare event*, Nuke thought. Both Y'din and O'em walked over and hugged Ti'sulh, then Nuke.

At the same time, Mictah stepped out into the desert evening. His eyes went wide, and he immediately dipped into a deep bow. "Erabon, my Lord! You are indeed here!"

Erabon walked to where Mictah knelt. Other Eremians poured from their encampment and gathered around, eyes filled with wonder. Nuke noticed, for the first time ever, that both eyes of each Eremian were focused on Erabon—and nothing else.

"Mictah. Arise, my son."

Mictah stood but did not look at Erabon. "My Lord. I am sorry I doubted." He shook his head, gave a quick glance at Erabon, and looked down again. "I have not been a good leader, I'm afraid."

Erabon lifted Mictah's face and had him gaze into his eyes. "What do you see, Mictah?"

Mictah's eyes watered. "I see love, my Lord."

Erabon smiled. "And that is all I have for you." He put his hand on Mictah's shoulder. "You are not the first to stumble in their responsibility. Yet the question is, what will you do now?"

"Whatever you require, my Lord." He bowed. "I am completely at your disposal."

"Mictah." Erabon's words were delivered with great love, but also with an instructive tone. "I do not desire to be just your commander, but your friend. I want service, but . . . " Erabon touched Mictah's chest. "Out of devotion, not out of duty."

Mictah gazed at Erabon, face blank.

"I have always desired a relationship with you and your people." Erabon opened his arms. Mictah looked at him, tears now flowing. He walked into Erabon's open arms, which then enveloped him in a tight embrace. "I love you, Mictah. Always have. Always will."

Mictah hugged back. "Thank you, my Lord. Thank you."

As Mictah stepped back and Erabon turned to the people, all bowed deeply or genuflected. Erabon again went to each one, embracing, wiping tears, talking, laughing. He picked up children, kissed them, tickled them, hugged them. He rushed no one and they seemed to adore him for it.

While this was going on, Mictah came over and greeted the rest of the group. Nuke introduced him to the rest of his friends.

"Nuke, you really came through. I'm sorry I proved so stubborn," Mictah said.

Nuke put his hand on Mictah's shoulder and laughed lightly. "You were not the only one, believe me." Zael and some of the others briefly told of what they initially thought and how their perspectives had changed. These stories created a strong bonding with Mictah and members of the other clans.

Before long Erabon was climbing the side of a dune so everyone could see and hear him. He spoke the same message he had to the other clans. All attention was glued to him and what he had to say.

Some of the children began to point to the sky.

Erabon followed their gaze. "Your children are showing you my authority. Who else could have Aphiah, Qerach, Ramah, and Sharab pass through your night sky?"

The people again bowed deeply. Erabon came down from the dune. "Arise, children. Arise and prepare. Your new home awaits."

One of the children again pointed to the sky. "Look at the star! Look at the star!"

Nuke knew this was one of the ships coming for the Eremians. Mictah turned to Bicca. "Go tell the others at the other settlements and bring them here. Use one of the fastest ships in our reserve. I'll have General Haktok accompany you."

Bicca nodded.

Mictah turned to Y'din. "Would you please assist?"

Y'din nodded. "Happy to do so."

Y'din left with Bicca to find the general.

For the next few days there was a flurry of activity as everyone prepared for their exodus and the beginning of a new life for them and their families. Y'din and O'em were the last to enter the ship. Ti'sulh and Nuke hugged both.

"It won't be long now before we're all together again," Ti'sulh said.

Y'din and O'em nodded and entered the ship, which rose quickly from sight.

Erabon held out his arms. "One last stop, my friends."

They locked arms once more. Nuke looked at Ti'sulh and smiled. She smiled back. He had not seen her this happy in a long while. Nuke felt his skin prickle, his body go weightless, and his vision blur . . .

. . . When his vision came back into focus, they were standing inside the first abode of the Myeemian underwater settlement.

Everyone was dressed in their traditional clothing. Nuke found himself dressed as he had been when on Myeem. So was Ti'sulh.

Before long there was a large commotion. As Myeemians passed by, they were at first curious, but upon seeing Erabon, they immediately bowed. Word seemed to pass quickly as more and more people crowded around. Everyone bowed at their first view of Erabon.

Ca'eb emerged from the crowd. When he saw Erabon, he immediately genuflected. "My Lord, Erabon. This is such an honor. It is you at last."

Erabon came forward and pulled Ca'eb to his feet. "You have been wise, Ca'eb, as you believed Nuke even despite others doubting."

Ca'eb bowed. "Thank you, my Lord. I have tried to prepare my people." He looked back at Erabon. "Now that you are here, their faith will be strengthened."

Erabon opened his arms and Ca'eb stepped into Erabon's embrace. He seemed to melt into the embrace as he hugged Erabon tightly.

Erabon greeted all the other Myeemians with hugs, wiping away tears, listening in a non-hurried manner, and speaking to many with words of encouragement.

Ti'sulh had Ca'eb greet all her friends who had accompanied her. The representatives of the other clans being present added even more credence to their belief Erabon had indeed returned, as many saw the others first before seeing Erabon for themselves. This was especially true of the other councilmembers Ca'eb gathered as he introduced them to the other clansmen before they could get through the crowd to meet Erabon.

This went on for several hours. Erabon came to where all the clan representatives and councilmembers were in discussion. "Ti'sulh, would you and Ca'eb accompany me to the other abodes so I can meet all of your people?" he asked.

Both nodded and smiled.

Erabon then turned to the other councilmembers. "Please prepare your people. They must leave this planet to prepare for their new home, which will be even better than this one, and they will now be in unity with the other clansmen and with me."

Each bowed and set out to spread the word. Erabon had them join arms again. Yet Ti'sulh, Ca'eb, and Erabon disappeared, and Nuke found him and the others once again reappearing. . . now on the island surface.

E'oa walked over to Nuke. "What's happening?"

"Erabon is preparing the Myeemians. They should surface soon. He looked up as the sun began dipping past the horizon, providing yet another spectacular sunset. The lagoon began to glow from the luminescent coral as the sky displayed the five planets that were arriving. *Erabon's timing is always perfect,* Nuke thought.

Michael came up to Nuke and gave a playful push on the back. "You lucky stiff."

Nuke looked at him, confused. "What are you talking about?"

Michael pointed at the lagoon. "Here you got to go swimming every day around beautiful coral. What did I get? Heat and volcanoes."

Nuke laughed. Z'zlzck walked up and threw his arm around Michael's shoulders. "And me, of course."

"Yeah, buddy. And you," Michael said with a chuckle.

Michael picked up the coral cross now hanging around Nuke's neck. "What's this? I didn't know you wore this." He looked closer. "It looks to be in the form of a cross."

Nuke nodded. "A gift from Ti'sulh. When I was first here, I told her about Mashiach and how he died. She had this prepared for me as a gift."

A grin came across Michael's face. "Of course she did."

Nuke rolled his eyes. "Oh stop."

"I like it," Z'zlzck said.

Michael jabbed Z'zlzck. "You suck-up."

Z'zlzck bumped Michael with his hip, almost knocking him to the ground. "You like it. I know you do."

Michael laughed. "Thanks for disjointing my hip, Bob." Michael held up his Zyhov necklace as well. "Looks like we both got souvenirs."

Z'zlzck put his arm around Michael again. "And you're mine."

Michael patted Z'zlzck's arm. "Thanks, Bob. I feel the same way."

The Myeemians began to come to the surface, walking through the lagoon and onto the island. Most looked up, amazed at the night sky. Nuke knew this was the first time to see this view for many of them, and he also knew none of them expected to see other planets in their sky. Many pointed at the sky as the ship descended, then hovered above the water, and finally extended a ramp to the island.

The Myeemians, hesitant at first, began boarding the vessel. The pilot stepped forward and encouraged them to enter.

As the families came forward, Nuke recognized one of the little girls. "Hi, A'iah!"

The little girl came over. Nuke bent down and she gave him a hug. "I knew I could trust your eyes." She looked up at Michael. "Eyes tell a lot."

Michael smiled and knelt next to her. "Oh yes. So what do my eyes tell you?"

She took her hands and placed them on both sides of Michael's face and stared into his eyes. "You miss someone. But you're still happy to be here."

Michael looked from her to Nuke and back. "Well, aren't you the perceptive one?"

She nodded. "I am."

Michael laughed. "And so modest as well."

A'iah looked up at E'oa. "I'm going to work with you one day. One day soon."

E'oa smiled. "I can't wait."

A'iah seemed to think about that. "You'll have to. But you won't have to wait too long."

E'oa chuckled. "Glad to hear it."

She waved goodbye and boarded the vessel.

Michael shook his head. "I feel like I just had a conversation with Erabon."

Nuke laughed. "She is something, that's for sure."

Both Michael and E'oa nodded.

Nuke was surprised to see Ti'sulh and Erabon walking to the beach through the lagoon. Although Ti'sulh was wet, Erabon was completely dry. Nuke chuckled to himself. *Why should that surprise me?*

Erabon hugged each of them again. "You all should board the vessel."

He smiled.

"My creative side is about to be shown."

THIRTY-NINE

ERABON CREATES

Everyone plastered themselves to the windows of the ship as word spread that Erabon was going to create. No one wanted to miss it. Thankfully, being the prophet of Erabon had its privileges—or maybe because the pilot turned out to be Kubim's nephew, Raphek—Nuke and his friends were allowed a fantastic view from the ship's bridge.

The first spectacle was Erabon himself. He seemed to fill the void of space in front of them. If, somehow, any of the clansmen had not been in awe of Erabon before, they likely were now. Nuke had seen nothing like this. He was sure no one else had either. Everyone's eyes grew large as saucers.

Erabon seemed to choregraph the creation of the new planet. He picked hunks of each planet and placed them together to form the new one. He took several mountains from Ramah and combined them into one large mountain, then made several more. He scooped snow from Qerach and capped one of the mountains with white and peppered others, forming a beautiful contrast between the purple of the mountains and the white of the snow.

He took the temple from each planet and combined them into one large temple, placing the structure on a ledge of the large mountain overlooking the lake below. Water flowed from underneath the temple and cascaded onto the rocks below in a type of waterfall causing rainbows to be seen in the midst of its spray. He scooped out an area at the base of the tall mountain and filled the deep indentation with water from Myeem and then placed the entire island structure with all its abodes in the middle of this lake.

Erabon scooped sand from Eremia and made beaches along several of the lakes. Next he took several of the floating islands from Aphiah and placed them from the lake below to the temple at the top of the mountain. The vine went from the lake below, through the floating islands, through the lake of the temple, and disappeared into the clouds. The vine's green leaves grew the entire way along the vine from the lake of the temple into the clouds, causing water to run down the vine and drip into the lake of the temple. Erabon then took several volcanoes from Sharab, juxtaposed them to the large mountain, then set them back far enough to create what looked like numerous hot springs at their base. Next he made large areas of ocean, desert, and plains.

Next he delicately took the wildlife from each planet and transplanted them to this new planet. Nemit was placed in the desert. The arnoclids were given a home in the snow. He found a place for each and every type of species.

Ti'sulh leaned to Nuke and whispered, "There's still parts of each planet left over. What do you think he will do?"

Nuke shook his head as he had no idea. He looked at her. "Why are you whispering?"

She gave him a blank stare and giggled. "I don't know. This seemed like such a holy moment, doing so seemed the proper thing to do."

Nuke put his arm around her shoulders and hugged her tightly. He felt the same. This was indeed a holy moment to savor.

Everyone stood in awe as they observed Erabon take the leftovers of each planet and create five spheres, setting them in orbit around this new world he had created.

Nuke mumbled to himself. "Five moons."

Ti'sulh looked at him. "What? What did you say?"

"He created five moons. Why?"

Ti'sulh shook her head. "We never had moons before. I'm sure he has a purpose."

Nuke nodded but was speechless.

Erabon then spread his arms wide as if to say he was done, that all should land. Their pilot set course for the new planet and sat the large vessel down at the base of the tall mountain near the large lake.

Soon they were all out of the ship and standing on their new world. Everyone's eyes were wide and mouths hung open. Nuke had never seen anything so beautiful. Color was everywhere with beautiful flowers and shrubbery. The mountains appeared majestic, and the floating land masses, still connected to the large vine, looked like steps leading up to the temple far above them. The large vine was supplied with life-sustaining nutrients from the water at the base of the large mountain from which it now grew. Everywhere Nuke looked the view was majestic, far superior to anything he could have imagined.

Erabon descended, first to the temple. He traveled down the floating land mass stairs to the lake below where most everyone was walking about. He stopped on the next-to-last step and spoke.

"My children, please enjoy all I have created for you. Scatter far and wide and wherever you wish. This whole planet is for you to enjoy. Your new planet Erabon is large enough and pro-lific enough to sustain you and your descendants for millennia until I design the next phase of our existence together."

Nuke wondered what the last statement was about. Yet if Erabon's future creation was more wonderful than what he had just created, he wouldn't be able to comprehend it.

It was a good while before Ti'sulh and Nuke could talk with Erabon. So many people were so grateful for all he had done; they were thanking him constantly. Nuke knew their talk could wait. In the meantime, they could enjoy this new planet. They walked around the lake, spent some time at the hot springs, and climbed partway up the mountain so they could see some of the land beyond the mountain. Everything was so well-pro-portioned and filled with diversity and color. There was noth-ing Nuke could imagine that would make this place any better. Seemingly, Erabon had thought of everything.

As the sun set, Nuke and Ti'sulh sat on one of the floating land masses and watched the spectacular display. The specta-cle was even more beautiful than the sunsets he had observed from Myeem. The reds and golds reflected off the lake making the entire area below them glow. Once the sun sunk below the horizon, the fluorescent coral shone again, creating a lovely ambience. Now Nuke could see there were luminescent flying creatures all over the mountain that made the whole mountain appear to twinkle as well as on the island in the middle of the lake, which now twinkled brightly against the blackness of the water.

Ti'sulh put her head on Nuke's shoulder. "I've never been at such peace. The beauty here is overwhelming." She looked up and smiled at him. "And to think we get to live here . . . " She chuckled. "Forever, I guess."

He patted her hand. He wasn't sure of that last part. For her, yes. This would be her home. Nuke wasn't so sure this would be his. He wasn't sure why he had that feeling. Maybe because Erabon had not discussed this world with him as he had with all the other clans.

Ti'sulh squeezed Nuke's arm. "Oh, Nuke. Look!" She pointed to the sky.

His mouth fell open. The five moons were visible and starting to glow. "They're beautiful," he whispered.

Ti'sulh nodded. "They will be a constant reminder of our service to him. They're the same colors we saw in his temples."

The colors were muted, and this gave them an ethereal look: blue, gold, red, purple, and white. Even in the night, Erabon added color and diversity. On the inside, Nuke sighed. This was truly a wondrous place. One he could never have hoped to dream about. Would Erabon allow him to stay?

Ti'sulh yawned.

Nuke grinned. "Getting sleepy, I see."

Ti'sulh nodded. "I think I'll go to bed. After all this time, being back in my own bed again will be nice. You know, I feel lucky my people got to keep everything familiar." She looked up and smiled. "Just with a few exquisite upgrades."

Nuke chuckled. "That's an understatement."

She nodded and yawned once more. "Coming?"

"I think I'll stay up a little longer."

"All right. See you tomorrow?"

Nuke nodded.

"You going to sleep back under the water also?" she asked.

"Probably," Nuke said. "It's the only home I know."

She kissed him on his cheek. "Sweet dreams."

"You too."

He watched her walk to the lake and dive in. He was happy for her. She would likely have the best night's rest she had had in a long time. He looked around again. Could he have this forever as well?

"May I join you?"

Nuke jerked around to see Erabon descending to where he sat. "My Lord."

He started to stand, but Erabon patted his shoulder. "Stay seated." He sat next to Nuke. "I see you have troubled thoughts."

"Yes, my Lord." Nuke knew there was no use trying to hide anything from him.

"You want to know if you can stay and have a life for yourself here?"

Nuke nodded again.

"You've lived in two worlds now, Yohanan. Which one is more important to you?"

Nuke opened his mouth but didn't know what to say. He had grown incredibly fond of Ti'sulh and his other friends here. Those he had once counted as alien, he now counted as friends. Yet he had friends and family back on earth, Triton, and even Saturn station. His mother must be out of her mind with worry. He didn't want that for her.

Nuke shook his head. "I don't know, my Lord. There's so much of each that I want to have."

Erabon nodded. "I can understand that. I, too, left one world for another." He smiled. "For several actually."

Nuke chuckled. "You do seem to get around."

Erabon threw his head back and laughed. "Yes, I guess you could say that." He turned more serious. "But I first left the one

I loved most for something which was more important than what I wanted." He looked into Nuke's eyes. "For *someone* who was more important."

Nuke nodded. "You sacrificed a lot for us." He paused. "And now you want me to sacrifice?"

Erabon shook his head. "No, Yohanan. Not sacrifice. But to do there what you did here."

Nuke cocked his head. "What do you mean?"

"I brought you here not only to give my people here perspective, but also to give *you* perspective."

Nuke squinted. He wasn't sure where Erabon was going with this.

"What was the biggest issue here with the different clans?" Erabon asked.

Nuke shrugged. "They didn't have the full picture. They clung too tightly to only part of the picture."

"Does that not sound familiar?"

Nuke thought about that.

"You don't have clans. But you do have different races, different religious sects, different worldviews. They each have a piece of truth, but most do not have the full picture."

"And you want me to help them put the full picture together?"

Erabon nodded. "There are some who are trying to do that, but many have lost their perspective. I'm hoping you feel you have found that perspective."

Nuke nodded. "Yes, I guess that is true."

"And do you have something others on your planet do not have?"

Nuke cocked his head.

Erabon held out his hands. "The hope that is to come." He leaned in. "You are living it, Yohanan. You are experiencing it. I want you to bring that reality to your people."

"Like my father?"

"I want you to complement your father. He has the knowledge, but you now have the vision and foresight of what will be coming. What you are experiencing here will one day be for your people as well."

"When?"

Erabon pressed his index finger into Nuke's chest. "When you have prepared them." He patted Nuke's shoulder. "Think about that."

"Can you tell me what you meant about something else?"

"What would you like to know?"

"You told these people they would live here until you have something even more splendid to share with them."

Erabon smiled. "Yes, but I've already told you in your Scriptures."

Nuke's eyes widened. "Really?"

"As I have prepared a Promised Kingdom here, I will prepare one on Earth as well."

Nuke nodded. "Yes, I know Scripture states that."

"And what comes after?"

Nuke cocked his head. "Eternity."

"Ah, eternity. Where all is connected into one." He smiled broadly. "One day, my whole universe will be connected without restrictions. What you see and what you experience here will be everywhere throughout my universe. Everyone will know everyone." He patted Nuke's shoulder and stood. "No restrictions, Yohanan. No restrictions."

Nuke looked up at Erabon. "And when will I return to my home?"

"When you have enough experience to remember and share."

Nuke thought about that and then turned to ask another question.

Erabon was no longer there.

FORTY

SETTLING IN

Nuke found the next several months both peaceful and exhilarating. He enjoyed time with Ti'sulh and all his friends. He didn't tell Ti'sulh about his conversation with Erabon the first night on this new planet. He had no idea when he would be leaving, so he didn't want that uncertainty hanging over Ti'sulh's head. He just hoped Erabon would give him time to say goodbye.

Structure was created. Leaders were chosen. Yet this time, leaders were chosen from across clans to preserve unity. Each clan's talents and capabilities—along with those of the various individuals—were taken into account for the greater good of everyone. Nuke remained a consultant to the leadership but didn't take an actual role. He thought that best even though others felt he should take a more permanent position.

E'oa was chosen as the official priest to lead everyone in the worship of Erabon. That was a unanimous choice and put E'oa in his element. A'iah was chosen as his apprentice. No one who knew her thought that strange. Ti'sulh became her mentor as well as E'oa himself.

Nuke and Michael spent a lot of time with Za'avan; he wanted to increase space exploration. That endeavor was slow going, though. Nuke assumed that because space travel had not been part of this culture for so long, the various elders had a hard time envisioning such efforts as no longer taboo. Erabon, however, had no problem with space exploration efforts.

In one of the meetings with Za'avan, Nuke brought up the topic of exploring the five moons.

Za'avan laughed but looked serious. "Nuke, I know this sounds miniscule compared to all you and Michael have done in your career, but to go to our moons would be a great step to help everyone here feel comfortable with us venturing into space."

Nuke held up his hands. "I have nothing against that. I'm on your side."

"Really?" He looked at Michael, who also nodded.

A broad smile swept Za'avan's face. "Great. Here is what I was thinking . . . "

Nuke chuckled to himself. Za'avan always had a lot of ideas. Yet getting the council to buy into them was not always so easy.

Nuke heard something about interstellar gates and came out of his thoughts; honestly, he had tuned Za'avan out since he had so many things on his mind. "What? What did you say?"

"I said, I would like to use your interstellar gates to create easy traffic between here and our moons. I think starting a settlement there would be something exciting to explore."

Michael chuckled. "Go slow, Za'avan. I suggest you first state you want to experiment with traveling from here to the moons and back." He shrugged. "Once they accept that concept and see it accomplished, you can move on to the next step."

Nuke laughed. "After all, it's not like you're under a time pressure or anything."

Za'avan chuckled. "True. I just get too excited."

A new voice entered the room. "You first have to get the gates."

All turned and saw Z'zlzck at the door.

"Bob, you eavesdropper," Michael said teasingly.

Z'zlzck chuckled. "Didn't know it was a secret."

Za'avan motioned for Z'zlzck to come in. "We could probably use your help."

Michael laughed. "See what you got yourself into?"

Z'zlzck sat next to Michael. "With you involved, I should have known better."

Michael punched Z'zlzck's shoulder. Z'zlzck grinned.

Za'avan ignored their bantering and went on. "I think we can use one of the large ships, put your jet inside, and you use it to tow the gates into the ship—and then we bring them back here."

Nuke's eyes grew wide. "Do you have approval to do that?"

Za'avan bobbled his head. "Well, not quite yet. Raphek, Kubim's nephew, is working on it. He's really excited about doing this and thinks he can convince Kubim to get the council's approval."

Michael laughed. "I know a guy who knows a guy."

Za'avan looked confused, but Michael and Nuke laughed.

Raphek burst into the room breathing hard. "They said yes," he said with a quick breath. He took a few more and announced it again: "The council said yes!"

Za'avan's eyes widened. "How did you get them to approve our idea so fast?"

Raphek shook his head. "I guess I caught them in the right mood."

Michael laughed. "I take back my sarcastic statement."

Za'avan began pacing the room with excitement. "All right. All right. Let's see." He looked at Nuke. "Your jet was stored in the mountain with the others, right?"

Nuke nodded. "As far as I know. My jet was left on Aphiah, but I heard it was placed in the mountain with all the other spacecraft."

Za'avan shook his index finger. "Good. Good. So, we have your jet." He looked at Nuke. "Unless you want to use another one?"

Nuke shook his head. He was accustomed to his own and didn't want to have to learn a different set of controls.

Za'avan nodded. "We'll bring another just in case we need it." He looked back at Nuke. "Probably don't, but just in case."

He looked at Raphek. "Supplies! How much do we need to bring?"

Raphek looked in thought for several seconds. "I'd say enough for twenty days. We can probably get there and back in about half that time or less, but that gives us some contingency."

Nuke turned to Raphek. "It took much longer for us to get here. Why do you think you can get there in less time?"

Raphek grinned. "Well, for one, we won't be dragging a planet along."

Nuke chuckled. "Good point. But still . . . "

Raphek shook his head. "I've been doing some further downloading. I can make the engine twice as efficient. Travel back will take only a fraction of the time we needed to arrive here."

Nuke raised his eyebrows and looked at Michael and then Za'avan. Michael shrugged. "Sounds good to me."

Za'avan grinned. "Let's get started then, before anyone changes their mind."

Nuke found it took them less than a week to get everything together. The night before leaving, Nuke sat with Ti'sulh watching the moons rise.

She put her head on his shoulder. "So, you now want to travel to our moons?"

Nuke chuckled. "Za'avan does. I just want to help."

She looked up at him. "Maybe I'll come too."

He rubbed her arm. "No real need. According to Raphek, we should be back in no time."

Her eyes widened. "Oh, so you don't want me to come?"

He chuckled. "Now, I didn't say that. Don't go putting words in my mouth. If you want to come, I'll make arrangements. I'm just saying we'll be back in short order."

Ti'sulh smiled. "Just checking." She sat back and put her head on his shoulder again. "I have some mentorship meetings with A'iah anyway."

Nuke rubbed her hand. "Don't worry. By the time you complete her lessons, we should be back."

He kissed her forehead and they sat and watched the moons, the fluorescent coral, and the twinkling mountain for quite some time.

Nuke was excited about getting back into space. In truth, he missed it. Although he certainly enjoyed the wonders of this planet, there was just something special about flying his jet among the stars.

FORTY-ONE

GATHERING THE GATES

W hile the ship was fast, there was still a lot of down time to be used. There was only so much planning they could do, but they did set aside a couple of hours each day for just that. Since they had the whole ship to themselves, the four of them made the vessel their playground. They kept in shape by turning running into a game. They did relay races to see who could run the length of the ship first, both in individuals and in pairs. Michael and Nuke taught Za'avan and Raphek the art of Capture the Flag.

Of course, they also made their silly moments into a game as well. They set up eating contests, burping contests, and even staring contests. By the time they were getting bored with the whole thing, they had arrived.

Just before they started on their goal, they met one last time to go over everything.

Za'avan looked at Nuke. "You still feel using only one jet is the best solution?"

Nuke nodded. "Yeah, I think so. With Michael being in the jet with me, he can watch the monitor while I do the maneuvers."

Michael looked at Raphek. "When we get the gates tagged together, open the large bay so we can pull them in and secure them. We also need to keep that part of the ship without gravity so they can travel better without us having to worry about their weight."

Raphek nodded. "Not a problem."

Nuke turned to Za'avan. "I know I said we don't need the second jet, but be sure it's ready just in case we need your help."

Za'avan nodded. "You got it."

As they left the conference room, Raphek and Za'avan went to the bridge, and Nuke and Michael went to the bay where the jets were stored. They each completed their normal pre-flight checks and climbed in.

Michael climbed in behind Nuke. "This may have been enough room for Ti'sulh, but this may put me closer to you than I ever thought I'd be," he said.

Nuke laughed. "Well, aren't you lucky?"

"Yeah, well I just hope you used enough deodorant today."

"Back at ya, buddy." He turned to Michael. "Double check that the interspatial transference device is back there."

"Yep. I have the device tucked in the corner here. Why do we have it on this mission?"

"Shouldn't need it. But just in case."

Nuke started the jet and let the craft hover a minute before pressing the throttle that propelled the jet forward and out of the storage bay. He did a couple of loops to get back into a rhythm.

"Easy there, bronco."

Nuke laughed. "I thought you liked loops."

"Oh, I love loops when *I'm flying*. Not so fun from the back seat."

Nuke chuckled. "OK. I'll be good."

Michael pointed at the monitor. "I see the gates. Go thirty degrees right."

Nuke did so and the gates came into view. "See them."

Nuke found the first step rather simple. He had to get the first gate tethered to the second gate. He did this by hooking the retractable arm on one of the cable loops and then tugging the second gate toward the first gate. Once he got close enough, he reverse-thrusted to stop the forward momentum of the gate. He then unhooked one end of the cable from the second gate and hooked that cable to the first gate. This tethered the two together.

Za'avan came on the comm. "Nuke, should you do the same for the other cables?"

"I don't think it's necessary," Nuke radioed. "We just need to get both gates into the cargo bay. We'll secure all corners once we're inside. Just be sure you have enough tethers to suspend the gates once we bring them to you."

"Already done. Just waiting for your arrival."

"Roger that."

Michael leaned forward to tap Nuke's arm. "May not need all three for the second gate, but we should probably use all three on the first gate so we can tow with more control."

Nuke thought about that. He wasn't sure that was completely necessary. Doing so would take longer but might save some time once they were in the cargo bay. Nuke nodded. "OK. You handle the retractable arm, and I'll focus on stabilizing the jet as you do so."

"You got it."

Nuke flew the jet to the first corner of the large triangle, the part of the gate holding the looped cable. Michael managed to unhook one end of the cable and attach it to the jet.

Michael tapped Nuke's arm. "One down. Two to go."

Nuke nodded. He flew to the second corner of the gate, careful not to have the first cable pull on the gate yet and cause the gate to shift or turn. "Be careful not to get the cables intertwined," he said to Michael.

Michael chuckled. "Doubting my skill?"

"No. Just reminding you to use it."

Nuke glanced at the monitor as Michael worked the retractable arm. He held the jet as steady as he could. Michael unhooked the second cable from the gate, but the cable slipped out of the hook and slowly drifted. Thankfully, the end of the cable drifted inward and not outward, away from the gate. This allowed Nuke to move the jet without making the first cable taut and pulling on the gate.

Michael hooked the cable on his second try and secured it to the jet. "Whew. That was a little tense."

Nuke nodded. He often thought about what initially caused these gates to activate accidently, bringing them both into this part of the universe. He surmised his head hitting the transference device the previous time was the culprit, but the cause could have been the gate getting jerked too quickly. He didn't want to try either theory again.

Michael looked at Nuke and patted his arm. "OK, buddy. Just one more to go."

Nuke nodded and slowly eased the jet to the third corner holding the last loop. Michael took more time for this maneuver as he unhooked the cable and secured it to the jet where the other two were attached.

Michael let out a long breath. "OK, Nuke. I think we're ready."

"OK, Raphek. We're heading your way. You can start opening the cargo bay doors."

"Opening now."

"Za'avan, stand by for anchoring this baby down once we arrive."

"On my way there now."

Nuke took the jet into a slow forward momentum. Once the cables were taut, he could feel the strain on the jet. He added more power to overcome the added mass but didn't want to add too much since he wanted a slow forward momentum. He glanced at the monitor showing the view from the back of the jet. All looked in order. The three cables went out from his jet from a single point to the three corners of the gate with the second gate being pulled with a single cable; it was now traveling in a parallel plane to the first gate. Nuke felt grateful all was going as planned.

He suddenly felt a small shake. "What was that?"

"What was what?" Michael asked.

"You didn't feel that? Check the cables. Something feels off."

Michael looked intently at the monitor and panned the aft camera. He shook his head. "I don't see anything wrong, Nuke." Michael patted Nuke's arm. "Relax. All's going fine."

Nuke nodded, but he felt uneasy on the inside. Granted, the shake was minor, but there shouldn't have been one at all.

Suddenly, a violent shake occurred. The jet was pulled off course. "What was that?"

Michael's voice now sounded panicked. "One of the cables broke."

The break caused the jet to get pulled in the opposite direction from the momentum of the free cable now traveling away from the gate. Nuke attempted to compensate by turning the jet back to its original position. Yet, this caused a stronger pull on the side of the gate where the two cables were still attached. This caused the opposite corner of the gate to move away from his jet and out of plane.

"Michael, where's the other gate?"

"It's moving up and around."

Nuke could now *feel* the pull of the other gate from its swing around the first gate. He did extremely fast mental calculations as to how to solve this dilemma. The best solution was to disengage the jet from the other cables, but he knew they didn't have enough time for that.

"Oh no."

"What's wrong, Michael?"

"I think the end of the first gate will hit the second."

Nuke swallowed hard. "That will . . . "

"Yeah. That will increase the speed and the centrifugal force the second gate is creating."

"Michael, I think our only option is to disengage the other cables."

Michael nodded. "OK. I'll work on that."

Raphek's panicked voice came over the comm. "Nuke, the second gate just activated. What are you doing?"

"What?" Nuke tried to peer up from the cockpit to see what was going on. "Where is it?"

"It's directly above you and swinging around heading for you."

"Michael, shut down that gate."

Michael fumbled to get the transference device. Nuke looked back to see Michael turning the device over and around. Michael shook his head. "Nuke, this device is not on. There's nothing to turn off."

Nuke tried to remain calm and think logically. "When the first gate hit the second, the jolt must have activated the gate."

His theory had to be correct, but that didn't help matters now.

"Any brilliant plans?" Michael asked.

"See if the device will connect to the gate. Maybe we can at least direct where we exit. As Michael quickly tried to work the transference device, Nuke could see the gate approaching. Its shimmering ripples sent a déjà vu moment through his mind—heightening his anxiety.

"Michael?"

Michael shook his head. "It won't connect to an activated gate."

Nuke knew that made sense even though he had hoped otherwise. "What about the other gate? Will the device connect to that one?"

Another jolt jerked the jet backward, causing his engine to stall. He frantically tried to get the jet started again, but all attempts failed.

Nuke glanced back at Michael. "Well?"

Michael shook his head. "It won't connect."

That didn't make sense.

"Nuke, the second gate is activated," Raphek said through the comm; his voice sounded shaky.

Nuke shook his head. Now he understood. With both gates activated, the device would not connect to either one.

"Nuke, I'm coming out to help in the other jet."

"No! No, Za'avan. Promise me you'll stay put until we get this sorted out." He could only think of Michael trying to help him the first time and getting caught up with his mishap. "Za'avan? Promise me!" Nuke all but shouted, his voice now emphatic.

"All right, Nuke. All right. Just . . . be careful."

Michael sighed. "It seems the torque of the cable attached to the gate was too much, causing the cable loop to snap off."

Nuke shook his head. Well, that explained the sudden jerk. He put his hand to his temple to try to develop a workable idea. He looked up and saw the free cable now coming their way. His eyes widened. "Michael!" Now there was panic in Nuke's voice. "Our only hope is for you to disengage the cables and do it as fast as possible."

"What's wrong now?"

"The free cable is coming our way. If it wraps around the attached cables, we'll be stuck no matter what we do."

Michael nodded and got to work on freeing the jet at the same time Nuke attempted to get the jet engine to reignite.

Nuke looked up; both the free cable and the activated gate were coming their way. He wasn't sure which would reach them first.

"There. Got it!"

"We're free?"

"Yeah. Can you get the jet started?"

Hope filled Nuke. He tried again, but with no success.

"Oh no!"

Nuke whipped his head back to Michael. "What now?"

"Freeing this end of the cable with the other free end made it act like a bola, causing this end to wrap around the other cable."

"And . . . "

Nuke then heard something hitting the jet.

"And the other end is now wrapping around the tail portion of our jet."

Nuke threw his head back and closed his eyes. Things were reaching an impossible point. "Michael, our only hope is getting the jet started and hope the cable is long enough for us to get to the other side of the gate before the gates come together."

Michael patted Nuke's arm. "Do it, Nuke. Do it!"

"The gates are closing!" Raphek's voice was clearly higher than normal.

"Working on it," Nuke replied.

Nuke tried again, and the engine came to life. He gave a "Yeah!" just as Michael did, and Michael delivered a quick pat to his shoulder.

"Now get us out of here!" Michael said, hope now coming through the panic in his voice.

Nuke gunned the throttle . . . but the cable just wasn't long enough. It pulled back on the jet. The only thing this did was cause the edge of the gate still attached to come to the other gate even faster. At this point Nuke didn't care; he kept the throttle gunned to try and pull the cable off the jet . . . but to no avail.

Nuke cut the engine, realizing their escape was hopeless.

"Za'avan, tell Ti'sulh . . . " He paused. "Tell her I'm sorry."

"Nuke, we'll find you. We'll find—"

Za'avan's voice turned to static as the two gates came together, sandwiching Nuke and Michael between them.

All Nuke saw was a shimmering bright light.

Déjà vu. All over again.

FORTY-TWO

NEW MISSION

Nuke awoke; he was disoriented for a time. Realization
dawned that he was in his jet. As he looked out from the
cockpit, he saw both gates nearby and deactivated. Sitting in
silence, his mind thought of Ti'sulh. His hope for a life with
her was gone. His eyes watered as he tried to reason with himself. After all, Erabon had said he would not have a life with
her. Yet the reality of that now hit his heart hard. His hand
went to his chest; his heart literally hurt.

"Yohanan, my son. I will always be with you."

Nuke heard Erabon's voice in his head. Was it his voice?
Surely it was, or he was going insane. Both seemed equally
possible, though. He wanted to believe the first was true.

I didn't even get a chance to say goodbye.

"And what would you have said?"

I . . . I don't know. Tears welled up in his eyes, spilled over
his bottom eyelids, and cascaded down his cheeks. *A kiss or a
hug would have been nice.*

"And that would make you feel better now?"

Nuke shook his head. *No. No it wouldn't.*

"My dearest Yohanan. I have always asked much from my prophets. Not because I loved them less or wished less for them, but because I loved them and knew they could bear more than most. The same is true for you—and my love for you. I know this feels like another sacrifice, and from your perspective you will likely always think so. But I have so much more in store for you. Now is a time for faith."

Nuke closed his eyes, causing more tears to run down his cheeks. Erabon had been faithful until now. He had to believe he would be again, going forward. *Yes, my Lord. I accept, if you can keep my heart from breaking.*

"I will keep all of you."

Nuke awoke with a start. Had he been asleep for this conversation? He shook his head. Had everything been a dream? He looked out the cockpit and saw the two deactivated gates. *Michael.*

He turned to see if Michael was OK. He wasn't moving. Nuke grabbed his arm and shook it. "Michael! Michael, are you all right?"

Michael stirred slowly. He put his hand to his head. "What . . . what happened?"

"We became a sandwich filling, unfortunately."

Michael groaned as he sat up, confused. "What?"

"We traveled in space."

Michael sat up farther, looked at the monitor, and then tried to look out the cockpit. "So, where are we?"

"I'm not sure. I just woke up." He looked out the cockpit. "I don't recognize the constellations." He shook his head. "No idea."

Michael looked at the monitor. "Well, we're still caught up in the cables of the gate."

Nuke thought about the first time. His solution for that dilemma would not work this time as the cable was physically wrapped around their jet.

Michael sighed. "I thought if we got sent back, Erabon would at least let us get back to our solar system." He rubbed the back of his neck. "This just doesn't make any sense."

Nuke nodded. He thought about the last conversation he had with Erabon. He apparently had a mission back home. *Or did I misunderstand what Erabon meant?* He sighed. "Yeah, I know. It doesn't."

Michael looked at Nuke. "Any brilliant ideas?"

Nuke gave a sarcastic chuckle. "Yeah, like the brilliant idea I had the last time you asked?"

Michael grabbed Nuke's arm. "No, Nuke. Really. You're the best problem-solver I know."

Nuke patted Michael's shoulder. "Thanks for the vote of confidence, but I've got nothing." He shrugged. "Even if we get free, who knows where we are?"

Michael nodded toward the instrument panel. "Have you tried to see if the computer knows where we are?"

Nuke shook his head. "I just assumed it wouldn't be helpful." He cocked his head. "But you're right. We should at least follow protocol." Nuke reached over and pressed a button for the computer to plot their position in space and, possibly, how far they were from Triton.

He didn't expect anything, but in only a couple of minutes, the computer pinged.

Michael's eyes widened. "That sounded like a positive ding."

Nuke nodded. "Yes, it sure did." He pressed another button and his eyes grew wide. He leaned forward and looked through the cockpit canopy and behind them. A smile crept across his face. He looked at Michael and chuckled.

"What? What is it?"

"Take a look." Nuke pointed where he was looking.

Michael gave Nuke a quizzical look. He climbed over Nuke to get a peek at what Nuke wasn't telling him. He looked, and his eyes widened. He patted Nuke's shoulder and laughed as he looked from Nuke back to the sky and then to Nuke again. "I knew Erabon wouldn't send us just anywhere. Alpha Centauri. We're at Alpha Centauri!"

"Our interspatial transference device should be able to get us home from here," Nuke said.

Michael settled back behind Nuke, a big grin on his face. "One jump and we're home."

Nuke's jubilation turned somber. "Only one slight problem. We're still tethered to the gate."

Michael's shoulders drooped. "Oh, yeah." Suddenly, Michael slapped Nuke's arm. "That's OK. That's what you did between planetary jumps."

Nuke wrinkled his brow, but then his eyes widened. "Of course. I was tethered to the gate and pulled it through the other gate." He shook his index finger. "That should work."

Michael nodded. "Before, we were trying to escape the gate. Now we only have to go through it."

Nuke pointed. "See if you can get the transference device to communicate with the gate we're tethered to."

Michael went to work. Nuke turned to check that all was in order so he could fire up the jet.

Michael laughed and slapped Nuke's arm again. "It's working. Nuke, it's working. The coordinates were already in the device. I only had to access them." He glanced up at Nuke and then back at the device. "It seems we'll exit just outside Triton's orbit near where we were before."

Nuke beamed. Hope was swelling within him. He crossed his fingers and pressed the button to engage the engines. They came to life. He looked at Michael and laughed. "It works."

Michael grabbed Nuke's arm and shook it. "One jump and we're home." He activated the gate.

Nuke looked at the shimmery surface. What engendered dread before now brought a sense of hope and exhilaration. He pushed on the throttle and took the jet through the event horizon. He felt himself becoming weightless. Light seemed to stretch and elongate around him . . .

The next thing he knew, his jet exited and the gate to which he was tethered came through behind him. He stopped his forward momentum once the activated gate's event horizon dissipated. As the gates went past him, he engaged his reverse thrusters and had the gates come to a complete stop.

Nuke looked back at Michael, a huge grin on his face.

Michael beamed back and slapped him on his shoulder. "You did it, Nuke!" He pointed.

Nuke looked up to see Triton in view; Neptune was past its horizon. His eyes watered. *Home.* They were home.

"Nuke! Michael! Is that one of you?"

Nuke recognized the voice of Jake. My, it was great to hear a familiar voice.

"Jake, is that you? This is Nuke. Michael's with me. Man, it's great to hear your voice."

Nuke heard a laugh and a whoop through his comm. Nuke laughed.

"Nuke, it's great to hear your voice. We thought we'd lost you. Where have you been?" He paused. "Never mind. We'll catch up when we get you back."

"We're kind of tied up, here, Jake. Can someone come rescue us?

"Two jets are on your way now."

Nuke saw them circling, likely assessing their situation.

"Man, you never make anything easy do you, Nuke?"

"McNamara? Is that you?" Nuke laughed. "Just giving you lazy guys something to do."

He heard laughter through his comm. "Yeah, I was really bored. Thanks for coming to my rescue."

Nuke chuckled. "Sure. Now can you come to ours?"

McNamara gave a hearty laugh. "No problem. I think the faster solution is to get you two out and into our jets. Then we'll deal with the whole gate entanglement issue later."

"So, how do you want to do this?" Nuke asked.

"How many suits do you have aboard? Can you both transfer out of your cockpit?"

Nuke grimaced. "Only one I'm afraid. Opening the canopy isn't an option."

Another voice came over the comm. "Is your jet functional, Nuke?"

"Yes, if we are untethered," Nuke replied, then paused. That voice also sounded familiar. "Haynes, is that you?"

"Hey, buddy. Sit tight. McNamara will get someone to cut the cable and I'll then guide you in."

Nuke smiled. "Sounds good."

Michael patted Nuke's shoulder while giving a broad grin.

Over the next several hours McNamara got a mechanic to cut the cable, and Nuke then followed Haynes back to Triton. At that point, Nuke and Michael were transferred into an isolation area. Jake now talked to them through the intercom watching through a clear wall that separated them.

"Sorry about this, gents," Jake said. "But we need to follow protocol to be sure you didn't bring back a toxic plague or anything."

Nuke smiled and nodded. "We understand. It's just great to be back."

Jake nodded. "OK. Hang tight. I'll check to see where we are and when the doc will get to you."

Nuke nodded and sat back. He looked at Michael. "So, what story do we tell them?"

Michael shook his head. "I'm not sure the truth will work in our favor this time. Rather than a detox room, we'll be in a padded cell for the rest of our lives."

Nuke scrunched the corner of his mouth and nodded. Michael was probably right. "When I really think about it, I'm not sure I'd believe myself either."

"I think our best bet is to just say we can't remember anything," Michael said.

Nuke cocked his head. "Why is that?"

Michael gestured toward him. "Do you know how long we've been gone?" He waved his hands. "I mean, do you know how long *they* think we've been gone?"

Nuke thought about that and knew the two may not necessarily be consistent. He thought back to Erabon changing the time of their arrival on each planet to match the time of each ship's arrival at each successive planet. Did he do the same type of thing here? Nuke wasn't sure. He didn't know if the Triton crew thought they had been gone for almost three years, as Nuke and Michael perceived it, or if the elapsed time was much shorter from the perspective of those on Triton. Nuke shrugged. "Your plan is probably best."

After a couple of seconds of staring straight ahead, Nuke looked back at Michael. "Do you think we could have imagined the whole thing?"

Michael gave Nuke a furrowed-brow look. "Do you think we dreamed it? But how would we have the same dream?"

Nuke bobbled his head back and forth several times. No, his memories definitely didn't feel like a dream, and he had never heard of two people having the same dream undergoing the same experiences.

Michael walked over to where Nuke sat. "Plus, we have tangible evidence. No matter what anyone tells us, we have our proof. We can always know we are sane." Michael reached down and held up the coral cross for Nuke to see, along with his Zyhov replica. "These . . . these are our proof. Our memories are real even if we can't share them with anyone."

Nuke nodded and gave Michael a weak smile. He was right. Keeping everything to themselves was a shame, though. They had a remarkable story. A thought came to him, and it made him smile to himself: *maybe someday I'll turn my adventure into a novel.*

The doctor came in suited up just in case they were carrying a biological threat of some kind. He checked them out from head to toe. Nuke had undergone physicals before, but never had someone looked at every square inch of his body and probed practically every possible entryway into it. Although a little awkward, he had endured worse. After that, and after what felt like a ton of blood samples, the doctor left them to themselves again until all the tests were run.

* * *

After staying in confinement for seventy-two hours and having to tell what they knew what seemed like a hundred times, Nuke and Michael were released with a clean bill of health, although they were to go for more follow-up in three months.

When they left confinement, Felicia was waiting. She threw her arms around Michael and planted a firm and long kiss on him. Michael gave her a hug after her kiss, and he looked at Nuke with his eyebrows bouncing up and down several times.

Nuke laughed and shook his head. Apparently, absence did make the heart grow fonder. Michael must have made a deep impression on her for her adoration for him to last three months—at least to her—in his absence. As the two of them walked off together, Nuke headed back to his quarters. Not his same quarters; those had been given to someone else after everyone had considered Nuke and Michael missing in action. Yet his new quarters looked almost identical to what he had before except for one major difference: as compensation for his misadventure he had been upgraded to a room with a personal latrine and shower. He laughed. He was moving up in the universe.

Jake stopped by. "Need anything?"

Nuke shook his head. "I'm fine. Thanks."

Jake pointed at him. "Low gravity racquetball tomorrow. No excuses."

Nuke smiled and nodded. "You're on."

As he settled onto his bunk, he knew he had to contact his parents. They had already been informed of his rescue, so they had time to recover before he called them. He picked up his tablet and called home. His mother answered. Her hand went to her mouth as soon as she saw him. The delay made this important communication difficult.

"Mom. Dad. I'm fine." He smiled. "Really, I'm fine. I've done a lot of thinking. I'm coming home for a while after my next checkup. It will be about three months from now, but I'll see you then."

He waited for their reply as he looked at his mother's tear-stained face and the gleam from his father's eyes, which now looked moist. Although a shaky one, his mother produced a smile. "Oh, Yohanan, we're so happy we'll get to see you."

Looking over his mother's shoulder, his father nodded. "I've missed you, son."

Nuke's eyes watered as well. His mother calling him Yohanan reminded him of his last conversation with Erabon.

"Dad," Nuke began, "I'm sorry. I was foolish in not listening to you. I now understand what you have been doing for the sake of others. I want to be a part of that . . . if you'll have me. I want to team up with you and spread the word of Erabon—I mean, of Mashiach—and tell others we need to be prepared for his coming." He chuckled. "I have a lot to tell you. So much. I'll ask for a transfer to the Saturn station and, later, a transfer to the moon station. That way I can visit more often. Eventually, maybe I'll be able to transfer back to Earth. We have a lot to do, Dad. A lot."

Nuke chuckled when his dad's face came into view. It was priceless to see his eyes go wide and a smile creep across his face. This time tears did come. "Yohanan. That makes me happy. Extremely happy. I can't wait to see you."

The transmission ended. Nuke set the tablet down and sat up on his bunk. He nodded. It felt right. It felt very right.

He picked up the coral cross and looked at it. Memories of Ti'sulh came flooding back. There was a pang of sorrow there, but he was filled with excitement about his future . . . here.

"I'll see you soon, Ti'sulh. Soon. When the universe becomes one." He smiled. "When the universe has no restrictions."

I hope you've enjoyed *Qerach*. Letting others know of your enjoyment of this book is a way to help them share your experience. Please consider posting an honest review. You can post a review at Amazon, Barnes & Noble, Goodreads, or other places you choose. Reviews can be posted at more than one site! This author, and other readers, appreciate your engagement.

Also, check out my next book, coming soon!

For more details, go to www.RandyDockens.com

—Randy Dockens

Ever consider what angels think about what goes on with us on Earth, or how they are involved?

Then come explore my next series:

The Adversary Chronicles

Discover stories from the Bible in a way not yet told.

He has many names: Lucifer, Satan, Devil, Adversary.

Read how he fell from the highest of places to where he is today, how other angels reacted to his actions, to creation, to Adam and Eve, and even to Noah and his family. Find a different perspective that will help you rediscover the awe of age-old Bible stories and give you a perspective you may not have considered.

The Adversary is alive and well. Come discover why.

(BEFORE FINAL EDITING)

SAMPLE CHAPTER FROM
REBELLION IN THE STONES OF FIRE

PART OF THE ADVERSARY
CHRONICLES SERIES

Rebellion in the Stones of Fire

ONE

Disturbance in the Force

Mikael approached two of his fellow warriors who were engaged in animated conversation. He had his left hand resting on the bejeweled hilt of his sword to prevent the weapon from impeding his fast gait. He nodded to them as he came to an abrupt stop. Both stopped their conversation in mid-sentence, looking at Mikael expectantly.

"Raphael, have you or Uriel seen Ruach today?"

Raphael gave a wry smile as he brushed his golden-colored hair back over his shoulder. His blue eyes twinkled with amusement. "Seen? Is that a trick question?"

Uriel chuckled but then stopped when he saw Mikael's extremely serious expression. Mikael didn't crack a smile.

"Mikael," Raphael said. "What's wrong?"

Mikael shook his head slightly. "I'm not sure." He too brushed his long blond hair, somewhat darker than that of Raphael's, over his shoulder. "Last time I saw him, he looked . . . different."

Raphael and Uriel looked at each other; both gave a slight shrug.

Raphael turned back to Mikael. "I'm not trying to be facetious, but how can you say he looks different? We can barely see him as it is. He's Ruach HaKodesh, Elohim's Spirit. He has a form, but he is pretty much transparent for the most part."

Mikael sighed. They were taking him too literally. "Yes, Raphael. But he produces a feeling, a presence, an aura . . . that is powerful yet calming."

Raphael nodded. "Yes, that's true."

"His aura, as we sometimes say, felt different—troubled— unlike any time before."

"Well," Uriel said, "he does have a great deal of stress to unite both the love and justice of our Creator so they can both exist within him." He shook his head. "Such stress likely takes its toll on him now and again. That's a lot of tension to keep harmonious."

Mikael rubbed his chin. "Maybe. This . . . felt different, though."

Uriel shrugged and patted Mikael on his shoulder. "We'll keep our eyes out for him and let you know if we find out anything or hear anything."

Mikael nodded to his friends. "Thanks. I'll let you know what I find as well."

Mikael walked on, wondering where to look, when he suddenly got the idea to head to the throne room. *Ruach.*

Ruach HaKodesh often sent telepathic messages to them to let them know the will of their Creator. Going to the throne room sounded serious—definitely not a place to approach lightly. There were only a few select Cherubim and Seraphim, special angels, who had access to the Creator in his throne room. Why would Ruach want him there?

The throne room was not hard to miss. Since the place contained the Shekinah glory of the Creator, his brilliance was so bright the light would penetrate any crevice existing in a structure. In addition, with the throne room being composed of various types of colored crystals, the place gave off a magnificent glow that could be seen from extremely far away. Not only was the throne room colorful, the area also sat on the highest place in the middle of the kingdom, a dimension in and unto itself. Mikael looked up and followed the path upward toward the glow—a glow he had always considered comforting knowing his Creator's presence was always with him. Now he would enter his Creator's dimension. That, he thought, was not as comforting.

As Mikael neared the throne room, he paused. Was he supposed to enter? There would be grave consequences if he entered uninvited. He looked around. His eyes caught a slight blur of something against the glow of the throne room. He approached.

"Ruach. I got your message. What is wrong?"

Only a vague outline of a person could be observed. Although transparent, he appeared like heat waves between an observer and an object. "Thank you for coming. I didn't want to alarm the others. You're the archangel, the leader of our Creator's heavenly host."

Mikael often wondered why he was the leader of an army. Shouldn't an army have an enemy? They certainly trained as if there was one. But everything here was so perfect. What was the need of such a force? Unless . . . Ruach was about to now tell him.

Mikael took a step closer to Ruach. He lowered his voice—he was unsure why he did, but doing so seemed the appropriate thing to do. "Ruach, tell me what's going on."

Ruach shook his head. "Mikael, I can't yet reveal what is going on. All I can say is, I have felt a change, and it's not a good change. There is a disturbance brewing. I can't tell you what it is or who it is, but . . . " His voice trailed off.

Mikael cocked his head. "But what? You can at least tell me where this . . . disturbance . . . is originating from, right?"

Ruach nodded.

"OK. So where?"

"That's why I called you here." Ruach's form turned toward the throne room.

Mikael looked from Ruach to the throne room and back, realization slowly dawning. In almost a whisper he said, "What? Here? But . . . why? How?"

Ruach turned back to Mikael. "That is why I need your help."

Mikael put his hand to his chest. "*My* help? But you're the one who can sense all. What do you need with my help?"

Ruach put his hand on Mikael's shoulder. Mikael could not see his hand there, but could feel it, as well as the warmth now radiating from his shoulder down into his very being. "That's the point, Mikael. The time of choices is approaching.

I need you to question the Cherubim to see what they know. If a rebellion is brewing, I don't want them to think I know."

Mikael's eyes widened. "Rebellion? Here? How—" He paused, his mind trying to catch up to such a thought. "How is such a thing even possible?"

Ruach shook his head. "It is a mystery. But a mystery you need to get to the bottom of."

Mikael slowly nodded, but then stopped. His heart sank. "Wait. You said 'them.' Why did you make this plural?"

Ruach seemed to look down and then back to Mikael. "It is plural, I'm afraid. The feeling I've received has gotten stronger over the last several days."

Mikael took a step back in shock. "I can't comprehend even one of us rebelling, much less several. Are you sure?"

Ruach slowly nodded. "Yes. I am certain."

Mikael glanced back at the throne room. "And you think the rebellion is from one of the Cherubim?" He shook his head. "They are the closest to our Creator. They reflect his glory back to him. How could rebellion be in one of them?"

"It is either one of them, or one of them knows something. You must find out what they know."

"But how do I do that? They are in the throne room almost constantly. They come out only rarely, and for short periods of time."

Ruach nodded. "Yes, that is true. And that is why you have my permission."

Mikael slightly cocked his head. "Permission? For what?"

"To enter."

Mikael's mouth fell open. "The throne room!?" His voice was full of disbelief. "But won't they know something is amiss if they see me in the throne room? Only the Cherubim and Seraphim are allowed."

"Others are allowed, with permission."

Mikael swallowed hard. As far as he knew, no one, as yet, had ever entered the throne room except for select Cherubim and Seraphim.

"The glow of one has faded," Ruach said. "Likely almost imperceptible, but perhaps you can notice so you will know where to direct your questioning. Don't approach directly. Not yet at least. Let's talk after your visit once you return. Don't engage. Just observe."

Ruach stretched out his transparent arm and directed Mikael's attention toward the entrance of the throne room.

Mikael's eyebrows raised. "You mean, *now*?"

"Is there any better time?"

Mikael knew the answer was no, but he wasn't sure he was ready for this step without further preparation. He started to ask if the Creator was expecting him, but caught himself as he realized Ruach HaKodesh was one component of the Creator Trinity. Ruach giving permission was the same as the Creator giving permission.

Mikael slowly walked toward the entrance of the throne room. Two large angels with broad shoulders and a muscular build stood next to the doorway. Each had blondish-colored hair and blue eyes that highlighted their tanned appearance. Both wore a sky-blue robe which contrasted with the golden sash around their waist and the other sash across their chest that was in place to hold a large, sheathed sword along their back.

"Hello, Azel," Mikael said.

Azel nodded. "Ruach has already informed me to allow your entrance."

Mikael nodded. "Thank you." He paused briefly at the entrance. Would the portal to this dimension open?

He briefly glanced at Azel, who simply gave a smile.

The entrance seemed to simply fade, revealing a myriad of colors within. Mikael swallowed hard and stepped through the opening and into a dimension few—if any—had ever been invited into.

ERABON PROPHECY TRILOGY

Come read this exciting trilogy where an astronaut, working on an interstellar gate, is accidently thrown so deep into the universe that there is no way for him to get back home.

He does, however, find life on a nearby planet, one in which the citizens look very different from him. Although tense at first, he finds these aliens think he is the forerunner to the return of their deity and charge him with reuniting the clans living on six different planets.

What is stranger to him still is that while everything seems so foreign from anything he has ever experienced, there is an element that also feels so familiar.

Available now!

THE STELE PENTALOGY

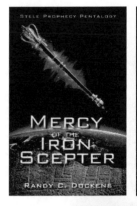

Do you know *your future*?

Come see the possibilities in a world God creates and how an apocalypse leads to promised wonders beyond imagination.

Read how some experience mercy, some hope, and some embrace their destiny—while others try to reshape theirs. And how some, unfortunately, see perfection and the divine as only ordinary and expected.

Available now!

THE CODED MESSAGE TRILOGY

Come read this fast-paced trilogy where an astrophysicist accidently stumbles upon a world secret that plunges him and his friends into an adventure of discovery and intrigue . . .

What Luke Loughton and his friends discover could possibly be the answer to a question you've been wondering all along.

Available now!

Why Is a Gentile World Tied to a Jewish Timeline?
The Question Everyone Should Ask

Yes, the Bible is a unique book.

Looking for a book with mystery, intrigue, and subterfuge? Maybe one with action, adventure, and peril suits you more. Perhaps science fiction is more your fancy. The Bible gives you all that and more! Come read of a hero who is humble yet exudes strength, power, and confidence—one who is intriguing yet always there for the underdog.

Read how the Bible puts all of this together in a unique, cohesive plan that intertwines throughout history—a plan for a Gentile world that is somehow tied to a Jewish timeline.

Travel a road of discovery you never knew existed. Do you like adventures? Want to join one? Then come along. Discover the answer to the question everyone should ask.

Available now!